A MAN OF LIES

A MAN
OF LIES

A NOVEL

BEN CRANE

PEGASUS CRIME

NEW YORK LONDON

A MAN OF LIES

Pegasus Crime is an imprint of
Pegasus Books, Ltd.
148 West 37th Street, 13th Floor
New York, NY 10018

Copyright © 2023 by Ben Crane

First Pegasus Books cloth edition July 2023

Interior design by Maria Fernandez

ISBN: 978-1-63936-409-1

10 9 8 7 6 5 4 3 2 1

Printed in the United States of America
Distributed by Simon & Schuster
www.pegasusbooks.com

For my Mickey,
who sees me.

PROLOGUE

So here's the short version of things: I did something stupid, some people got hurt, and I'm about to try something far worse. If you want the longer version, there's some things you need to know first.

My name is Barrett Rye, and I am a confidence man. I've been other things before. When I was eight I wanted to be a magician. When I was sixteen I started working in organized crime. Now, nineteen years later, I'm a professional trickster.

I'm going to make you a promise, right here at the start of everything. It's probably the most important part of the story, so if you can only remember one thing, remember this:

Nothing I say is the truth.

Of course, if you can only remember one thing, then you should put the book down now. You're going to need to remember a lot more than that. If you think you're up to the task, though, I have one more promise, nearly as important as the first:

Nothing I say is a lie.

"But, Barrett," I hear you say, or at least you would if we were capable of having an actual dialogue, "how can that be? How can what you say be not the truth and not a lie?"

"Well," I say to you in this imaginary conversation, "that's the trick of it all. If I told you that, I'd give up the whole game."

FRIDAY

FRIDAY

CHAPTER 1

Barrett Rye, 10:22 P.M.

Perhaps we should start in Brock's gambling den, a private club in the back of a garment warehouse in downtown Omaha. An old man sits in a defunct break room, and if you know the password, he'll let you through a broom closet to the space behind, a modern recreation of a prohibition speakeasy. There are six tables inside, two each for poker, blackjack, and roulette. Brock has filled the room with wood paneling and richly cushioned seats. The serving girls wear cocktail dresses and ferry drinks from the bar. The dealers wear crisp cummerbunds.

There's a trio of legal casinos right across the river in Council Bluffs. People come to Brock's for the thrill of the criminality—a moment of excitement in milquetoast lives—or because they are desperate. Brock is more than happy to accommodate them all. The whole room smells of musk and sweat layered with cheap booze and stale cigars, and overwhelming it all is the acrid bite of adrenaline in the corners of my mouth.

There are six of us at the table, but only two matter. There's a hair over three thousand dollars in the pot, and we're the only two left in the hand. The first might be the largest human I've ever seen in person. He's a nearly seven-foot wall of muscle whose eyes sit too close together beneath his encroaching brow. I'd never want to see him across from me in a darkened alley, but at a poker table? A sucker is born every minute, and this man has a face that screams his idiocy to the world.

As for his opponent, well, what can I say about him? He's handsome—of course—but in a casual way. A way that makes you think he could be your friend. "You're already twelve hundred into the pot," he says, grinning a salesman's smile to the bruiser across the table. "What's three more?" He straightens the cuffs on his perfectly tailored suit.

I'm about to do something profoundly stupid. I'm going to cheat. I might not have become the magician I dreamed of being as a kid, but I know how to vanish a card and replace it with another. Months of planning come down to this one move, but if this bruiser can't get it through his steroid-addled brain that he needs to call, it all will have been for nothing.

It's not about the money on the table here. I need orders of magnitude more than that if I'm going to convince Enrico Scarpello, the head of the largest criminal syndicate in Chicago, not to kill me. But if I'm going to get that money, I need this man to call.

The big man studies his cards a moment more, as though they might have changed since he last looked at them, then pushes his chips to the center of the table and turns over the two pair I knew he had.

And now, if you watch closely, you'll catch me. The moment of truth. Here comes the move.

"Kings and tens? That's good. But not quite good enough."

The four guards whose sole job is to keep the games here honest don't spot it when the flush is turned over. But somehow the giant idiot who hasn't managed to string more than three words together all night does. The cards on the table are not the cards I was dealt.

He stares at them. His forehead wrinkles, skin pinching together around an old scar. His hand darts out, faster than you'd think possible. The whole casino stops for a heartbeat, and there is no sound but the rattling of a roulette ball. Two bouncers materialize at the tableside.

My arm strains. There is no fighting him as he turns both of our hands up, working to expose them to the room. It's only then that I see the card. I haven't quite managed to get it all the way down inside the sleeve. There is the tiniest corner of the off-suit jack—the actual card I was dealt—poking up above the cloth.

I feel the gasp ripple through the crowd more than I hear it. The audacity of cheating in Brock's house is staggering. The bouncer's grip descends, and I rise to my feet.

Brock Schmidt, the man himself, comes out from the back rooms. He is a compact man, dressed to match the gangster aesthetic of his establishment, but despite his small size, he commands attention with an easy authority.

"I swear to god, Brock. I don't know how that card got there."

"Be quiet. I'll deal with you later," Brock says. "I want everyone here to know that cheaters are dealt with in the harshest possible terms." Brock turns to the giant, leaning back to take in the man's full height. "Will you join me in private to discuss how we can make this right, Mr.—?"

"Barrett," the man says. "Barrett Rye."

Yeah. The big fucker? That idiot bruiser who can barely talk? That's me. I told you—never the truth, but never a lie. I learned early on that my size might draw attention, but while plenty of people look at me, nobody sees me. They think my identity ends with my biceps, so my brutishness is the best disguise I have. Nobody wants to think they got outsmarted by the guy who has more muscles than brain cells.

Sorry. I was in the middle of something.

"I didn't do anything," my opponent protests, and he's right. I slipped the card up his sleeve as I grabbed his wrist. "Come on. You all know me."

"Yeah, Richard," one of the bouncers says. "We do."

Richard slumps. The full extent of how fucked he is sinks in. As the bouncers escort him away, I let Brock lead me after them.

"What about my chips?" I ask, looking back at the small pile I had at the table. One of the serving girls is neatly transferring it to a plastic tray.

"Don't worry, Mr. Rye," Brock assures me. He's stopped trying to look me in the eye. It's too much of a strain on his neck. "Your money will be kept safe. Every dollar accounted for. I don't believe I've seen you in here before."

He won't come out and ask me who I am, but I can feel him trying to figure me out. How did I notice what all his people missed?

"No," I say. "I just moved here."

"None of my men saw Richard swap that card."

I shrug. "I don't like cheaters."

"No," he laughs. "I don't think any of us do. If you ever need work, I could use an eye like yours." I'm sure having someone who looks like me on his staff would help burnish his image as well.

"I've got work," I say. My tone doesn't leave room for a follow-up.

"Too bad. In the meantime, we have something of a bounty system around here." He withdraws an envelope from his jacket pocket and holds it out to me.

"A what?"

"A bounty. Five thousand dollars to anyone who helps uncover a cheat. This is only the third time I've had to pay it out."

"Huh," is all I say as I take the envelope. I had known about the bounty program, of course. But I don't want Brock to know that.

The lush appointment of the games room gives way to institutional space in the den's back halls, and Brock tries to direct me to his office. I watch the bouncers lead Richard in the other direction, out to the dark alley behind the building.

"Is that not satisfactory?" Brock follows my gaze.

Silence, I have found, is one of the most powerful tools I have, and so I am silent. I let my frown speak for me. My hands flex slightly. My shoulders tense. Brock wants me to follow him away from the door, but that's not where I need to be. I wait for him to have the idea himself.

"You don't like cheaters," Brock says, feeling out my words. I don't respond. I let the silence work. "They make you angry, and you'd like to express that anger."

I smile back with as much cruelty as I can muster.

"That sounds reasonable to me." Brock turns from his office and leads me into the alley.

CHAPTER 2

Two Months Ago

Enrico Scarpello, the man who ran organized crime in Chicago, had asked me to join him in his office. Most collection guys wouldn't be meeting with him personally, but I'd been working for him since he was a street boss, so I didn't think anything of it. The guys out front waved me in when I arrived.

The old man sat behind his desk, looking pristine as always. He was laughing at something Mickey had said. Mickey was sitting across from him with an accounts book open between them. That was when I knew something had happened. There was no good reason for me and Mickey to be meeting with Scarpello together. Plenty of bad reasons, but no good ones.

Mickey turned, and his smile dropped a fraction of a degree. His lips drew closed across his slightly crooked front tooth. He hadn't known I was coming either. Two bad signs. I kept my face neutral. No reason to give away my concern. There was still a chance that this was something banal. We'd been careful. We hadn't left any sign of what we were doing.

"What's up, boss?" I asked.

Scarpello looked at me, and I knew how fucked we were. "Thank you for joining us," he said. His eyes flicked over my shoulder.

I felt her moving behind me, but I knew better than to look. Scarpello was in control. Whatever he wanted was going to happen. There was a faint stirring as the door closed, and Laia Quintana took up a position beside me.

Laia was a soldier, like me, but the similarities ended there. She was a gun for hire, and her presence meant Scarpello no longer trusted his own organization. She was a small woman, barely a hair over five feet, but as much of a mistake as it is to ignore me for my size, it's worse to do the same to her. She'd tracked guys halfway around the world based only on a whisper. We'd never gotten along, but I respected the hell out of her.

"What's going on, boss?" I asked again as Laia quickly—but thoroughly—patted me down. I tried to keep my expression empty.

"He's clean," Laia said. She slid a chair into the backs of my legs. I rolled forward a bit but stayed standing.

"Sit down, Barrett." Scarpello's tone was conversational. Of course, he didn't call me Barrett. I had a different name then. But I'll keep it consistent here, for your sake. "You've done a lot of quality work for me over the years. You're one of my best earners, squeezing money out of stones I'd given up hope of ever producing, and that alone is enough to win you my admiration."

Mickey was staring forward, his gaze locked onto the space just below Scarpello's chin. He had never been one for conflict or confrontation. It was one of the things I loved about him. He never let this world we lived in harden him. That wasn't what I needed right then, though.

"But my affection"—Scarpello was still talking—"you earned with time and dedication. This world isn't what it was when I was coming up. But you I could always count on. You're like a sledgehammer. I wouldn't try to do algebra with a sledgehammer, but when you need something wrecked, it's always gonna be there for you. You understand what I'm saying?"

"Not really."

At the sound of my voice, Mickey snapped out of his reverie. "Boss," he said. "Whatever you think is going on—"

"Now Mickey here." Scarpello silenced him with a gesture. "Mickey is a whole different sort of creature. He's more like a ferret. Did you know you can train a ferret? They can do tricks. You can even put one to work. But it doesn't matter how well you feed it or how often you play with it, it's still nothing but a fancy weasel. If it sees even the slightest opportunity to advance its furry little life, it'll take it. It doesn't care how bad it hurts you. It doesn't even care if it hurts itself. You put one in a cage and prop the door open with a bit of food, the dumb little shit will eat that food and slam the door on itself every time, even if it knows it's sealing its own fate."

I barely felt the needle as Laia pressed it into my neck—it didn't need to go deep—but the anesthetic burned as it entered my bloodstream.

I swung behind me, favoring speed over accuracy, and Laia must have miscalculated just how fast I could move, because my elbow caught the side of her head.

Mickey came to his feet a second after I did. "Barrett," he said. He was afraid. We'd both known this might happen. "You're bleeding."

I ran my hand over my neck. It would heal. Just a pinprick.

"Did you two really think you could get away with this?" Scarpello was still seated, still looking at us calmly. "Did you really think you could steal from me, and I wouldn't notice?"

"We didn't steal anything," Mickey said. "My books are clean."

"Of course your books are clean. You're smart, Mickey. But you're not smart enough."

The anesthetic was working quickly. I had maybe thirty seconds. No time for anything subtle or clever. It always came down to violence in the end. I took a step toward Scarpello.

Except I didn't. Not quite.

I thought I did. My body moved as though I had, but my feet remained rooted in place, and I toppled over. Maybe I had less than thirty seconds before the drugs took hold.

I hit the ground badly and, doing a quick test of my extremities to see what I could still move, came up with an answer of nothing. I was flat on my chest, my head twisted so I could just see Mickey. The fear in his voice was giving way to full-blown panic.

"Barrett," he said again as he knelt next to me.

I tried to say something to Mickey. To offer him some reassurance, but my mouth wasn't working. All that came out was a bubble of drool.

"Out of respect," said Scarpello, walking around the desk, "for your many years of service to this institution, I will give you one chance to make this right."

"Yes!" Mickey looked up at him. "Anything. Whatever you need, we'll do it."

My vision was starting to darken. The room narrowed down to Mickey and Scarpello and now Laia, standing again beside them.

"Not you, Mickey. You've played your hand, and you've played it poorly." Scarpello looked at me. "Remember this, Barrett. Remember what happens when you forget that you work for me."

Laia drew her sidearm. It was a small piece, a .22LR pistol. You might trust it to take down a raccoon, but not to stop an attacker. She didn't need it to stop an attacker, though. Only a ferret.

I tried to scream. I strained against the numbness that was taking my body away from me, but that battle had been lost before I knew I was fighting it.

"Barrett," Scarpello said as he stepped around Mickey to look me in the eye, and the blackness crawled in from the edges of my vision. "I want you to remember this moment."

"Barrett," Mickey looked away from Laia. He didn't want to see it coming. His eyes met mine. I was supposed to be his protector. I would keep him safe. He had given me everything, and I had given him—

Laia fired three times into his back. The subsonic rounds were pitiful. Mickey deserved a cannon fusillade to send him off, and instead he got this. Three little firecrackers. His eyes went wide, and he fell beside me. His face bounced off the carpet and turned away. I was grateful for this small mercy, that I did not have to watch him go. I couldn't bear the weight of his disappointment in my failure. His hand lay next to mine. I wanted to reach for it. To offer him that small comfort as his life spilled out onto the rug around us.

But I could not give him that. All I had was my failure. The knowledge that when it mattered most, I not only could do nothing but was glad that he couldn't see me. That I didn't have to see him. I wonder now if I could have reached his hand. If I could have tried harder. If the paralytic wasn't the only thing holding me back.

As the black swept down, the last thing I saw was Scarpello leaning over me. I felt dry fingers on my cheek.

"Get me my money."

CHAPTER 3

Peter Van Horn, 10:25 P.M.

The beam from Peter Van Horn's flashlight glints off the coin as it spins. A damp coil of blond hair falls across his eyes as he catches it. He resists the urge to check the result. Instead, he pushes the errant lock back beneath his patrolman's cap, leaving his fate in suspense.

He stands in the darkened third floor of the U-Store-It, a self-storage facility in a mediocre part of town. There is neither enough crime nor enough money to warrant the expense of hiring off-duty police, but management says it's important, and they're willing to pay. They won't fix the rattling in the beleaguered A/C unit, but they'll shell out for a real badge and gun to walk the halls of rolling steel doors.

Most of the officers who moonlight here stay in the lobby, tucked in a corner where the parking lot attendant can't see them, and do whatever it is a person does when they've got an eight-hour shift and nothing to keep them honest.

No one would know if Peter did the same. The building has no interior cameras. But he is paid to patrol, and he can't afford to risk

13

the money. He leads a frugal lifestyle, but a uniformed cop's starting salary hasn't gone up in Omaha in eight years, while the price of nearly everything else has. Add in the debt from his brother's end-of-life care, and these side jobs are the only thing keeping him ahead of the increasingly angry calls from the bank.

So he patrols, and he makes a game of it to pass the empty hours. At each intersection and every stairwell, he flips a coin to determine what route he takes and to see how quickly he can cover the entire building. This time, the first two floors took less than fifty minutes, but now he's stuck in a loop on the third floor among the climate-controlled units. When he reaches stairs, a heads tells him to climb, while tails keeps him on this level. He's flipped eight tails in a row.

The coin sits in his closed fist. Surely it can't be tails again. Nine would be absurd. This run could still come in under a respectable two and a half hours if he can get up to the next and final floor. If he can flip a heads. He uncoils his fingers.

Tails.

It isn't the end of the world. It will be nice, he admits as he wipes at the sweat gathering on his forehead, to spend a bit more time in these cooled hallways. The fourth floor is an oven. Better to stay here.

The key to success is to redefine failure.

After a few steps, though, he pauses. He had thought the rattling was just the A/C fans fighting against the summer heat, but the clang echoing toward him now is something else: slow and careful footsteps.

"Hello?" There's a childish warble to his voice. He grabs the railing, flecked paint and spotted rust scratching at his palm, and leans out over the opening. There is nothing but the darkness between the stairs as they switchback to the ground, twenty-odd feet below.

He steps away from the banister. As his light pulls back, he swears he can see it flashing off something brassy, not the white paint of the handrail but a warm yellow reflection. It's probably a trick of his mind. Like the footsteps. It's only the boredom catching up with him. Even so, he reaches for his taser.

He has it half drawn when he is washed in light.

His first thought—and he will ponder what this says about him later—is one of petulant anger. You can't burn the lights at night. He doesn't think about the danger implied. He doesn't search for cover. His training disappears, and his mind is filled with the storage manager's voice and her overpowering perfume, floral verging on saccharine.

"No overhead lights," she told him before his first shift. "They are on only when we're open. Company policy." Her chins jiggled in time with the waggling of her finger. She could stand to walk the darkened stairs a time or two herself, Peter thought before reprimanding himself for the unkindness.

It's all moot, though. The overhead lights aren't on. A flashlight blinds Peter, and the manager's wrath is the least of his problems.

"Hands in the air!" A voice of authority. The source of the light.

Peter finds himself complying. The voice told him to raise his hands, so he does. Someone else is in charge now. The cuffs of his shirt slide up his forearms. It's been a struggle his whole life to find clothes that fit his lanky frame.

Peter squints into the light but can see only the vague suggestion of a human form. Tall and broad. A straight line from armpit to ankle. The shoulders begin to move. Up and down, in time with the thrumming of the A/C.

"Christ, Petey," the figure says. "You're pale enough, you'd think I'd already shot ya."

Peter knows that voice, with its lilt of cruelty hiding beneath mirthless laughter.

"What are you doing here?" Peter asks.

Owen Oster, one of the senior patrolmen on his shift, lowers the flashlight, his mouth quirked somewhere between a smirk and a sneer. Owen is shorter than Peter but has thirty pounds on the younger officer, and his aggressive confidence has a way of shrinking whoever he's talking to. He joined the force right out of high school—it seemed the easiest way to continue winning respect and adulation—and after twenty years hasn't risen above the rank of patrolman. He's never seen much need to.

"I'd ask you the same thing," Owen says. "Police are supposed to give orders, not take them. It's what that's for." Owen shines his light at Peter's belt and the pistol hanging off it.

"Right. Sorry," Peter says, jamming his taser back into its holster.

"I'm just fucking with you, Petey." Owen claps Peter on the shoulder. "You gotta relax, or this job'll send you to an early grave." With gentle but irrefutable pressure, Owen directs Peter to the other stairs, the most direct route back to the lobby.

Peter takes a calming breath. He doesn't like being caught unprepared, and he certainly was not prepared for this, but getting his hackles up now won't fix anything.

"What are you doing here, Oster?" Peter goes back to the question. Back to the script.

"I've been looking for you. Why don't you just stay by the front door?"

"We're supposed to patrol the building. That's what the client wants."

"The client doesn't know shit about what they want. That's why they hire us. Anyone wants to rob this place, they'll come through the front, hit the lower levels, and get all the cash out of the leasing office. Meantime what are you doing? Dicking around up here, working twice as hard to do half as much."

"You came out here to berate my professional technique?" Peter sweeps his hair back under his cap.

"Sarge didn't call you?"

"No," Peter says. He checks his phone to be sure. No missed calls.

"He said he would. Sent me to relieve you. You've hit your hours for the week."

More company policy. The department allows its officers to moonlight for only twenty hours a week, and their records on this are meticulous. They get a cut of the officer's pay. The uniforms, weapons, and badges are city property, after all.

"That's bullshit." Peter doesn't like to swear. He's been practicing—he needs to curse to survive on the force—but the words don't feel natural. "This is my first night this week."

"I can only tell you what Sarge told me. I'm supposed to send you home and finish out the night for you."

"These are my hours," Peter protests. "I barely get any to begin with. How does he think I hit twenty?" Sarge's policy is that the more senior an officer, the more priority they get in selecting jobs, and Peter has no seniority.

"Someone must have misfiled a time sheet." Owen shrugs. "You know what the department is like."

Peter still has his phone out. He starts to pull up Sarge—properly Sergeant Phillip Nowicki—in his contacts.

"You want to wake him up over this?" Owen casts a skeptical eye at Peter.

"Didn't you just talk to him?"

"That was two hours ago. I had to get dressed, get over here, and find you."

"I need these hours, Oster." Peter feels like a boy begging his father for a quarter to put in the gumball machine.

"You'll get it sorted in the morning," Owen says around a yawn. "Besides, you seem a bit stressed. The time off will do you good."

"The extra pay will do me good," Peter snaps.

Owen's expression softens. "I remember starting out. If you need money, let me know. We're all brothers in the badge, right? There's easier ways to make a few bucks."

A thread of danger lurks behind the casualness in the offer. Peter knows that Owen and his partner are in somebody's pocket. The whole station knows, but so long as they get their paperwork in on time, nobody seems bothered.

"I just want my hours."

The corruption in the force bothers Peter, but in the same way that kids in Africa with worms burrowing through their feet bother him. It's sad, but he has neither the power nor the inclination to do anything about it. If Owen forced him to choose between open conflict or dipping into the dirty water—well, Peter has never been one for fighting.

"I tell you what," Owen says. "I've got a shift later this week at some private thing downtown. You get this sorted out with Sarge before then, and I'll give you that. Help make up for tonight. Yeah?"

Peter is still on edge. The pieces don't line up. He knows he didn't mess up his paperwork, and Sarge's filing system is more precious to him than his children. There's something more going on here, but he is out of objections. And at the end of the day, so long as he gets his hours, he's satisfied.

"Sure," he says. "Thanks, Oster."

"Call me Owen, yeah?" Owen drags a chair into the corner of the lobby.

In his car outside, Peter realizes he should have asked Owen what Sarge was doing on duty so late and why he called Owen about it. But for all that Owen's story doesn't make sense, there is one bit of truth in it. Waking up Sarge would be a mistake. Peter can clear it up in the morning. Satisfied with this plan, he drives away, waving cheerily to the parking guard, who gives him a curious tilt of her head as she lifts the gate arm.

It isn't until he's almost halfway home that he realizes he didn't see Owen's car anywhere in the parking lot. Another curiosity to add to the list. Another question to be answered in the morning.

CHAPTER 4

Jim Pickens, 10:28 P.M.

Hello?" a voice calls down from above with a querulous pitch. Conrad uses an arm to hold Jim Pickens back against the wall. At least, Pickens thinks Conrad is the man's name. He was never formally introduced to the surly cop or his partner.

"Stay back," Conrad whispers as a flashlight plays across the stairs around them. "And stay quiet."

Pickens fixes Conrad with his best withering glare. It was Conrad's clunking footsteps that drew the attention of the guard.

Conrad appears unmoved in the face of Pickens's scorn. It seems very little could move the stout wall of a man. A trio of crooks in his nose and extensive scarring across his meaty knuckles stand testament to those who have tried, and failed, to do so in the past.

The flashlight recedes, and voices start to filter down as Conrad's partner, Owen, talks with the guard up above. Pickens is glad to have been left with the quieter of the pair. Conrad strikes him as the more honest. He wears his cruelty on his sleeve. As the voices head away, Conrad lets him go.

"Unit 327," Conrad says, gesturing for him to take the lead.

"I know," Pickens replies, voice straining as he hefts the heavy duffel containing his tools. Conrad lifts the empty bag that will, if all goes well, carry away their prize. "I got the same briefing you did."

The two make their way in uncompanionable silence up to the third floor, guided only by the scant light spilling through the barred windows. They stop at one of the largest units in the building, nearly twenty feet across and secured by a trio of heavy shackle locks, each of a different design. Pickens smiles. It's been too long since he had a challenge.

"Can you give me a light?" he asks.

"Not until we get the all clear from Owen." Conrad's focus is on the hallway.

Pickens just shrugs and unrolls his leather tool case. Carefully nestled inside is an array of tension bars and rakes, plus a variety of hooks, shims, and devices whose names, much less purpose, are beyond the officer's ken.

A light bouncing around the corner presages Owen's return. Conrad tenses, one hand on his service weapon, until his partner comes into view.

"Any trouble with the kid?" Conrad asks.

"I thought he was gonna cry when I sent him home. Looked like I just told him his puppy had cancer."

"Were we ever that dumb?"

"Me?" Owen laughs. "No. You took a few more hits to the head, though."

"Keeping you safe from the line." There is more vitriol than Pickens would have expected from the cop.

Owen smiles, hoping to defuse his partner's anger. "For which I will be forever grateful."

From below them, kneeling before the three locks, Pickens clears his throat. "Can I get some light now?"

"I thought you were the best," Owen says. "Could get into a bank safe with your eyes closed."

"I am, and I could," Pickens says. "But unless you want me to scratch these cylinders and leave proof we were here so obvious even you couldn't cover it up, I'd suggest you give me a light so I can see what I'm doing."

"I'm just messing with you. Don't get your panties twisted."

Pickens hates working with cops, the openly dirty ones most of all. A dirty cop is a dangerous variable, liable at any moment to lash out and assert their respectability. Pickens, regardless of how well he dresses or finely he talks, will always be just a thug, an uppity Black boy grasping beyond his station. Pickens, to their mind, is a criminal because it is in his bestial nature, while the dirty cop is only dirty because the world would not otherwise give him what he is duly owed.

Pickens sets to work, lest he say something he regrets.

The locks are good, custom jobs from skilled designers. Every obvious weakness has been closed. But for a talented picker, there is never a question of if a lock can be opened. Only how quickly. Thanks to solid intelligence letting Pickens know what he'd be up against tonight, it takes him eight minutes.

"Et voila," he says with a flourish as the third latch releases.

Owen just stares at him. "We can go in now?"

Pickens nods and starts putting away his tools. "Damn fine work there, Pickens. I've never seen a pick so clean," he says to a tension rod. "Oh, why thank you, Pickens. How kind of you to say."

"Wait," Owen says, pulling on a pair of nitrile gloves. "Your name is Pickens?"

"Mm-hmm."

"And you pick locks?" That's Conrad.

Pickens rolls his eyes, though he keeps his head down so the cops can't see it. "We've still got work to do tonight."

As Owen opens the door, the smell of dust and oilcloth, old wood, and plastic sheeting washes out across them. The three men stare into the storage unit. Six hundred square feet, all of it packed, floor to ceiling, with art.

It is a haphazard and chaotic collection. No common interest, theme, or origin unites the pieces. A dozen busts line one wall, their shapes barely discernible beneath a drop cloth. Racks of paintings are piled up against crates. A huge Turkish rug is rolled up in the back, running the width of the room.

Owen moves first, reaching out for a Pwoom Itok mask, his expression mirroring its bulbous eyes.

"Touch nothing," Conrad whispers to him.

"I'm wearing gloves."

"Those were our orders."

Owen relents silently, focusing instead on Pickens. "Let's get this done."

"He said it's in the back," Pickens says, shouldering his bag of tools once more and taking the empty bag from Conrad.

"I know what he said. Conrad, can you keep watch out here, make sure the kid doesn't come back?"

"Sure," Conrad says. "But don't touch anything back there."

"Come on, man. They'll never miss one little thing." Owen points to a wavy bowl of blue-and-green glass. "What about this?"

"The hell are you gonna do with a Chihuly?"

Pickens doesn't look up, not wanting the cops to see his surprise that Conrad recognized the artist.

"I was gonna eat some Cap'n Crunch," Owen says with a grin. "Who the fuck's Chihooey?"

"Chihuly," Conrad corrects him. "Don't you remember ninth grade? That field trip to the Joslyn Museum? They had a bunch of his shit there."

"No," Owen says. "I don't remember a ninth-grade field trip." He steps back from the bowl, though, his hands raised in surrender. "I was just joking around. I'm not gonna take anything."

It doesn't take Pickens long, despite the clutter, to find what he's looking for. The safe is solid-looking but otherwise unremarkable. It is black steel, several feet to a side, with a dial and a handle on the front. There is a small patch of open space, just enough room for the door to swing open, where Pickens starts unloading his gear, assembling his portable drill press.

"Give me a hand with this?" he asks.

The main body of the boxy tool is nearly as large as the safe itself and hangs from four mounting arms. Owen grunts in surprise at the weight of the thing, but together they hoist it into position above the safe. Once Pickens is satisfied that it's secure, he waves Owen away.

"Shouldn't it be on the front?" Owen asks. "Where the door is?"

"No," Pickens says. "The front is the strongest part. This safe was designed to be mounted in cement to protect the top. It'll be easier to go in through there and get at the lock from behind."

"Why wouldn't they put it in cement, then?"

"Because whoever installed this just bought the heaviest, most expensive safe on offer without paying any attention to the actual situation they'd be using it in."

Owen nods sagely, as though he had known this all along and was merely testing Pickens's expertise.

"This might get loud," Pickens says, offering Owen a pair of earplugs.

Owen waves them away. "Do what you gotta do."

Pickens shrugs, puts in his own plugs, and sets to work.

Metal screams beneath the drill bit as Pickens operates it with a steady hand. He then uses a punch rod guided by a fiber-optic camera to reach inside and manipulate the safe's inner workings. Owen and Conrad barely have time to grow bored before there is a heavy thud as the locking bolts retract and the door falls open.

"Is it in there?" Owen asks.

"Give me a light," Pickens says. "Let's find out."

Owen crouches beside Pickens, and the two men look into the safe. Owen's face falls.

"There's another safe," he says. "I don't get it. Why's there a safe inside the safe?"

"Redundancy," Pickens says. "Like the three locks outside. Each was different, needed different tools and different skills to open."

Owen stares at the safe, unsure exactly what Pickens is saying. "Are you gonna open that one, too?"

"Yes," Pickens says. "But not here. Back at Holzmann's." Pickens carefully slides the safe into the extra duffel. While he breaks down and packs away his drill, Owen and Conrad go through the storage unit, ensuring that they've left no trace of their presence.

The three men leave the same way they came, through a hole in the fence behind the U-Store-It's loading dock, where Conrad's Jeep is waiting for them.

Pickens is only in Omaha for this job, and Holzmann was insistent that he be driven everywhere by his trusted people. A rental car might leave a GPS trail of Pickens's movements, and cabs would be even worse. So Pickens has another thirty minutes of the cops' presence to enjoy. They seem content to ignore him, though, and he is more than happy to return the favor.

He watches, instead, the changing landscapes as Conrad drives them away from the industrial environs surrounding the U-Store-It. Wire-topped fences around broad, boxy buildings give way to wide streets, strip malls, and subdevelopments, and ultimately—as they leave the city proper and Route 6 turns into a freeway—to striped green fields of soybeans.

CHAPTER 5

Barrett Rye, 10:29 P.M.

I may not have been here before, but I know this place. This temple to misery where all the shit that makes the shiny and polished casino run is tucked away, out of sight. Richard is already on the ground, protecting his face from the two bouncers. Brock calls them off, and I take their place.

I take no pleasure in hitting Richard Sands. I tell myself—and I know this is me rationalizing—that I am not beating him for me. I am beating him for the girlfriend he sent to the hospital three times in two years. I'm beating him for the working girl whose nose he broke after that girlfriend finally took out a restraining order. I'm beating him for the trail of misery that he leaves in his wake, though I know that I, of all people, shouldn't be throwing stones on that account. I've made my living hurting people, only a tiny fraction of whom deserved it. But at least I'm trying to change. That's why I'm here.

"Stand up," I say. I don't enjoy this, but I need them to believe I do. I grab Richard's lapel and drag him to his knees. A seam in his jacket gives way. It's a fine-looking piece, but the stitching is cheap.

"I didn't do anything," he wails.

I hit him in the face, and he crumples. He tries to crawl away from me. I just want to finish what I came for and get out.

I grab his jacket again, but he slips free of it. There's something heavy in it. He looks back over his shoulder and sees me rifling through his pockets.

"Hey!" he calls. His mouth is bleeding, and a red mist accompanies the cry. I feel like I'm going to be sick. "Stop that!"

In the right breast pocket I find a lump of metal a bit larger than a quail egg, with a little button and an LED light at one end, a loop for a keychain at the other. It is smooth and cool against my fingers. I lift it out, and his eyes go wide.

"That's mine!" he shouts.

Everything I've done tonight was to get me here, to get this little ball of steel. This is how I'll get the money I need to get Scarpello off my back. Brock and his bouncers are looking the other way, bearing witness to nothing at all. I hold out the metal spheroid and gesture for Richard to come take it. He crawls back to me, his hand outstretched for the silvery bauble.

"Please give that back."

My fist closes around it, and I slug him in the jaw. He falls again. I don't want to hear him whimper anymore. I walk back to Brock, keeping the metal hidden in my palm, as he wraps up a conversation with his pit boss.

"I think I'm done," I say.

"Of course," Brock says, paying no mind to Richard on the ground behind me. "The pot from your last hand has been awarded to you, and we've taken the liberty of cashing out your chips." He passes me another, smaller stack of cash that I slide into the envelope alongside the bounty.

I cover the palmed egg with the envelope and drop the whole thing into my pocket.

Brock's eyes stay on the abraded skin of my knuckles. "Perhaps you would like to wash up before returning to the game?"

"I'm done for the night," I say. I got what I came for.

◆

When I was eight years old, I wanted to be a magician. When I was eleven, puberty hit with the strength of—well—me. By the time I was twelve, I was five foot six and just shy of a hundred and fifty pounds. I was six-eight when I dropped out of high school. There are only so many things that the world says a man of my size with skin that looks like mine can be, and I was never one for team sports. I don't like relying on other people, and I hate them relying on me. With no diploma and no demonstrable skills, it wasn't long before I got into trouble, and when Scarpello offered me a way out—a way to earn respect—I leapt at the chance.

CHAPTER 6

Jim Pickens, 11:23 P.M.

Elkhorn is a wealthy enclave on Omaha's western flank. Oversized ranch homes hang back from the streets, peeking around landscaped copses of maple and hornbeam. Henry Holzmann has built his headquarters here, ensconced among Omaha's finest citizens, on a four-acre lot surrounded by a twelve-foot fence. His is the only property in the development with such a wall—the neighbors prefer to display their wealth—and it required a special dispensation from the HOA for him to build it.

"I've got your delivery here," Conrad says to the intercom at the gate. With a buzz, the pedestrian door opens, but the iron and wood slab that bars the driveway remains unmoved.

"We never go onto the property," Owen says before Pickens can ask the question. "It keeps everything cleaner."

"Right," Pickens says. "It's been a pleasure."

Two men come out of the gate and silently help him with his gear.

"I've got this one," Pickens says, holding the safe close as he follows the men onto the estate.

A small guardhouse stands just inside the wall, and the driveway bends lazily across the wide lawn toward the house. It's a two-story mansion with half-timbered walls over a brick base. The grounds around it are kept clear, and a stone path circles the whole property. Holzmann had wanted to have floodlights installed but decided that the increased security was not worth the additional scrutiny it would draw from his neighbors.

At the front door, another guard frisks Pickens before leading him to the boss's office, where Holzmann waits with his lieutenant, Benny D'Angelo.

Benny stares at the little safe as Pickens places it on Holzmann's desk. It doesn't look like one of the most secure safes in the world. It doesn't even look stronger than the ones they put in the hotel closet to hold your wallet and passport while you're down at the pool. He touches it and feels the steel flex beneath even gentle pressure.

"Do not touch," Holzmann says without looking at his lieutenant. He stands at the bay window in the back of his private office. His rigid posture belies his age, and careful military tailoring conceals a growing paunch and slope to his shoulders. Despite having spent the overwhelming majority of his life in America, he has guarded his Berlin accent.

"He won't break it," Pickens says. "You can do whatever you want to the skin. It's only once you get inside that you need to be careful." Pickens is setting up his drill press once again, hanging it this time, as Owen had originally expected, from the front of the safe. He marks five spots around the dial and places a guard exactly twenty-four millimeters from the end of his drill bit.

Holzmann nods sagely. "The policemen did their work?"

"They did." Pickens keeps his tone carefully flat. Owen and Conrad would not have been his first choice in partners, but they had, as promised, kept security away.

"Good," Holzmann says. "It is important to choose men on whom we can rely and to put aside all other considerations. Most important is the trust which we must have in our lieutenants." He turns from the window to observe Pickens's reaction to this wisdom, but Pickens remains focused on his work. Holzmann points to a framed print on the wall, one of several military portraits, of a baby-faced young man in a high-collared uniform with a swept-back shock of dark hair. "Carl von Clausewitz. One of the most brilliant strategic minds humanity has ever produced. Prussian, of course."

"What the boss is saying"—Benny leans over to Pickens—"is that when you want something done, you gotta pick the right guy."

Holzmann strides across the room, arms locked in place behind his back. "It is good we hired Herr Pickens for his technical skill and not his philosophical insights."

"I just don't see what I could add to the great masters. Clausewitz, Bismarck, Moltke." Pickens gestures to each of the portraits in turn.

Holzmann pauses in his pacing, surprised and pleased. "Very good, Herr Pickens. And now you will make me very happy to open that safe."

"You have the key for me?"

Benny replies more quickly than Holzmann can. "You said you could open anything."

"Sure," Pickens sighs. "I can open it. That's trivial. The key doesn't unlock it. It disables a security core at the safe's center. If this door opens even the tiniest crack before that core is disconnected, the whole chamber floods with a mix of nitric, hydrofluoric, and hydrochloric acids. Anything inside will be reduced to slag. The only way to prevent that is with the key."

"Why would someone do that?" Benny takes a careful step back, as though his presence might trigger the device.

"If you have something you would rather destroy than lose," Holzmann says. He looks again out the bay window. Pickens is not the only guest he is expecting tonight. "Call Herr Sands. He should have already been here."

Benny puts the call on speaker for Holzmann's benefit. It rings six times before Richard Sands answers, and when he does, it is clear he's in pain.

"Where is the key, Richard?" Benny asks. There is a long silence before Richard responds.

"So about that—there's a bit of a problem."

Benny looks to Holzmann, who frowns but says nothing.

"What kind of problem?" Benny prompts when Richard doesn't continue.

"I had the key, and I was on my way to you guys when this fucking goon—"

Holzmann's face sours, and Benny interrupts the story. "Language, Richard."

"Right, sorry. So this goon, biggest mother—" Richard catches himself. "Biggest guy you've ever seen. Big as a truck. This guy corners me in an alley, sucker punches me, and takes the key."

Holzmann and Benny huddle in a whispered conference before Benny returns to the phone. "Why would he want the key? You said it's just a metal ball."

"I don't know, but I'll get it back." Even Pickens can hear the desperation in Richard's voice.

"And how do you plan on doing that?" Benny asks.

"I got the guy's name. Barrett Rye."

At a gesture from Holzmann, Benny ends the call. "What do you want to do, sir?"

"Put our police friends on it," Holzmann says after a moment's consideration. "I want to know everything about this Barrett Rye."

CHAPTER 7

Eight Months Ago

Mickey and I were in bed together. He was tracing the curve of my pec and chuckling to himself.

"What is it?" I asked.

He looked up at me, and I felt all over again the wash of fear and joy that always came when he looked at me. His smile was so pure. I had done nothing to deserve that smile. What right did my hands—my filthy, bloody hands—have to touch his skin? He flushed red. "You're looking at me like that again."

"I am not!" I don't know how he saw through me so easily.

"You are," he said. "But I don't mind." He laid his head against my chest. His stubble scratched me as he smiled.

"What were you laughing at?" I pressed. "Don't think I didn't notice you change the subject."

"Double negative." He tried halfheartedly to push away from me, but I held him close. He liked to feel my strength.

"I'll double your negative."

"What does that even mean?" He laughed. God, I could live in that laughter. I don't give a fuck if that doesn't make sense. It does to me.

"What were you laughing at?"

He grew quiet and smiled again. "It was nothing."

"Oh, it must have been real bad," I said. "Now you've gotta tell me."

"I was just thinking that you—" He put a hand on my chest. "This is really stupid." I was silent. He went back to idly playing with the lines of my chest. The blush moved across his neck. "I was just thinking that you've got bigger tits than most of the women I've been with."

Later, as I was falling asleep, I felt him moving behind me. Shifting. Unable to get comfortable. There was something on his mind, but I knew I couldn't push him. He would share when he was ready.

Eventually, I heard him take a deep breath, let it out, and say, "Hey, Barrett?"

"Yeah?"

More silence as he thought through whatever he needed to.

"You still awake?" He was stalling.

"Yeah."

"How long do you want to keep doing this?"

I felt my heartbeat accelerate. I was sure he could feel it with his arm thrown around me. Could feel the sweat prickling up on my back. How long did I want to keep doing this? I'd never been with someone like Mickey before. Never let anyone know me like Mickey did. I wanted to keep doing this for as long as he would allow it. Unless that wasn't what he meant. Maybe that wasn't what he meant? Please let that not be what he meant.

"Keep doing what?" I tried to keep the nerves out of my voice.

"This work." It wasn't what he meant.

I rolled over to face him. "I dunno. This is just what I do."

35

"It makes you miserable," he said, and he was right. I did hate it, but it was all I'd ever known. I didn't let myself think that life might have more to offer than misery served up at Scarpello's altar to greed. I had never thought I could have someone like Mickey either, though.

"What else would I do?"

"Whatever you want," he said. "We could go legit. I could get a CPA license. We could leave Chicago. Go somewhere new. There's nothing here for us." He was talking quickly, trying to not leave a moment of silence for me to fill with a *no*.

"Where would we go?" I asked.

"I don't know. Where do you want to go?"

I wasn't sure. I'd never imagined leaving. This was just who I was. I was a mob enforcer, a professional boogeyman. But now Mickey was making me think about it, and I knew—as surely and as desperately as I knew that I wanted him—I knew I wanted it. Whatever he was offering, so long as it wasn't here and wasn't this, so long as it was with him, I wanted it.

"I want," I started. The words fought to stay inside. As soon as I said them, I could never take them back. Never pretend they weren't there. I didn't like the work, but I had Mickey to make it bearable. And if I said no, he would drop this. That would be the end of it. We would continue our lives, continue our work, continue being miserable in all things except each other.

Maybe that was enough. Who was I to think I deserved a life with everything? I had found Mickey. Should I not be satisfied with that? I took a breath to tell him no. We shouldn't dream of what we can never have. I felt his arm tighten as he held me closer, and I realized that he hadn't breathed since I last spoke. He was as afraid as I was, but he had been brave enough to ask the question. The least I could do was answer it.

"I want to leave with you." Saying the words raised gooseflesh down my arms.

Mickey let go of his held breath. "I can get us new documents. Set us up far away, and we can start again."

"How quickly?" I asked. Now that the hope was there, the idea of returning to work pained me.

"It'll take time," he said. "We need to be careful if we want to do this right. And I'll need money to get us started."

"Then let's get you some money," I said. And that's what we did.

◆

None of that is important right now, though. The why and the how of getting from there to here. What matters is that the five-thousand-dollar bounty from Brock is nice, but it barely even registers against what I owe Scarpello, and certainly wasn't worth the risk of slipping a card up Richard's sleeve. I am playing a longer game now.

You learned, or at least I did from a childhood of heist movies, that a con requires cleverness and wit and, above all else, a joyful capacity to lie. To not just present untruths, but to drown the target in such overwhelming inundations of charming bullshittery that the facts can't withstand the patter. It also requires a plan, the more convoluted the better, that leaves the victim trapped in a twisting labyrinth, helpless to piece it all together in the aftermath.

Maybe that works for some folks, but I've got a different take. Running a con is not about lying, nor is it about planning. There are too many pieces in play to predict them all, and anyone who says they can is lying to you. A con artist isn't a conductor; they're a tickler.

Do you know those fishermen who stand in a river with no equipment, watching as the fish swim past in their chaotic multitudes?

They study the fish, searching for patterns in their movements and waiting for the precise moment that one swims right beneath their legs, and then they strike. If they time it right, they can run their hand beneath the fish, grab it by the gills, and lift it wholly out of the water. That's tickling, and that's what I do. I watch the chaos, waiting for the right time to strike.

I might try to nudge the fish one way or another, but I can't control the whole school. So the thing at Brock's wasn't about the five thousand dollars. It was about creating a situation where I could get what I was really after, which was that little ball of polished steel I'd taken out of Richard's pocket. That, I knew, was valuable.

I couldn't have just stolen it off him, though. That would have drawn too much attention. I needed to look harmless, or at least as harmless as someone like me can look. Hapless, more like. Just an innocent idiot who'd stumbled into something beyond my meager comprehension.

I'd left them enough clues to track me down. I'm in the water, arm cocked back and at the ready. Now I wait and see if the fish will swim to me.

SATURDAY

CHAPTER 8

Cass Mullen, 6:47 A.M.

F uck you," Cassiopeia Mullen mumbles at the shrill buzz of her alarm. Her eyes won't open in the morning light. It takes her several seconds to come out of her dream and place herself. She's in her bed. Her phone is beside her on the TV table she uses for a nightstand. Pawing at it, she knocks it to the ground, and then follows it herself as the sheets, tossed away in the restless heat of the night, tangle and catch at her ankles.

"Fuck," she hisses, kicking free of the fabric. She can see the phone. The screen is dark, but the blaring of the alarm continues. It isn't coming from her phone but from the intercom box in the living room.

Her own face reflects back at her in the black of her TV screen. From this angle she almost can't see the cleft that pulls her lip toward her nose. She almost can't see the thing that will forever mark her, forever mar her.

Almost.

She will always be the freak with the fucked-up face, the one with the family too poor to afford the basic surgery to fix it. No matter what else she does, she will always be that first.

"Fuck right the fuck off with that noise!" she shouts. But the buzzing continues. The world doesn't care how loudly you rage at it. It will only change when you grab and twist and force it to fix its shit.

"You OK, Cass?" A voice from the next room. "I heard something fall."

"Yeah, Jonny Boy. I'm fucking fine." She glances back at the bed. At least Vic seems to have slept through the whole fiasco.

She's gotta stop sleeping with Vic. It gives the wrong impression. Makes them think they're all equal here in her little gang.

She's been telling herself this since they were fifteen, but seven years later, nothing has changed. With her blood up after a successful burglary, it's hard not to drag him to her bed. It would be easier if he weren't so fucking good at it. If he weren't just stupid fucking hot.

The intercom buzzes again.

"Who the fuck is here at six fucking A.M.?"

"I dunno," Jonny Boy says through the door of her room.

"Well find the fuck out!" She pulls on some shorts and a tank top. It looks like she's up for the day. Vic rolls over in the bed behind her, and she pauses briefly. Christ, but the man is gorgeous. He spends too much time at the gym, but it is time well fucking spent. With the sheets on the ground, he is fully on display.

Beautiful, compliant, without a single ambition beyond whatever she needs him to do. Why can't they all be like him?

Jonny Boy cracks open her door and breaks her from her reverie. The fat man is looking at Vic in her bed. She can't figure out whether he's jealous of Vic for getting to fuck her, or jealous of her for taking Vic away from him.

"It's Richard outside," Jonny Boy says. "Says he's got work for us."

"Fuck Richard," she says, picking her way carefully from her room, around the spent vape cartridges and forgotten take-out containers, to the front door.

Jonny Boy moves to the kitchen and last night's pizza on the counter.

"There anything left?" she asks him.

"Just one slice," he says. He pulls it from the box and holds it out to her. "You want it?"

"Fuck no," she says. "Trash that shit. Fuck, man, that's how you get salmonella or some shit."

Jonny Boy looks at the slice forlornly, his sad little face falling into a sad little frown, before tossing it. Hers might be the most pathetic second-story crew in the city, but at least they follow orders. She jams the button on the intercom.

"The fuck do you want, Richard?"

There's a pause before Richard responds, trying to figure out, no doubt, what tack to take. He usually meets her vitriol in kind, but you don't get to wake a person up at the ass crack of dawn and then get twisted when they're a bit short.

"A pleasure as always to hear your dulcet tones, Cassiopeia." His voice crackles through the box. "How are you this fine morning?"

"I'm fucking tired, Richard. You know what time it is?"

"No. I don't. I've had a night, and you're gonna want to hear what I've got for you."

"I swear to Christ, if it isn't scald-your-dick hot, I'll fucking murder you, waking me up this early."

After buzzing Richard in, Cass orders Jonny Boy to throw on a pot of coffee while she gives her mouth a quick rinse with some Listerine. She gives it a five-count after Richard knocks before she takes a seat on the one detritus-free section of the sofa and gestures Jonny Boy to let him in.

"Jonny Boy! How's it going, big guy?" Richard doesn't wait for a response, sliding past Jonny Boy's prodigious girth and into the apartment. Richard's vanity has always kept him immaculately assembled, but he's here now in a torn suit with a swollen lip crusted with blood.

"Jesus Christ," Cass says. "The fuck happened to you?"

"Like I said, it's been a night." Richard searches the room for a spot to sit amidst the trash.

Jonny Boy grabs a towel from the kitchen counter—the fuck is a bath towel doing there? Cass really needs to have a word with the boys about keeping this place presentable—and lays it across a chair for him. Richard perches, instead, on the arm of Jonny Boy's favorite recliner.

"Where's pretty boy?" Richard asks. "I don't want to have to explain this twice, and time is of the essence here."

Cass yells for Vic, and a moment later he comes out of her room, as naked as the day he was born.

"Hey, Richard," he says with a smile. "How's it going?"

"Not too fucking good." Richard grabs the towel that Jonny Boy had offered and tosses it to Vic. "How's it going with you?"

"I can't complain." Vic wraps the towel around his waist and sits down next to Cass, his leg resting against hers. She glares at him, but he doesn't seem to notice. This is why you don't fuck your crew.

Jonny Boy drags a beanbag out of the bedroom that he and Vic usually share and collapses into it.

"All right, Richard," Cass says. "We're all here. Tell me what the fuck this is about."

"Somebody stole something of mine," he says. "You three are going to get it back."

"We're gonna need more than that," Cass says when Richard doesn't provide any further details. "What got stolen?"

"A key."

Vic exhales heavily beside her. "Oh, man," he says. "I locked myself out of my house once. My abuela's house, actually, but still—"

Cass puts a hand on Vic's shoulder, trying to quiet him. He's a steady hand in a scrap, and his devotion to the crew is beyond reproach, but he doesn't contribute much to a conversation. He leans into the touch, and she jerks her hand back.

Richard raises an eyebrow. She shouldn't have touched Vic, but having done that, she sure as fuck shouldn't have pulled away from it. She can feel the heat rising in her cheeks.

"I called a locksmith," Vic says, looking from Cass to Richard and back when neither responds. "Have you tried a locksmith?"

"We're talking now, Vic," Cass says. "Tell me more about this key."

Vic quiets and settles back into the couch, resting his arm against hers. She tries to ignore it, then leaves for the kitchen. For a cup of coffee.

"It's the key to a safe," Richard says, twisting around on his perch to keep her in view. "A little electronic fob, like a car remote."

"I'm guessing you stole it from your job?" Cass asks. Richard's silence is confirmation enough. "Why not steal another?" Coffee in hand, she comes back into the living room but doesn't return to the couch.

"'Cause this thing is one of a kind. It has a chip with a code on it that's not stored anywhere else in the world."

"All right," Cass says. "We'll get you back your special key, but first you gotta tell me, who'd you steal it for?"

Richard glares at her. "I stole it for myself. I'm working on something."

"Right." Cass points to the door. "You don't want to tell the truth, you can fuck right off."

"I've got plans of my own, you know."

"All the time we've known Richard Sands," Cass says to Jonny Boy, "he ever strike you as the sort to do something on his own initiative?"

Jonny Boy thinks for a second and then shrugs. "I guess not?"

Richard is pissed off. Cass can see that much. He wants to lash out at them, but he came here asking her a favor. The man might sell snake oil, but part of that is knowing when not to push, and Cass is not one to be pushed right now.

"Fuck it," Richard says. "I stole the key for Holzmann. He's got a safe he needs to get into, and he knows I'm the man to do it."

"Clearly not." Cass says it before the thought is fully formed. There's no need to antagonize Richard further, but there it is, the insult let fly.

"Fuck you," he spits at her. Vic is on his feet and across the room. More things are happening than she can process. Vic lost the towel in his haste and stands now, inches away from Richard, in all his naked glory.

"You wanna kick my ass, Vic? Go the fuck ahead. It'll be the perfect goddamned capstone to a perfect fucking night." His lip has started bleeding again.

Jonny Boy looks up at the two of them. His eyes are too round, two dumb little circles giving him a look of perpetual injured shock. He starts lumbering to his feet, but he takes his time about it. If there's going to be a beatdown, he knows he should be a part of it, but he's got no true love of violence. On her less generous days, Cass wonders why she keeps him around, but he's always stuck by her. That's gotta count for something in this world.

"What do you want me to do, Cass?" Vic doesn't take his eyes off Richard.

"It's too early to fight," Cass says. "You're bleeding on my chair, Richard. Jonny Boy, go get the Band-Aids. Vic, I need more coffee."

Vic grabs the towel from the floor and takes Cass's mug. "You want any, Richard?" he asks, all malice vanished. Richard shakes his head and wipes the blood from his face with a torn cuff.

"So what's going on with this key?" Cass asks. She sits back down, hoping to let a bit of the tension out of the conversation.

"Holzmann hired me to get it. I borrowed it from work. It was from some custom job they did years ago for this paranoid old fuck. We've got the only copy in the world and no way to make more of them. I was supposed to grab it from the lockup, run it to Holzmann, and get it back to the office before we open in the morning."

Jonny Boy comes back from the bathroom with a couple of butterfly bandages and a cotton ball. "You want me to take a look at that?" He reaches out to dab at the blood oozing from Richard's lip.

"I'm fine." Richard pushes the cotton away.

"He's got a gentle touch," Vic calls from the kitchen.

Richard ignores him. "So I got the key last night but had a while before I was supposed to deliver it. I wasn't gonna go early and spend a couple hours sitting around doing nothing, so I went to Brock's to burn off some nerves."

"Please tell me you didn't fucking bet the key," Cass says.

"You take me for that much of an idiot?" Before Cass can respond, Richard continues. "Don't answer that. We're getting along too well. But no, I didn't bet the key. I was feeling good, on a hot streak, when this fucking goon got it in his head that I'm cheating. And no, before you ask, I wasn't. But this guy grabs my arm and, fuck if I know how it got there, pulls a goddamned card out of my sleeve."

"At Brock's?" Vic comes back with Cass's coffee and sits again beside her.

"Right at the goddamned table. So they drag me out back, and as I'm getting the shit kicked out of me, this fucker goes through my pockets and decides that Holzmann's key is his just recompense."

"Brock's a businessman," Cass says. "Just buy it back."

"He wasn't Brock's goon. He was just some fucking guy."

"So you want us to track down some random dude?"

"I already did the hard part for you," Richard says. "The fucking idiot introduced himself. Said his name was Barrett Rye. Then, as I was wandering the streets trying to figure out what to do, just before my phone died, I looked him up on Facebook. He's set to public, and his whole page is selfies of him in his apartment, and—and this is the best part—I know the fucking building. I put their security system in."

"All right," Cass says. "So we head there, get your key back, and that's it?"

"That's it," Richard says. "You can make five thousand dollars before breakfast."

"You have five grand on you?" Cass asks. When dealing with Richard, it's always best to get paid up front.

"No," Richard says. "But this Barrett fucker does. I saw Brock hand it to him as a reward for spotting the card in my sleeve. All I want is the key. Anything else you can find is yours."

Jonny Boy looks to Cass. They could use the money, and it sounds like an easy enough job, but before Cass can accept it, Vic interrupts.

"What's in the safe?" he asks.

Fuck, that's a good question. Cass should've thought to ask that. This is what happens when she does business at six in the fucking morning. She puts a hand on Vic's leg. "An insightful fucking question, Vic."

Richard runs his tongue across the scab forming on his lip. "You want the five grand or not?"

"Not enough for me to risk myself or my boys when we've still got unanswered questions."

"Come on, Cass," Richard pleads, and she knows she's onto something if he's fighting this hard not to give her an answer. "Five grand is way over market for a grab-and-go."

"Yeah, it is," she says. "But this isn't just a grab-and-go, is it? This is a grab-and-go for a one-of-a-kind key to a one-of-a-kind safe that Holzmann wants into. So again: "What's in the safe?"

CHAPTER 9

Peter Van Horn, 7:49 A.M.

P eter Van Horn's childhood was spent surrounded by death, watching his brother waste away, one labored breath at a time. His parents had tried to shield him from it, but they, tired from the long nights at the hospital, died in a car crash, leaving just the two boys—now young men, if only barely—and the cystic fibrosis.

He is free of that now. He hates to think of it in those terms, but there was an undeniable relief to the arrival of the end. His brother's suffering had finished. Now all that's left is Peter and the guilt and the debt.

He lived when nobody else had, and it was meaningless. He knows better than most that he only has so many days on this earth, and every heartbeat that passes in waiting is a heartbeat he can never reclaim. It is an insult to those who died to waste even a single moment here. So he tries to wait as little as possible. To infuse each day with intention. The world might be capricious, but it will not force him to be still.

At least, that's what he wishes he had learned. Brushes with death were supposed to fill you with purpose. All Peter got from it is anxiety.

It's too much to demand the absolute most from every moment. With every day that goes by, each more pointless than the one before, the weight of all that unused potential builds up higher, the pressure deepens, and Peter is left increasingly paralyzed by the knowledge that his brother would have dragged more from this life than he has.

His shift starts at eight A.M., but he makes sure to arrive early. A few third shifters glance his way, but nobody will meet his gaze. The desk sergeant sends him up to the top floor. Captain Dumetz wants a word.

Something catastrophic must have happened with the filing system if the captain is getting involved. He usually has as little to do with the daily lives of patrolmen as Peter does with setting citywide policy. Still, Peter feels a bit of relief as he rides the elevator. Whatever is going on, it will be resolved soon enough.

The captain isn't in yet, but, his secretary assures Peter, he is at the top of the morning agenda. No magazines sit on the coffee table for him to peruse, so instead he catalogs his unanswered questions. Why were Sarge and Owen both on duty so late? How had his paperwork gotten so badly misfiled? Why wasn't Owen's car in the parking lot?

Captain Dumetz arrives precisely at the top of the hour but doesn't glance at Peter. The secretary gives a sympathetic smile as she follows Dumetz into his office. Peter listens to their voices, muffled beyond the point of words, through the closed door. He runs his hands through his hair a few times, willing it to stay out of his eyes. The voices quiet, and Dumetz's secretary returns.

"Just a moment more," she says. She reminds him of the nurses after they'd read a disappointing test result but had to wait for the doctor to deliver the bad news. Two more minutes pass before the door behind Peter opens and his shift commander and Sergeant Nowicki come through. The secretary waves them in to Dumetz's office and resumes her typing.

At some signal unseen to Peter, the secretary looks up from her screen. "They're ready for you now," she says.

The captain's office is large. A wide desk covered in folders dominates a corner, between a wall of filing cabinets and a window overlooking the motor pool. The captain, shift commander, and sergeant are all on the other side of the room at a conference table with ten chairs, a projector, and a speakerphone. The three men look up as one when Peter enters the room. Each has a slim folder in front of them.

"Officer Van Horn," Dumetz says. "Thank you for joining us. Please have a seat. You were working last night in uniform at a self-storage place down by the river, is that right?"

"Yes, sir," Peter says. "The U-Store-It. They contract with us to have it patrolled every night."

Dumetz scans the contents of his folder quickly. He has a thoughtful quality to him that Peter appreciates in a superior officer.

"All right," he says. "You've got a clean record. Your sergeant tells me that you're a good worker. Not his brightest star, but you can be relied upon to do the job. You have no commendations, but you've also had no complaints filed against you. So, Officer Van Horn, I want you to think carefully about your answer to this question, because right now, we're all on the same side, trying to sort out a big old cock-up. With that preamble out of the way, Officer, won't you please enlighten me as to what the fuck happened last night?"

Peter takes a breath. The three men watch him intently. You don't get to command positions like theirs without some real skill at finding the truth. Together, they'll figure this out. He summarizes the events of the previous night as efficiently as he can. Sarge gives no reaction to his own indirect appearance in the narrative, though the shift commander does glance at him curiously. When Peter is finished, he sits back and folds his hands in his lap, content that his part in this drama is complete.

Dumetz sits forward in his chair as he speaks. "Did you call your sergeant to confirm that there was an issue?"

"No, sir," Peter says. "As I said, sir. It was very late, and I didn't want to disturb him."

"Why would the sergeant be dispatching somebody that late?" Peter's shift commander asks him. "His shift ends with yours at six."

"I wondered the same thing," Peter says. His hair falls across his eye, and he forces himself to remain still.

Sarge clears his throat, speaking for the first time in the meeting. "There's no issue with your paperwork. And I didn't send Owen out."

"And," Dumetz continues, reading once again from the folder, "the gate guard at the storage facility reported nobody else in or out of the facility all night. Just you."

Peter is quiet for a moment, unsure how to respond. Dumetz presses a button on the speakerphone and, when his secretary answers, asks her to get Officer Oster for them.

While they wait, Peter says, "I'm sorry, sir. I guess I don't understand what's happening. I thought I was here to talk about an issue with the filing system."

"There's no issue with the filing system," Sarge says, defensive of his domain.

"No," Dumetz says, and as he meets Peter's eye, the civility and kindness that he had regarded him with earlier are gone. "We're here because last night, while wearing the badge and uniform of the city police of Omaha, you walked away from the facility that you were guarding."

"I didn't—" Peter starts, but he is cut off by the secretary on the speakerphone, announcing that she has Officer Oster on the line.

"This is Owen Oster." Owen's voice crackles out of the machine.

"Owen, it's Sarge. Where were you last night?"

"Last night? Conrad's sister is having a baby. She had a bunch of girlfriends over to celebrate, so me and Conrad took her husband out."

Peter is going to object, but a glare from Dumetz silences him.

"And Conrad can back you up on that?" Sarge asks.

"He should. His brother-in-law, too. What's going on?"

"Thank you, Owen," Sarge says. "That's all."

Dumetz hangs up the call and sits back to consider Peter. "Officer Van Horn, when you walk out of this room, I want you to drop to your knees and thank Jesus, Allah, Yahweh, the Buddha, and every other deity you can come up with that nothing more happened last night. If anything had been stolen, then we would have been responsible, and I'd have gotten every last penny out of you before I cut you loose. Instead, your dereliction has only put at risk one of this department's most lucrative and long-standing contracts, rather than guaranteeing its destruction. You are being placed on a desk handling administrative tasks. Professional Oversight will want to speak with you soon."

Peter knows, beyond a doubt, that Owen Oster had been at the U-Store-It. He knows that he followed the appropriate protocol and that doing so is synonymous with doing the correct thing. He hadn't wanted to be a cop—he had actually wanted to be a librarian—but once he learned that the force had a protocol for everything, he realized he could be happy here. You follow the flowchart from A to B to C, and at the end is success.

Peter had followed the protocol.

But here he is, in the captain's office, being referred to Professional Oversight. This is not the way the world works, yet it is how the world is working. If he were a different person, he might curse and swear and decry Owen's lies. He might declare the whole system corrupt and storm out in righteous fury. He might do any number of different things to defend his innocence, were he any number of different people. But

Peter Van Horn is not a different person. Peter Van Horn is who he is. He is the man who, when confronted with a minor question, will seek out an answer, but, having been shown that his entire understanding of the world is false, does nothing at all.

Dumetz looks at him from across the table, waiting for him to respond in some way. "Do you have anything else to say in your defense, Officer?"

Peter's lips purse. He opens his mouth. He closes his mouth. He pushes his hair off his brow. "No, sir," he says, at last.

CHAPTER 10

Peter Van Horn, 8:27 A.M.

I n the bullpen downstairs, he sits at a computer. He turns it on but does nothing further. People move around him. They whisper. Word has gotten out. A few try to engage him in conversation. They ask how he's doing. He says he's doing fine. They tell him to keep his chin up. He'll get through this. The union will take care of him. He nods and turns back to his computer. Before long they leave.

There's no protocol for this. Eventually, Sarge will come over and assign a task to occupy his time while the wheels of the investigation turn. For now he has nothing to do but accept the empty reassurances of his colleagues. He knows their views of him are changing. Before today, he had been, as Dumetz said, a perfectly acceptable officer. Not exemplary, but not embarrassing. He was the reversion to the mean, made flesh. Now, though, he's being moved to a new list—the list of those, like Owen and Conrad, who are on the take. He will not be looked down on, and he will be protected without question or hesitation by his fellow officers, but he will forever bear that mark.

As though summoned by his thinking of them, Peter sees Owen and Conrad across the bullpen. Owen is on a computer as well. Conrad catches Peter's eye and waves. Peter doesn't think there is any kindness to it. Owen calls somebody on his cell, then scribbles something down, and the two men leave.

Owen left the database program open. He is still signed in. He should have signed out before leaving. That's what protocol says to do. Peter crosses the bullpen to do it for him, but he notices something strange when he sits at the computer.

Owen is not signed in as himself, but as Melissa Fulli, another officer on their patrol. He could not have done that accidentally, and she wouldn't have signed in here herself. Peter saw her on the far side of the room.

On another day, Peter might have walked away. This isn't his problem to solve. But this isn't that day. The structures that Peter has used have failed him. Do what you are supposed to do, he had told himself, and all will be well. But that hasn't worked, has it? And if he's being honest, it isn't just the last day that has shown that to him. His whole life stands testament to the failures of his systems.

On another day, Peter would have done nothing. Today, he calls up the last database entry that Owen had been looking at. It is a USPS Change of Address form, filed in Chicago a month ago, requesting mail be forwarded here to Omaha. He doesn't recognize the name on the form. He'd never heard it before this exact moment, but Owen and Conrad had looked the guy up and tried to cover their tracks while they did it. Maybe he'll know what is going on.

Or maybe it will be a waste of time, but Peter has nothing better to do. Owen and Conrad had gotten this name and address and left in a hurry. Peter writes them down, logs out Melissa, and walks out of the station. He has a mission now. He is going to find Barrett Rye.

CHAPTER 11

Eighteen Months Ago

Scarpello used a decentralized system for his collections. An enforcer—someone like me—would be sent out after a delinquent debt. We called them wellness checks. Methods were left up to the individual's discretion. Scarpello was a big believer in the wisdom of the perspective from the ground, plus no orders for violence could be traced back to him if he never gave any.

After collecting, the enforcer would report to an accountant—someone like Mickey—and turn in the cash. The accountants each kept their own books and washed their own cash. Once the money was clean, it would be fed into one of Scarpello's front companies and washed a second time. All of this left him with a relatively high overhead, having to go through at least two complete laundering cycles before the money got somewhere he could use it, but it also kept the boss himself at a significant distance from the criminal activity, and each accountant's individual cell of enforcers and fronts could be burnt off should it become a risk to the larger operation.

Mickey wasn't my accountant. If the system had been working as intended, the two of us would have never met. But his guys had needed help on a stubborn job, so I was called in. Mickey knew the target was holding out, but his team couldn't figure out where the cash was hidden.

So I let Mickey's guys beat the hell out of me in front of the target, a surgeon who'd started using to keep his hands steady and lost track of the line separating the functional addicts from the common chaff. He helped patch me up, and the two of us got to talking about our mutual dislike for that crew. I let the surgeon think he was taking the lead in the conversation. He suggested I might get a group of friends together to rid us of a mutual problem.

I agreed out of self-preservation, but my friends were honest workers who deserved pay for their specialized labor. Terms were quickly agreed to. Once the surgeon produced the money, my friends failed to materialize to protect us from Mickey's guys.

Out of everyone I'd ever worked with, Mickey was the first to truly see what I'd done. It scared me, at first, to be looked at as more than muscle. But there was something exhilarating to it as well. I hadn't felt this way since high school, the last time I tried to do magic for an audience. When he looked at me, he didn't see the part I was playing. He saw me, and he saw everything that I was capable of being, and he made me see it too.

We were together for almost a year before we decided to run.

Laundering is a slow endeavor. It takes time to feed the money through the various cash enterprises that conceal its origins, and there is a certain amount that disappears at every stage, the cost of doing business. Mickey took advantage of those inefficiencies and ran a pyramid scheme on himself. He skimmed the clean money coming out for us and let dirty money through to make up the difference, using tomorrow's receipts to cover today's debts. We'd be gone before any of the IOUs punching holes into Scarpello's financial records would come due, before there was any reason to have the slightest suspicion that anything was amiss.

We weren't going to do it for long. Just until we had enough to disappear.

CHAPTER 12

Barrett Rye, 9:00 A.M.

My phone rings at nine A.M. precisely. I let it ring four times before I put down my tools and grab the phone off the wall. I might be the only person in the city under sixty with a landline. If you're looking to be tracked down, the local phone listing is an effective tool.

The man on the other end tells me to be at the Bob Kerrey bridge in thirty minutes. They make it clear that there will be money in it for me, and I agree. The bridge is close by, leaving me enough time to finish up my work before going.

I hadn't seen the key before last night, so I wasn't sure exactly what I would need. Now, with it in hand, I had spent the morning molding two lumps of plastic resin into pretty good matches for the size, shape, and weight of the key. Each is coated with a suspension of powdered tin in a layer of cyanoacrylate, leaving them with a sandy silver coating.

Before heading to the bridge, I put them into an aluminum electro-plater I set up in the kitchen. In about an hour's time I should have two passable duplicates of the key. They won't be perfect copies, and they won't do shit to open the safe itself, but they should be a fair stand-in, at a glance, for the real thing.

I decide to walk to the bridge and avoid the morning traffic. I've got plenty of time, and the exercise will calm my nerves. I keep to a slow pace, not wanting to arrive dripping sweat. The heat of the summer has been building with heavy humidity trapping the warmth at night, leaving the air a brackish soup. The forecasters are saying it will break soon, with a low-pressure system coming down from the north to release the pent-up energy.

The Hyundai Accent passes me three times before I realize I'm being tailed. It's not that important, though, so I let it go. I'm looking to be tracked down. Why should I worry that it's working?

As I turn off Riverfront Drive and start toward the looping ramp that leads up to the half-mile bridge that arcs across the Missouri, a man in a suit falls into step beside me. He's about ten years my senior and carries himself with the confidence of a fighter. His jacket is but-toned closed, and I can see the sweat breaking out across his forehead and the back of his neck. He can't open the jacket, though, without flashing the 9mm holstered beneath his left arm to the world.

"Are you Barrett?" he asks. I nod, and he takes my arm and directs me away from the bridge. "Come with me."

"What's this about?" I ask, keeping my tone light.

"Just be cooperative and you'll walk away from here a richer, happier man," he says. His arm swings as he walks, causing his lapel to gap away from his chest and give me a view of his gun. It's an unnatural, but practiced, movement on his part. He wants me to know that he is armed.

I could take him in a fight, if it comes down to that, even with the gun, but I give up nothing by letting him think that his little show of force has intimidated me, and so I demure.

"Sure," I say. "Whatever you say."

He leads me to a cart where Holzmann waits with a cup of coffee in each hand. It's my first time seeing him in person, and he looks smaller than I expected. It would be easy to dismiss him as just one more rich old white man in a city with far too many of them. That would be a mistake.

Holzmann's reputation in Chicago, insofar as he has one, is as a competent local boss who favors rationality above all else. He can be ruthless when the situation demands it but sees outright violence as a means only. His strength comes not from the fear of those beneath him but from his ability to keep open conflict off the city's streets, something that has, in turn, kept the police away from his operations. He is a useful tool when moving goods through Omaha, but a minor player in the grand scheme of Midwest crime.

He had the good fortune to expand an inherited shipping concern with ties to the Italian mafia into the world of vice just as Berkshire Hathaway and its associated firms brought billions of dollars into Omaha. In the last four decades he became the sole purveyor of illicit distractions in a city with far too much money in far too few hands. He has been wanting to grow beyond the biggest little town in America since the turn of the century but never put together the power to expand outside the city limits.

There is very little as dangerous as a smart and ambitious man restrained, and right now I am the thing standing between him and enough wealth to claim legitimacy on a national scale.

If he thinks for even a moment that I knew what I was doing when I took this key—that I intentionally stole from him—he will kill me. So I have to convince him I have no idea what's going on. I'm just a dumb lunk, a recent transplant to the city who went to a poker game and got distracted by a shiny bauble. If I can make him buy that, I'm set. Otherwise—well, this is gonna be a short story.

"Thank you, Benny," he says to my escort as we approach. Benny gives me an admonishing look—he and his gun will be close by—and steps away.

There is a moment of appreciation that most people go through when they first see me. A gradual widening of the eyes as they track up my body. Everyone knows a tall person. They think they know what big looks like. But there is a difference between your coworker who has to duck their head when they get into a car and the truly large.

After the surprise and wonder, Holzmann decides he knows who I am. He might not have anyone my size on his staff, but he has dealt with his share of bruisers, and we tend to be made from the same mold.

Having finished his appraisal, Holzmann offers me one of his cups of coffee. "Thank you for joining me on such short notice, Herr Rye. I didn't know if you take it with cream or sugar, so I leave that to you, but good coffee is rare in this city, and you certainly don't hold it now." He scoops three spoonfuls of sugar into his own cup and stirs.

"Thanks," I say and follow his lead. He's using a ploy I've used myself before, and I can hardly fault him for it. Benny surely isn't the only soldier present, and Holzmann knows why we are here while I, presumably, do not. His deference will let him gauge my intentions. If he shows weakness and I push a false advantage, he will snap down in an instant.

Before he continues, he leads me away from the coffee cart and the light traffic of joggers making their way along the riverfront. Away from the crowds. Away from witnesses.

"You are no doubt a busy man, and so I will keep this brief," he says. "You have come into possession of something of mine, and I would like it back."

I give him my best blank stare. "I have?"

He smiles, and his eyes flick to my side. I follow his gaze to see another grim-faced man watching us from twenty feet away. Benny is about thirty feet in the other direction. Too far for me to reach before he could draw and fire. The third man lengthens the odds even further. I'm not planning on trying to fight, but I let Holzmann see me doing the calculations. It's what he expects of me.

"Do not worry," he says, resting a hand on my forearm. "There is no reason that this should be anything other than a mutually beneficial situation. I don't care how you came to have my key. All I care about is getting it back."

I transfer the coffee to my left hand and reach into my pocket. Holzmann doesn't respond, but Benny tenses in my peripheral vision. I stop moving, and Holzmann waves Benny off. Slowly, I draw my hand out with my keychain.

"All these are mine," I say as I look at the keys. "Apartment. Car. Mailbox."

Holzmann gives me a tight smile and pushes the keys away. "Not one of those. This is a special key. A small metal device. I believe you won it last night in a game of cards?"

I let my eyes widen slightly. Now we're on the same page. But then I frown. "Mmm," I say. Noncommittal. "That maybe rings a bell."

Holzmann's face darkens. "Do not mistake my politeness for patience. One must always be polite in diplomacy, even in declarations of war."

Benny has taken a step closer.

I swallow. "Declarations—is this—" I look at the ground. Let him think he won the negotiation. I've pushed back just hard enough that he feels like he worked for the victory.

"Only if you want it to be." Holzmann pats my arm comfortingly. "War is not profitable for anyone but the gravediggers. But this is the wonderful thing about this country, is it not? Everyone is here to profit. So let us a find a way for us both to be enriched. You have my key, and I desire it back. Would you say fifty thousand dollars is a fair price?"

The coffee falls from my hand, my fingers rendered temporarily senseless by the number. "Shit," I say, hopping back as the hot drink splashes my feet. Benny tenses at the sudden movement, but I keep my hands visible. "Did I get you?" I squat down to wipe the coffee off myself.

Holzmann chuckles. "I take it this number is acceptable to you?"

"Yes," I say. "Very. I don't have the thing with me."

"How prudent. Shall we reconvene here in, say, three hours to handle the exchange?"

The money from Brock's bounty was nice, but not worth all of this. Fifty thousand dollars, though? That's getting closer to what I'll need.

Holzmann and his men leave first, with the Hyundai that tailed me falling into line behind their Mercedes SUV. Once they're out of sight, I hurry back to my apartment. I have only three hours to get ready. It's not much time.

The first thing I do is check on my fake keys. The aluminum isn't yet thick enough that I'd trust it. They need a bit longer. That's fine.

The apartment I'm renting is a moderately sized one-bedroom in a converted factory downtown. In two years, the city hopes, the building will be filled with tech bros and kombucha drinkers, but for now most of my neighbors are call-center drones who moved to the big city to escape dying farms. The gentrifiers are content to stick to Old Market and Midtown.

My desk, where I've been making the fake keys, sits next to a window that opens onto the fire escape. I've got a small table by the kitchen—such as it is, with just a microwave and a two-burner stove built into the counter—and a couch and armchair set up in front of a TV. A stack of free weights stands against the interior wall.

In the coat closet, a bank of monitors shows the feed from security cameras I hung at the building's front door, in the hallway, over the alley behind my unit, and inside the apartment itself. I can see it from anywhere in the apartment except the bathroom and one corner of the bedroom, and I can, if needed, close the closet door to conceal it from any visitors.

I've done my best to decorate the place in keeping with my persona. I put some boxing posters up on the cinder block walls with sticky tack and hung some sweaty socks and towels on the backs of the chairs around my table.

After cleaning my gear off the desk and putting out a layer of haphazardly arranged mail, I check in on the keys again. They'll have to do. I hide one of them behind a poster where I chipped off the front of a cinder block. The second one I glue into the hollow center of a novelty top hat keychain, which I hook onto my own keys.

I had gotten the key off Richard without incident, and the trail I left for Holzmann had worked beautifully. He's on the line for fifty grand. And fifty grand would be nice. But I can get more. I need to get more. Fifty thousand dollars won't be enough to get away from Scarpello. Maybe he'd accept it and let me spend the rest of my life working off the remainder, but I can't go back to that.

Holzmann thought he was going to get this key last night, and I delayed his gratification. This has left him frustrated. I am going to make him desperate. I am going to make him beg me to end his misery. He will offer whatever amount is necessary to stop the destruction that I wreak.

I don't know the details yet, but I'm not worried. I have three hours to figure it out. What I need is an agent of chaos, somebody fearless and wild to throw Holzmann's entire organization into disarray. Somebody who'll do exactly what I ask of them without ever realizing that they're working for me. And the perfect candidate is about to present herself.

CHAPTER 13

Cass Mullen, 11:38 A.M.

Cass hates Vic's van. The thing fucking screams criminal. The only thing that could make the white panel monstrosity more conspicuous would be an airbrushed scene of wizards and pegasuses on the side. Pegasuses? Pegasi? It doesn't fucking matter. She'd almost prefer that. It would be trashy, but people wouldn't want to call the cops if they saw it parked on their corner. Instead, they're in this lightly rusted, white box with tinted windows and a real hey-kid-you-want-some-candy vibe.

At least Vic keeps the interior clean. The seats up front are well vacuumed, and the floors are free of trash. The benches in the back have been stripped out and replaced with a futon. Polyester sheets, printed to look like batik silks, line the walls.

"Everybody ready?" she asks. "We do this fast. Don't give him a chance to think it through. Get the key and get out."

They're parked outside the building where Richard said this guy lives. It doesn't look like much. One of the many interchangeable low-rise apartment buildings that cover the city.

"What's the plan?" Jonny Boy asks, gathering up the wrappers from his breakfast. They'd grabbed some drive-through on their way over. Vic didn't want anyone eating in the van, but his desire to placate Jonny Boy's hungry whining proved stronger than his need to keep his sanctum free of the smell of grease.

"I just fucking told you the plan," Cass says.

If she had a halfway decent crew, then she'd be done with petty jobs like this, but she can't get a real crew without a real score, and she'll never get a real score working with these amateurs. But they are what she has, and she'll be damned if she lets their weakness hold her back.

She pops the glove compartment and pulls out the Hellcat they keep there. The tiny pistol is comically small, but it shoots fine, and with twelve rounds to play with, even someone as incompetent as Jonny Boy is bound to hit their target.

"Let's go," she says. "I'll run point. Vic, you're backing me up. Jonny Boy, you're the wild card."

"What about the shotgun?" Vic points to the long storage crate he has bolted to the wall across from the futon. Inside is a change of clothes, a pack of condoms, a couple bottles of knock-off Gatorade, and an AR-style semiautomatic 12-gauge. Whatever the Hellcat lacks in intimidation factor, the military-looking weapon more than makes up for.

"Leave it," Cass says, getting out of the van. "We won't need it. There's three of us and one of him."

As they walk to the front door, Cass gets herself ready for what they're going to do. It doesn't take much to find the anger she needs to threaten violence. Still, though, she is a bit nervous. She gets nervous before any job. Not about her own performance, but about her boys'. Vic and Jonny Boy are always a question mark.

Vic can be relied on to do what he's told. He is more dog than man, enthusiastic and eager to please, loyal to a fault, and willing to protect his packmates with deadly force. But he also lacks all ambition for a life beyond the one he has. He has his crew. He gets three meals a day, a warm place to sleep, and the occasional tumble in her bed. What more could he want?

Jonny Boy—sweet fucking Jonny Boy—is a different story. If she hadn't known him since middle school, the two of them finding mutual commiseration from the bullies that made her life hell before she learned to bite back, she'd have left his dead weight behind years ago. Plus, Vic likes having him around, and the bastard is a bull in a fight once you get him riled up. When he starts throwing that mass around, it's gonna do some damage.

They'd left Richard at her place. The poor fucker needed the rest, Cass had said. She hasn't told Vic and Jonny Boy yet, but they aren't bringing the key back to Richard. Cass is done dealing with middle management. If she wants to get anywhere in this city, then she needs to stop working for little shits like Richard Sands. As soon as she gets the key, she's heading straight to Holzmann to sell it to him directly. Once he knows that Cass is the sort of person who gets shit done, she can get into the big leagues.

"Do we need masks?" Jonny Boy asks as they get close to the building.

"No, Jonny Boy," she says. "We don't need masks. You two fuckers want to roll up on this guy in broad daylight with masks on and shotguns out? How the fuck you think that's gonna look?"

Jonny Boy just shrugs.

"How's it gonna look?" Vic asks.

"It's gonna look like a fucking robbery," she says.

Jonny Boy is quiet a moment longer. Cass can see him struggling. He wants to ask her something else, but he doesn't want to get yelled at again. Cass takes pity on him. Never say she isn't a merciful boss.

"Yes, Jonny Boy," she says. "It is a fucking robbery. But that doesn't mean it has to look like one. We go in, we politely ask for the key back, and we go on our way."

"And our money?" Vic asks. "What about the five grand?"

"Oh, that?" Cass smiles at her boys. "We fucking take that."

Barrett Rye is listed on the front door. Unit 204. She hits the button by his name.

"Got a delivery for Rye," she says, and the door buzzes open. She uses her sleeve to wipe the button down and open the door, then follows Vic and Jonny Boy into the building.

"You take this," she says to Jonny Boy, holding the gun out to him.

"Come on, you know I hate those," he says.

"You want to get paid, don't you?"

"I'll take it," Vic says, reaching for the little pistol.

"No," Cass says. "Jonny Boy gets the gun. He's the wild card. A wild card is scarier with a gun."

"Fine," Jonny Boy relents, taking the pistol and wedging it into his waistband. "I don't want to hurt the guy, though."

"You won't have to. Just do your fucking job."

CHAPTER 14

Cass Mullen, 11:45 A.M.

t's a small building with only six apartments on the top floor. Unit 204 is at the end of the hall. With a final glance at her boys to make sure they're ready, Cass gives the door a pound.

"Barrett Rye!" she calls. "Open up!"

She hears the deadbolt slide back and the security chain release and is already stepping forward as the door opens. She's used to being one of the shorter people in a room, but she's not ready to be below the guy's sternum as she pushes into his apartment. He's the sort of tall that can make an NBA player look small, and he's ripped to boot.

Dirty towels hang over his bedroom door. Mail sits in piles on the table. Right in the center of the table is an envelope with cash spilling out of it. This might be even easier than she'd anticipated.

"Who are you?" Barrett asks, sounding like he's straining every cell in his brain to form the question. As he follows Cass into the apartment, Jonny Boy and Vic file in behind him.

Jonny Boy heads straight for the kitchen. "Oh, you know this guy has a stocked fridge," he says. As the wild card, Jonny Boy's task is to keep the target off balance. Cass will talk, Vic will look scary. Jonny Boy just needs to be unpredictable.

Cass pulls out a chair at the table and sits down. She learned that from *The Godfather*. Marlon Brando sits through that whole movie, and he's scary as fuck. Why? Because he's the boss. He doesn't need to stand up, and neither does she. Vic posts up behind her, and she looks up at Barrett Rye.

Barrett, for his part, looks confused. Confused about who they are. About why they're there. About what Jonny Boy is doing digging through his fridge. Cass watches the gears turn and grind.

"Holzmann said I had three hours," Barrett says, glancing at a clock.

Cass and Vic share a look. This guy is supposed to be a civilian, so how does he know Holzmann?

"Oh, fuck yeah," Jonny Boy calls from the kitchen, pulling out a brick of something wrapped in deli paper. "Smoked turkey! Thin-sliced, too."

If this Barrett guy knows Holzmann, then they can't just rob him. She needs to figure out who he is and how he's connected. Clearly he's muscle of some kind, but is he a trusted agent? Is he just a nobody? How badly did Richard fuck them on this?

"He sent you to pick up the key, right?" Barrett asks, trying to fill the silence. "I just met him this morning. He was gonna buy it from me. He was supposed to give me three hours."

It's always nice when the idiots answer your questions without you having to ask them.

"That's how Holzmann is," Cass says with the knowing shrug of the lackey. "He gets impatient."

Barrett nods and leaves to get the key for them. With his back to her, she reaches for the envelope of cash on the table. She has a hand on it when he stops. She's just let go when he spins on a heel to look back at her.

"You got my money?" he asks. It takes her a moment to realize he's asking about the payment he has been promised by Holzmann.

"Yeah," she says. "You got the key?"

Barrett's brow furrows as he looks from Cass to Vic to Jonny Boy. None of them are carrying anything. "Where's the cash?" he asks.

Cass grabs a pen and a scrap of junk mail off the table. She scribbles some random numbers down. "Your money," she says, waving the paper in the air.

Barrett's brow furrows further. "That doesn't look like any fifty thousand I've ever seen."

"It's a new system Holzmann is using," she says. "This is a bank account with your money in it. Can't be traced. We get the key, you get the digits."

She can see Barrett thinking it over, deciding whether or not he buys the lie.

"You're out of mayo," Jonny Boy calls from the kitchen. Barrett's confusion clears, saved from the complexities of bank accounts by something concrete and present.

"There's more in the cabinet," Barrett says. "Left of the fridge."

Cass listens to Jonny Boy rummaging through the cabinets as Barrett takes a step toward her. Barrett reaches for the paper, but she pulls it back. "Show us the key, then you get paid."

Barrett eyes the paper. Cass can see his pulse in the veins along his neck. He's close enough that he could easily grab it. Hell, he could grab her, but she's got Vic beside her, and Barrett might have fifty pounds of muscle and a foot of height on him, but Vic can hold his fucking own.

As Barrett's eyes slide over her other shoulder, she knows that Jonny Boy has come back to join them as well. She can hear him chewing the wet sandwich he's made, the mayo slurping between folds of turkey slices and the flaps of his lips. But he also will have left one hand free—he knows the drill—resting too casually on the grip of the Hellcat.

"Just give us the key," she says. "I want to pay you as badly as you want to get paid. We've all got shit to do today."

Barrett looks from her to the paper to the gun. "I should call Holzmann," he says, taking a slow step away from her.

She comes to her feet, holding the paper out again. "That would be a mistake," she says. "Just hand over the key."

Jonny Boy puts his sandwich down behind her. She knows he's twisting his baby face into the fiercest grimace he can muster. Vic pops his knuckles.

"Can I ask you something?" Barrett asks. He's stalling now. Trying to find a way out. "Do you know what's in the safe?"

"It doesn't fucking matter," Cass says. The question of the safe and its contents is a problem for another time. Right now, she needs to get the key and get out.

"I know. I'm just curious. It's not like I'd be able to do anything about it."

"So just give me the fucking key," Cass says, but what she's thinking is that he's right. There isn't anything he could do about the safe. No matter how big he is, he's still just one guy. A whole crew, though? For the right prize, who knows what a crew could pull off.

"Last chance to do this as friends," she says.

There is a fulcrum around which every situation rotates. A point which has, to one side, the weight of all that came before and, on the other, the potential of all that will come after. Cass watches as Barrett passes that point, his expression hardens, and the outcome becomes fixed.

So be it.

Vic launches himself around the table, leading with a shoulder, hoping to bowl the big man over. Barrett absorbs the full force of Vic's momentum.

He rocks back on his feet, but doesn't fall. As Vic starts showering blows into his sides, Barrett wraps both arms around Vic and lifts him into the air. With a grunt, he drives Vic back, slamming him into the wall.

As Vic crumples, Jonny Boy, always a half second late on the draw, clears the pistol from his waistband. While he fumbles with it, Barrett grabs a glass of water from the table and throws it across the room. It doesn't break, but does catch him in the neck with a wet thud.

Jonny Boy drops the pistol as he gasps for air, and Barrett closes the gap. Kicking the gun aside, he lays a roiling combination into Jonny Boy's gut, finishing with a blow to his chin. Cass can hear Jonny Boy's teeth slam shut.

Across the room, Vic struggles to get his feet beneath him. He must have knocked his head into the wall. This is getting out of hand.

With Barrett distracted, Cass comes up behind him. She isn't much of a fighter, but she's gotten into a few scrapes in her time. She doesn't have Jonny Boy's weight or Vic's strength, so when she hits, she has to hit smart. Barrett's height puts his kidneys right below her shoulder. Right in line for a straight jab. She lines up the punch and sends it home.

It's like punching a brick wall, but the giant arches his back around the blow. It has clearly hurt. She ducks aside as Barrett turns, swinging his arms out blindly to sweep her away.

Which is all the separation that Jonny Boy needs to fall forward. It is a guileless, though effective, move as his prodigious weight collides with Barrett's side. Barrett is already off balance from his quick turn to find Cass, and his knee buckles beneath Jonny Boy's collapse. The two men tumble to the ground, and Jonny Boy only needs to make himself still to trap Barrett beneath his mass.

Cass spots the Hellcat and grabs it. "That's e-fucking-nough," she says, pointing the gun at Barrett. She wishes it had a hammer she could ratchet back to drive home the threat.

Barrett looks up at her. He's stopped fighting, but there is still defiance in his eyes. Big guys don't like losing. They sometimes need to be taught a lesson more than once for it to make it through their thick skulls. Fine. She can do that.

She presses the muzzle of the gun to his forehead. His eyes cross, tracking the weapon, and the thrill of victory courses through her. This is the part she loves. The part where they realize that they've been beaten and that she was the fucker who did it to them.

"Want to reconsider?" she asks, smiling down at him. The smile tugs at the tough tissue that bifurcates her lip.

A slimy drop of pink, blood and saliva mixed, rolls from Barrett's mouth.

"Fuck you," he says.

She steps back and looks to Vic. His eyes seem to be focusing again, and he glares at Barrett. She gives him a nod, and he kicks Barrett squarely in the side.

"Where's the fucking key?" she asks.

Barrett can't look away from the gun. He's about to break.

"Get up, Jonny Boy," she says. "No need to get brains on you."

Jonny Boy never likes to see people get hurt. As he stands, he takes one last, sad look at Barrett. "This isn't worth dying over, man," he says.

And Cass watches the last bit of resistance bleed out of the giant's eyes.

"It's in the wall," Barrett says, gesturing toward his bedroom. "Behind Clay/Liston."

Vic rips the poster down to reveal a small alcove carved into the wall. From there he pulls out a little ball of silvery metal. He tosses it to Cass. It's a strange little thing for all the trouble it has inspired. But it's hers now.

"This could have been so much easier for all of us, but you had to go and make it fucking difficult," she says, shaking her head with theatrical sadness. "Now I'm willing to put this unpleasantness behind us, but I think that an apology is in order. Perhaps a small offering"—she grabs the envelope of cash from his table—"as a gesture of goodwill."

If the fucker had just given her the key when she asked, he wouldn't have had to get kicked. But she does have to admit, it always feels better when they fight.

CHAPTER 15

Cass Mullen, 12:12 P.M.

Things are quiet in the van. Vic drives—she made sure his eyes were working right before letting him get behind the wheel—Jonny Boy eats his sandwich, and Cass studies the silver ball. It has a nice heft to it. Clearly it is a well-constructed object, whatever it is. It doesn't look like a key or the car fob that Richard had described. It's more like a tiny metallic bird egg, the progeny of some futuristic space pigeon.

She stares at herself, reflected in the fun-house mirror of the little egg's convex surface. She can't get Barrett's words out of her head. Richard offered them five thousand for the key, but Holzmann was paying Barrett fifty. Even that wouldn't be enough for Richard to risk his job, though. A job that had earned both of them quite a bit of money as he got prime intelligence on the worst-secured houses in the city.

Which means Holzmann must be paying more than that for this little ball, and Holzmann never overpays for anything. Which leads again to that same question: What's in the safe?

And the inevitable follow-up: How can Cass get it for herself?

"I didn't want to hurt anyone," Jonny Boy whines from the back of the van, pulling Cass out of her plans.

"He made us do it," Vic says, slowing down for the turn onto their street. The big van doesn't corner too well.

"I know," says Jonny Boy. "I just don't like it."

Fuck this. Cass deserves a real crew, some real fucking workers who don't need to be coddled back together every time they get in a fight. With that, she could rule the whole fucking city. To do that, though, to get out from under these two albatrosses that she's been dragging around her whole fucking life, she needs money.

"Turn around, Vic," she says. "We're not going home."

"We're not?" he asks, but he does as he's told.

"What about Richard?" calls Jonny Boy from the back.

"Fuck Richard," she says. "That fucker let us walk in there blind, he can wait a little bit longer. I need somewhere quiet. Somewhere I can think."

"What about my abuela's house?" Vic suggests. "Out by Saddle Creek."

"That place still have a pool?" Jonny Boy asks. "I could go for a float."

Cass looks at him, incredulous. "Why wouldn't it still have the pool? The fuck you think is gonna happen to a fucking pool?"

"I dunno," he says. "Maybe they filled it in when she died or something."

Cass had started the morning with a plan to become Holzmann's personal fixer. Now she has the seed of a new idea. Fuck working for the boss. She should be the boss herself.

CHAPTER 16

1951

Maxwell Novak received two things of note on his seventeenth birthday. The first was a letter from the army informing him that his father had perished while serving honorably in Korea. The second was a two-thirds stake in his father's steel mill. The letter did not inform him, though subsequent conversations did, that his father had been killed by friendly fire, taking seventeen rounds from a confused sentry team after his patrol had gotten turned around and approached their base from the wrong direction. Maxwell thought it meaningful that his father had been shot seventeen times, it being his seventeenth birthday. He did not believe that there was such a thing as a coincidence.

This is, of course, complete bullshit. Coincidences are real. The world is full of random chance, and if you smash enough numbers together, patterns will emerge. They have no meaning. They are not the universe trying to communicate with you. They are just the infinite monkeys at their typewriters. But Maxwell was a believer.

His older sister and two younger brothers, each having received a one-ninth stake in the steel mill, attempted to contest the will which so unequally divided their father's estate, but the elder Novak's preference for his eldest son was well-documented, and the will had been duly signed, witnessed, and filed with the necessary authorities prior to his death.

Maxwell's relationship with his family never recovered, but the steel mill flourished. In 1955 he bought out his siblings and began expanding. As the postwar boom waned, and the hippies and the communists destroyed the American economy, Maxwell shuttered the mill in Gary, Indiana, and moved the company's operations south. First, he opened a plant in Texas to provide specialized parts to Boeing, and then another that worked with Texas Instruments to create the bodies that would hold their revolutionary integrated circuit chips.

He frequently visited Korea, searching for the meaning behind his father's death. What he found instead was an underutilized workforce. He opened his first factory in Gwangju in 1975, and while there were rumors that he had stolen manufacturing techniques, the Korean legal system was willing to look the other way so long as he was bringing in money. By the turn of the twenty-first century, Maxwell Novak had quietly become one of the wealthiest men in the country on the back of a distributed manufacturing network that nobody had ever heard of.

He moved his headquarters from Texas to Omaha, hoping that the wealth that had followed Warren Buffett there would surround him with a higher class of people. Those who might appreciate his genius. Instead, he found only those looking to take ever more advantage of him.

As death approached, his paranoia grew. Everyone near him was only there to live off his leavings. He was a miserable man with nothing to recommend his company beyond his exorbitant wealth.

He had learned from the exhaustive probate of his father's estate the importance of a carefully managed death plan. His will was meticulously constructed to lay out exactly what his intentions were. Upon his death the company was to continue operating as before, and most of his money would be poured back into it, ensuring that it would carry on as a testament to his siblings' failures.

He had put together an extensive collection of art, surrounding himself with the greatness lacking in the world around him. He carefully guarded this collection, having purchased it for his enjoyment alone, and his will was clear that this was to continue upon his death. The entirety was to be preserved and stored, out of sight of the world. Its very existence was to be kept secret, with only the occasional sale to fund its continued maintenance.

After his death, the firm he had retained to execute his will determined that the collection would need to be appraised.

In 1885, Tsar Alexander III of Russia needed an Easter present for his wife. Wealth was of no value to her, but she treasured novelty deeply, so he hired a jeweler to construct a surprise for her. Fabergé delivered to the tsar an enameled gold egg that split open to reveal a gold yolk. That yolk opened further, hiding a multicolored hen, that itself contained the final surprises: a ruby pendant and a diamond crown. The tsarina was delighted with the gift, and Alexander commissioned eggs from the Fabergé house annually, a tradition carried on by his son, Nicholas II, until the Bolsheviks executed him.

The exact number of eggs created is a point of some dispute, though it is generally agreed that fifty-two Easter gifts were commissioned by the tsars. The locations of forty-six are known. It had only been forty-five until 2012, when a scrap dealer bought what he thought was a replica at a flea market. He intended to flip it to a gold merchant to be melted down, until he realized the truth of what he had. It was only just saved from the crucible, and later sold at auction for thirty-three million dollars. If one of the six still-missing eggs were to be found today, it could sell for twice that.

Novak's collection was housed in an unassuming storage facility, spread across dozens of units. His estate paid for the building to be under constant guard by the local police force. The appraiser they hired had a reputation for both accuracy and confidentiality.

When the appraiser opened the safe inside the other safe in the back of storage unit 327, he didn't believe what he was looking at. But after dedicating a week to it alone, he was forced to conclude it was the Nécessaire, a Fabergé egg last seen in 1952 when it disappeared into the private collection of someone identified only as "A Stranger." The appraiser held one of the great lost treasures of the world. And then he resealed it inside two safes under a dusty drop cloth behind a corrugated steel door, to sit, unknown, for decades to come.

He tried to stay quiet. That was the job, after all. Through conversations with colleagues and loved ones, he said nothing. When asked directly once, a few drinks in at a lively cocktail party, what the most exciting appraisal he had ever done was, he lied.

However, later that night, he was talking with one of the servers, an attractive young woman with an amateur's enthusiasm for fine jewels, and the words came spilling out. She smiled and chucked him on the shoulder, feigning disbelief. She would have heard about something like that. He pitched his voice low and leaned in close as she held her ear to his lips. He told her that he had been sworn to secrecy, but that, on his honor, in a storage facility just off the river there was a Fabergé egg.

She did what the girls who worked for Holzmann always did when they came across a piece of particularly juicy intelligence during their duties, and her boss began to plot. His entire career he had been denied the legitimacy and respect that should have been his by right. But no more.

If the appraiser's reputation for secrecy was stellar, though, and even he was not able to keep this under wraps, then the criminal network of informants and contractors that supported Holzmann's operations had no chance of containing it. He needed to act quickly. And he did. But he needed help, and one of the specialists he reached out to happened to have known Mickey and let slip about the egg, which is how I came to be in Omaha, looking for enough money to buy Scarpello off my back.

I failed Mickey once, and I might never come to terms with that, but he died trying to get us both out. He saw what I never could, which is that there was more that I could offer the world than pain.

I just need to dole out a tiny bit more, and I can be free of it forever.

I'm telling you all of this for a reason. I want you to understand the amount of money at stake here. Holzmann is looking at an eight-figure windfall, and not only do I need more than the fifty thousand he offered me, but he can easily afford to pay it and still come away from this a staggeringly wealthy man.

I'm not too big to admit my faults. I don't want you to think that I'm callous or greedy. I am vain, but I am not those other things. They say you can't put a price on human life, but that's not true, is it?

John Stuart Mill's utilitarianism argues for the greatest good for the greatest number. The needs of the many, so says Spock, outweigh the needs of the few. Surely it is defensible to sow a little bit of suffering now to avoid a far greater amount later. That's what I tell myself, at least.

My plan is simple. Cause chaos. Holzmann wants the key, and he wants it quickly. Every moment he doesn't have it is a moment his plans might fall apart. When some other player might learn of the egg's existence and swoop in to take it.

So every moment that I don't give him the key might be the critical moment when things turn against him. That threat of someone snatching away his prize hangs above him in terrible suspension. The longer I can delay, the more desperate he will become. The more desperate he becomes, the more he will be willing to pay to end that desperation and remove the sword from above his head. This is why I sent Cass and her crew after him.

He could decide to use force, but Holzmann is a man of rationality. The cost of attacking me and the fallout from that violence would be more than the cost of simply paying me. With sixty million dollars on the line, he'll take the simpler path and pay me the couple hundred thousand that I need.

I want to make one other thing clear as well. I know you think you've heard this story before. You think you know how it's all going to end. You're wrong. This doesn't end with me having the egg. Even if I could hang on to the key, get my hands on the safe, and somehow get it open, I would still need to find a buyer for it. Priceless Russian artifacts aren't the sort of thing that you can take to your friendly neighborhood fence. And I'd need to convince Holzmann not to kill me over the whole thing.

So no, I'm not going to walk away from this with a Fabergé egg. It'd be a hell of an ending, and I'll be the first one to admit my fondness for such, but it is not my ending. All I'm looking for is enough money to let me be the man Mickey saw when he looked at me.

CHAPTER 17

Jim Pickens, 12:33 P.M.

The sun is brutal. The whole city has been boiling. At least, Jim Pickens thinks to himself, watching the heavy black clouds growing in the west, some relief might be coming.

Pickens is usually brought in for a single task—which he performs quickly and expertly, and for which he is compensated at a rate commensurate with his skills—and then released again for that favorite pastime of the freelancer: searching for his next gig. But Holzmann is keeping Pickens close by at all times. As soon as he gets the key, he wants Pickens to be there to open the safe.

Currently, Pickens sits on a bench near a sweeping footbridge that spans the Missouri River, waiting for the man who is supposed to sell them the key. Holzmann is next to him, holding a paper bag with fifty thousand dollars. Benny is nearby with his favorite goon. Pickens thinks the man's name is Wade. At one P.M., with a glance at his watch, Holzmann gestures for Benny to join them and lend him his cell.

"I wish to speak with him directly," Holzmann says. "I want him to understand the scope of the error he has made."

Pickens tries to stand and give them privacy. He shouldn't be here. He shouldn't know Holzmann's business, nor does he want to. He is only on this bench to verify that the key is genuine. The fewer other details he knows, the happier he will be. But Holzmann waves for him to stay, and Benny lays a hand on his shoulder.

"Hello?" A man answers Holzmann's call.

"For the longest time," Holzmann says, without further greeting or preamble, "I only slept with whores. Do you know why that is, Herr Rye?"

Pickens has to admire the man's flair for the dramatic.

"I was terrified of being embarrassed," Holzmann continues when their key salesman, Rye, does not respond. "It is my greatest fear, you know? Public humiliation. The good thing about a whore, Herr Rye, is that she will never leave you sitting in the park with your dick in one hand and a bag of cash in the other."

There is silence on the line for a moment. "Well fuck you too," Rye responds. "If you're gonna gloat, at least make sense."

"Obscenity is the refuge of little men. Watch your tongue, and give me my key."

"Your guys already took it."

Holzmann sits up straighter, a feat that Pickens would have thought impossible a moment before. "I promise you," he says. "My people did nothing of the sort."

"Well three of them just left here with your key."

"Describe them to me," Holzmann says, the performative anger of his little whore speech giving way to real wrath.

"They were young," Rye says. "Three kids. Fat guy named Jonny Boy. Pretty guy. There was a woman in charge."

"The woman," Benny interrupts. "Was her face messed up?"

"I guess so. Not too bad, but sure."

"That's Cassiopeia Mullen," Benny tells Holzmann. "She's nobody. A house-burglar with a sloppy crew. Jonny Boy Wright and Vic Velasquez. They'll all be caught and put away within a year." Benny pauses, mentally confirming a detail before he continues. "But she has done work with Richard Sands before."

Holzmann sucks his teeth, processing this new information. Pickens wishes again that he had been allowed to step away. He doesn't like to get involved with petty local conflicts.

"We're done," Rye says, his patience apparently expired. "Whatever this bullshit is, I'm done with it." The line goes dead, but Holzmann has already moved on. He grabs Pickens by the elbow and starts leading him back toward their car. Benny gestures to his man, Wade, and the two fall in behind them.

"You want me to take her?" Benny asks. "We're not far from the place she and her crew usually hole up."

"Check it out, but keep your distance," Holzmann replies. "Herr Sands did promise he would make things right. If she's working for him, he'll come crawling out of the mud with the key. If she's on her own, then we'll make her the same offer we did Rye. Don't move against either of them until I send reinforcements."

With a salute, Benny tosses the car keys to Wade and departs for his mission. The rest of them start the drive back to Holzmann's estate.

"Mister Holzmann," Pickens says, once the Mercedes has left the city. "I understand these delays are beyond your control, but I do need to bring up the details of my fee with you."

Holzmann turns from the window to consider him. "Of course, Herr Pickens," he says. "I hired you for an evening's work, and that has stretched into far more."

"I have every faith in your ability to get me what I need to complete this job, but the scope of my commission has grown." Pickens chooses his words carefully, keeping his inflection as level as he can. Nonthreatening. Unassuming. But aware of the value he brings. "For longer-term work like this, I charge a day rate, plus a hazard percentage, as you now have me operating in the field."

Holzmann's face is a flat mask. Pickens fights the impulse to keep talking. If he hadn't spent the last twelve hours with the man, he might be concerned or feel ignored as Holzmann turns to the window, but this is simply how he thinks. When he finishes his private deliberations, he will deliver his answer.

For the next five minutes, Pickens enjoys the blast of cold air coming from the vents. The cream leather seat is cool beneath him. He marvels at the full suits that Holzmann and his men wear. Their only sartorial concession to the heat seems to be the choice of cotton over wool.

Eventually, Holzmann says, "I like you, Herr Pickens. I bear you no ill will for pressing when you have me at a disadvantage. I should be disappointed if you did not. A man must be compensated for his time. Benny will ensure you are paid appropriately."

When they arrive at the Elkhorn estate, Pickens goes straight to the office at the back of the house where the safe is being stored. He already drilled out as much as he could. The safe is, for all intents and purposes but one, open. All that remains is to throw the handle, retracting the bolts holding the door closed, and open it.

Of course, if he does that now, the contents of the safe will be destroyed. But once he has the key, he can open it in seconds.

Reassured that all is in place, he returns to quietly waiting. From this room, he has a view through a windowed door into the backyard. The men who patrol the grounds use the guesthouse, a few hundred feet away, as a staging ground, and the intervening space is kept open. Pickens does his best to ignore them and their guns, and instead watches the approaching storm cross the sky to meet the sun.

Holzmann joins Pickens shortly and spends the afternoon conducting business from here.

At four o'clock, when there is still no word from Richard Sands or Cassiopeia Mullen, Holzmann calls Benny for an update. He's been staking out Cass's apartment. Nobody's been in or out, but he has seen movement behind the curtains. Her opportunity to come to him willingly has passed. Holzmann sends Wade and a few men out to take the woman.

CHAPTER 18

Cass Mullen, 1:24 P.M.

Vic and Jonny Boy want to spend the afternoon in Vic's grandma's house, sitting by the algae-filled pool or sleeping on the plastic-wrapped houndstooth furniture beneath paisley walls. It's a pleasant, three-bedroom place on a quiet street with a walled-in yard. It's nicer than Cass's apartment, and it makes her feel claustrophobic. It smells like old lady. When they arrive, she asks Vic why he sold the bed, looking at the yellow rectangle of rug in the corner of his grandma's bedroom, the only section of carpeting still its original color.

"Abuela died in that bed," he says, as though that explains it.

"Of a heart attack," Cass objects. "The bed was fine, and it's not like she was using it anymore."

"Goddamn, Cass," Jonny Boy calls from the kitchen. "The bed wasn't fine. She'd just died in it. You don't sleep in the bed someone died in."

"Oh," Cass says. "She shit herself, didn't she? A lot of people shit themselves when they die."

"It's just about respect," Jonny Boy says. He's cut up an orange and put some cheese and crackers on a plate for them. It's Kraft singles and store-brand Ritz, but from the smile on the guy's face you'd think it was a Michelin-star charcuterie. "It's where she took her final rest."

Vic grabs some crackers. "Thanks, man," he says, giving Jonny Boy a squeeze on the shoulder. "It was her bed, you know? It wouldn't feel right to keep using it. Wherever she is now, I want her to know that I love her. That I miss her. How would it look if I just threw her away and slid into her bed?"

"You took her fucking house, though," Cass says. "Is that really different?"

Vic has a way of looking at her that used to upset her but now just makes her sad. Like he's surprised. Surprised not only that she would say something so awful but also that he can still be surprised by that. He should have learned by now that she's a bitch. She didn't ask to be born like this. She wishes, sometimes, that she didn't have these ambitions. Life would be simpler if she were content to accept its bullshit. If she would settle for a boring fuck and start spitting out babies.

But that's not what she wants. That's not who she is. And if she has to be a ruthless bitch to get what she wants, then so be it. She came here to figure out a plan. To find some way to turn this key into their fortune. But Cass Mullen isn't a planner. Cass Mullen is the bad motherfucker who gets shit done.

"We shouldn't have come here," she says. "We've got fucking work to do."

"I thought we were gonna go swimming," Jonny Boy whines, looking toward the back of the house where the nasty green pool is.

"Well we're fucking not," she says, grabbing an orange slice on her way to the front door. "Not right now. First we gotta get paid."

Richard is upset when she calls and tells him to sit tight for a while longer, but he agrees in the end. What other choice does he have?

CHAPTER 19

Peter Van Horn, 3:26 P.M.

P eter can barely hold his eyes open. Only anxiety keeps him going, and that is a poor motivator when what he needs is to sit still. He's been driving all over the city, and all he wants is to lie down and take a nap. He can't, though. He has work to do.

Peter's world turned, overnight, from one where everything had a place and there was a procedure for any situation into a nightmare of contradiction and paradox. Owen Oster was lying about what happened at the U-Store-It. This was a problem. Peter knew he was not the right person to fix this problem. He also knew that nobody else would. His bosses made it clear that they only wanted a scapegoat, and Peter was convenient.

Peter had many questions, and answering questions usually brought him peace, but he didn't know how to answer any of these. Why was Owen at the storage center? Why had Owen needed him gone when nothing had been stolen from the facility? Why—and he did admit that this question was not new, but it had taken on a new urgency—did a mid-tier self-storage building too cheap to properly light its own hallways shell out for police protection when they could have a mall cop for a third of the price?

Peter had spent his life within the shared set of rules and boundaries that define a functioning society. In exchange for this, he had been repeatedly crushed beneath the heel of an uncaring universe. Society's strictures are not rules, but a self-inflicted handicap the weak ensconce themselves in, and the strong turn to their advantage. He was done with it.

Amped up on this revelation, he left the precinct, got into his car, and drove to the address registered with the USPS for Barrett Rye. He parked across the street, where he could keep an eye on both the front door and the fire escape hanging from the building's side.

While waiting, he looked the man up online but couldn't find a link between Barrett and Owen Oster. Barrett looked like a recent transplant to Omaha. He was a personal trainer whose body itself was all the advertising his services would ever need. He had no clear connections to the police or criminal organizations. There were no friends or family in common between him and Owen. Yet Owen had wanted not only to know where this guy lived but also that nobody else would know he was looking for that information.

Peter didn't have to wait long before Barrett himself came strolling out the front door. Peter knew from the pictures that Barrett was big, but seeing him in person was something different. The guy certainly had the look of a criminal about him. On top of his sheer size, there was a dullness to his expression that Peter had come to recognize, and his nose had the crooks and bulbs of a man who had been in his fair share of fights. His skin was dark, but not black, with traces, perhaps, of Mongolia. Maybe those huge people from down in Australia. Peter didn't know enough to say. This didn't mean he was criminal, Peter quickly pointed out to himself. It was just an observation.

When Barrett was a block or so ahead, Peter pulled into the morning traffic. There was no way to avoid passing him, and Peter was too worried about Barrett getting into a car and driving off to leave his own vehicle and follow on foot. So instead he allowed himself to pass his target and looped around the block to pick him up again. When Barrett turned into the small park by the Kerrey footbridge, Peter parked and watched.

He didn't recognize the old man Barrett met with, but from the presence of two armed guards, Peter suspected he was organized crime, though he might also be one of Omaha's wealthy investor class taking his personal security too seriously. Peter wished he had learned a bit more about the criminal players in the city he was protecting, but there had been no reason for him to do so. He spent most days issuing traffic tickets.

As Barrett left the park and the old man got into a Mercedes, Peter was left with a choice. He could continue following Barrett, or he could hope that this old man might lead him to something else of interest.

He flipped a coin, then set off to follow the Mercedes.

It circled the city aimlessly, stopping once at a cafe where the old man had a cup of coffee before returning to the bridge in the early afternoon. Peter watched as the old man went into the park, accompanied by his guards and a young Black man in professional clothing who had been driven out to meet them. Peter wondered why he had actively noted Barrett and the Black man's skin color, but not that the old man and his guards were all white. One more addition to his list of failings.

They sat on a bench for forty-five minutes before the old man made a phone call. One of the guards left on foot, and everyone else left in the Mercedes. Once again, Peter had a choice to make. Follow the old man who seemed to be in charge of whatever was going on here, or abandon that route to follow the guard. Again, he was being asked to make a critical decision while having absolutely no information.

So he flipped a coin and stayed with the old man.

Which is how he came to be in Elkhorn, watching nothing happen at a gated house. After nearly eight hours in his car, he was forced to relieve himself into a bottle that now sits behind him. He had grabbed some granola bars and a bag of peanuts before beginning his surveillance, but those ran out while the old man was getting his coffee. He would like to run the plates on the Mercedes, but he has nobody at the station he trusts.

He's not sure how much longer he can keep this up. Hunger or the need for sleep will eventually overtake him. While he spent most of the morning enlivened by his newfound purpose, as the hours wore on, that energy flagged. It's hard to maintain the thrill of taking action when all he's doing is sitting in a car, watching an immobile gate.

With each passing minute, that enthusiasm, seemingly summoned from the ether, evanesces just a bit more. What is he doing here? His job is on the line, under threat because he stands accused of abandoning his post, and his reaction had been to walk away from the police station, away from the desk he had been assigned to, to follow a civilian without the faintest shred of evidence because he thought that one officer had used another officer's credentials to look him up.

He should have gone to Sarge when he saw Owen using Melissa Fulli's login. He should have called Sarge last night when Owen relieved him, or gotten Owen to put it in writing. He should have done a lot of things, but instead he came here.

This is a fool's errand. He'll go back to the station, he decides. The best he can do is beg for Sarge's mercy. He'll tell Professional Oversight the truth when he speaks with them, and they'll sort it out. It shouldn't be on his shoulders to unravel this mystery. He doesn't have the skills for this. He's not the right man for this job.

The anxiety that has been coiling in his chest since he first heard the footsteps in the stairwell begins to unwrap. It is a physical relaxation that begins behind his shoulder blades and spreads down his limbs. He closes his eyes and takes a breath. This is not his responsibility. He just needs to do as he's told, and the truth will win out.

He holds the breath for a two count, feeling his heart slow. He hadn't realized it had been beating rapidly, but it was a steady staccato throughout the day. It begins to fade, and he lets the breath go, letting his cares and anxieties go with it.

In. Hold. Relax. Out. Peter Van Horn is filled with the surety of the justice of the universe. He will find a way through this darkness. His diligence will be recognized. All will be well.

CHAPTER 20

Cass Mullen, 4:06 P.M.

They're back in Vic's van, parked on the side of the road up the street from Holzmann's estate in Elkhorn. This is the sort of place they should be. Wide streets. European cars. A house you hire a cleaning service and a gardener to maintain. These lawns aren't mowed. They're manicured. A beat-up old Hyundai sits four lots away, standing out almost as much as Vic's shitty van. Cass feels bad for whatever poor domestic worker goes with the car. From the looks of the storm coming in, they're gonna have a miserable fucking drive home tonight.

"I don't see why I couldn't skim the pool and go for a swim," Jonny Boy says from the back. "We're just sitting around. We coulda done that just as well back at Vic's place."

"We're not fucking sitting around," she says. "We're staking the place out."

"Oh. Well, it feels a lot like sitting around."

"How many houses have we broken into, and you still need me to explain this shit to you? We wait for them to leave or go to sleep, and then we move."

"I still don't think we should do this," Vic says. "Holzmann was gonna pay the big guy fifty Gs for the key. We should just sell it to him."

"And then he gets what's in the safe? Fuck that. We're taking everything."

"Holzmann will kill us."

"He won't have a chance. We'll get the safe and leave town. Start over somewhere new. We can roll into LA the richest motherfuckers there. How about that, Jonny Boy? Everyone in LA's got a pool, and you can go to Disney World every day instead of having to drive three hours out to Six Flags."

"Disneyland," Jonny Boy says.

"What?"

"Disney World is in Florida. We could go to Disneyland."

"Fine. You can go to fucking Disneyland," Cass says. "And Vic, you want to see someone play besides the fucking Huskers, right?"

"I don't want to go to LA," Vic says. "I like Omaha. Abuela is buried here."

Cass has been giving these two too much slack recently. They're starting to question her, and she can't have them thinking this is a democracy. "Then you can fucking stay," she says. "But we're doing this. Now get ready, both of you."

Jonny Boy starts going through the storage box, loading shells into the shotgun's magazine. "This isn't a normal house, Cass. Holzmann's got guards and shit, and there's only three of us."

"The storm will cover us," she says as she checks the action on the Hellcat. "We just gotta go in fast. Before they realize we're there, we'll get the safe and be gone." She puts the key into the glove box, where the pistol had been. If something goes wrong, she wants it out here as a bargaining chip.

"Hey, Cass," Vic says, pointing toward Holzmann's house. "Something's happening."

Cass looks up. There is, indeed, something happening. The front gate opens, and two black sedans pull out. "Stay low," she says. The sedans turn toward them.

"He knows we're here," Jonny Boy says. "Richard told him."

"No," Vic says. "He wouldn't do that."

Cass isn't so sure. She lowers her seat, hoping to stay out of their view as the cars approach. The sun reflects off their windshields, keeping her from seeing their passengers. How many of Holzmann's men is she going to need to deal with? She's got twelve rounds in the Hellcat. If she can start shooting first, she can take a few of them out, maybe drive the rest off.

She slides into the footwell. If Holzmann's men are going to open fire blindly, they'll focus their attention where the bulk of her mass should be. She might be able to dodge the worst of the volley if she stays here.

"Give me the shotgun," Vic says. He's laid his chair as flat as it will go and reaches back for the gun from Jonny Boy. Good. Cass would much rather he have it. She's not sure Jonny Boy would be able to pull the trigger.

"Hey, Vic?" Jonny Boy says, handing the gun over.

"Shut the fuck up," she hisses at him. The sedans are fifty feet away and closing.

The sun isn't down yet. The storm hasn't arrived. She'd been counting on those to cover their noise and fragment Holzmann's forces. They need to do this quickly. Deal with whoever is coming and get into the estate before Holzmann realizes that his little ambush has failed. They'll have no margin for error, but she can pull this off.

She inhales deeply, willing her pulse down. The lead car is thirty feet away. She slowly lets the breath out. She's a decent shot, but the tiny pistol is unreliable, and she's shooting from the hip through the side of the van at an ambiguously placed target. She needs the car close if she wants to make this count. Twenty feet now. At ten she'll take the shot.

"Be ready," she whispers to Vic.

A cloud passes over the sun, the first hint of the encroaching storm, and the glare drops away. She can see the driver. His eyes are forward, not on her. The passenger looks away, gesturing at nothing. Both are Holzmann's men, but they're paying her no mind. The back is empty.

Vic shifts beside her, rising up to fire. She throws a hand out. "Wait!" she calls, willing command into her voice while trying to stay quiet enough that she doesn't draw attention from the passing sedan. Vic falls back into his seat.

The second sedan passes, just like the first, without a glance toward them. Two more soldiers heading somewhere else. Cass watches them go, and only once they turn the corner and leave her view does she slide her finger out of the trigger guard and make the Hellcat safe.

"Fuck," she says, drawing the word out into an exhale. "They weren't coming for us."

"Where were they going?" Jonny Boy asks.

"How the fuck am I supposed to know that? Christ, Jonny Boy. Use your fucking head."

The storm is getting closer. Soon it will be time for them to move, and the universe seems to be reaching out to Cass. It knows it has given her a hard fucking go of it. But it is ready to make amends.

"It's good news," she says. "Holzmann's sent his men away. The place will be empty."

"Yeah," Jonny Boy says. "I guess you're right."

The rest of the storm's approach passes with agonizing slowness. Waiting for the cover of darkness and the distraction of thunder is critical, but she doesn't know how long those four men will be gone.

The storm inches closer, and the sun sinks further behind the clouds. Jonny Boy hands out balaclavas.

When the rain lets loose, Vic sets off with a wooden ladder under his arm and the shotgun strapped to his back. He scales the wall around Holzmann's compound, and two minutes later the pedestrian gate out front pops open. Cass and Jonny Boy hurry through to find Vic holding two guards at gunpoint.

He has already disarmed and gagged them, and it's a good thing, too. If they were to talk, they'd scare Jonny Boy with threats of Holzmann's retribution. Instead, all that they can offer are drooly, muffled grunts.

"I thought the place was empty," Jonny Boy says. "You said Holzmann sent all his people away."

"They're just watching the gate," Cass says. "And Vic took care of them. The house will be open." Vic frowns at her but doesn't say anything. She has no idea if it's true, of course, but by the time Jonny Boy learns otherwise, it'll be too late for him to back down.

Cass checks the guardhouse for an alarm panel they might have hit. Instead, she finds and snags a bundle of riot cuffs. One pair locks each guard's hands behind their backs, another binds their ankles together, and a third attaches those two sets to each other, effectively hog-tying the men. She locks them, gagged and bound, in the little structure. Cass grabs their pistols—no need to use her own when Holzmann so helpfully provides—and hands one to Jonny Boy.

"Hey," Vic says, holding out the shotgun to Jonny Boy. "Trade you? I'm the better shot with that."

The three of them, already soaked by the rain, hustle toward the house. Cass points to the front door.

"Head in there. Sweep the house. Don't give them a chance to react." She has to pause as the thunder makes all communication impossible for a moment. "I'll go around back and catch anyone trying to run. We meet in the middle, and we're gone in five minutes."

With a nod, Vic takes off for the front door, and Jonny Boy, after giving her one final sad look in the hopes that she will call the whole thing off, follows.

CHAPTER 21

Jim Pickens, 5:03 P.M.

A t five o'clock, the storm arrives. The sun is still well above the horizon, but the clouds roll across it and bring an early twilight. When the rain comes, it comes suddenly, a furious torrent of water.

The men in the yard scramble for cover, trying to shelter beneath the building's eaves before acquiescing and moving into the guesthouse. From there they can still watch the yard and be at the main house quickly.

When the first bolt of lightning strikes nearby, it shakes the building to its foundation. Holzmann glances outside with disapproval, upset at nature's audacity. As the peals of thunder continue, one every minute or so, and visibility through the window is reduced to mere feet by the sheeting rain, Holzmann's frown deepens. He should have been celebrating his triumph by now, toasting the new growth and respect that the safe's contents would afford him.

The first crack of gunfire might be mistaken for another thunder-clap, but as a dozen more shots and a scream of pain follow in rapid succession, there is no doubt as to what is occurring in the front of the house.

"Get down," Holzmann says, though Pickens is already flat on the ground. "Protect the safe." Holzmann goes into a cabinet and comes out with a rifle.

This is not what the locksmith signed on for. His criminality lies in the quiet patience of a puzzle, not the frenetic destruction of a firefight. But there are soldiers between Pickens and the danger. Trained men who know how to handle themselves wait on the other side of the solid door, ready to defend him.

There is another quick burst of gunfire. Closer than the last one. Pickens curls behind the solid workbench. At any moment the gunmen could burst through the door and kill him. He never should have come here. Someone is begging for their life. Words nearly indistinguishable through phlegm and panic. Pickens wishes they would be quiet.

"Control yourself," Holzmann hisses at him. All traces of his accent have disappeared. Pickens closes his mouth, and the begging stops. "War is a trial of moral forces by means of physical ones. If we do not break, they cannot defeat us."

Pickens stares at Holzmann. The old man has placed himself behind the door which leads to the house. Should the gunmen try to come here, they will find Holzmann and his rifle at their backs.

More gunfire, closer than before, drives him again to the ground. Then a scream of profound pain tears through the wall. It is formless in its agony. It is shock and suffering stretched beyond the capacity of words to contain. It falls in pitch as the lungs and vocal cords that sustain it give way to the inevitable demands of the body.

And then a crash as the door flies in on a wave of splinters. Pickens just has a chance to see Holzmann's eyes widen as the slab of wood swings around, knocking the rifle off target and slamming him into the wall. A massive man stands in the doorway. His face is obscured by a balaclava, but the whites of his eyes shine through with rage and pain. He is massive not in height, but in girth. A gun, all black steel and hatred, hangs from a strap in his fingers, but he pays it no heed. He takes in Pickens, cowering on the ground, and then passes over him, following Pickens's gaze to Holzmann, recovering from the shock of the blow behind the door.

Holzmann lowers his rifle, but the intruder catches the barrel in one solid fist. He tears the gun from Holzmann's fingers and tosses it clear. Pickens sees in the old man's expression something that he has clearly not felt for a very long time. Holzmann is afraid.

There is something perverse about it. Something private. Pickens turns away from the old man's shame. The rifle lies, ignored, on the far side of the room. He could get there before the attacker could stop him.

But Pickens has been saying all day that he shouldn't be here. He wants nothing to do with this. He was brought here to open a safe. When it comes time to do so, he will gladly execute the terms of his agreement. Until then, he is a houseguest who has overstayed his welcome and now finds himself in the middle of a domestic spat.

There are two doors out of this room. One, which has just been half torn from its hinges, would take him back into the house, toward the screams and the gunfire. The other leads to the backyard, to the storm and the fury of nature. He'll take his chances with the lightning.

CHAPTER 22

Cass Mullen, 5:07 P.M.

The rain runs down Cass's face. She can't see a fucking thing as the holes in the balaclava gather the water into her eyes. Fuck it. She'll be out of the city soon, and she wants Holzmann to know it was her that fucked him. She rips the mask off.

Even without it, visibility is shit. The universe must still be looking out for her, though, because she meets no resistance as she heads into the backyard. She ducks beneath an eave as another clap of thunder rings out. It would be fucking rich if she got this far only to get fried by lightning.

Three doors lead from the backyard into the house, but she doesn't have long to wonder which one hides her prize, as the nearest opens. She presses herself against the wall of the house, hoping to stay out of view of whoever is coming.

A Black man she's never seen before crawls into the grass. He is underdressed for one of Holzmann's men, wearing khakis and a short-sleeve white shirt with a collar and tie. Usually they wear full suits, really leaning into the whole mafioso aesthetic, but this guy looks more like a computer geek than a goombah.

She steps into his field of view and raises the pistol. He looks up at her from the mud with wide eyes. He looks terrified. Terrified means malleable, and that's good enough for her.

"Who the fuck are you?" she asks.

The man stares at the gun. "People call me Pickens," he says.

"OK, Pickens. Where's the fucking safe?"

He glances back over his shoulder. Just inside the door, resting on a workbench, is a black box, about the size of a shoebox. She smiles and says a silent thank you to whatever celestial being she owes for this one. She pushes Pickens ahead of her and back into the house.

This room is spacious. A desk is set up along one wall, and a small table sits in the corner with a stack of papers and a brown paper lunch bag on top of it. The safe, in the center of the room, is surrounded by tools. Near the shattered remnants of the interior door, his gun forgotten on the ground beside him, Jonny Boy stands over Holzmann. He has pinned the old man to the wall with one forearm across his chest and the other raised back to slam a fist down into the cowering crime lord's face.

Holzmann's eyes, wide with panic, fall on her as she slips fully into the room. This is the most feared man in the city. She has never met him, and if she didn't know that this was his estate, she might not recognize him. Holzmann is a force. His power is a constant in Omaha. But this man before her is desperate. He is pleading. He is broken. And he has been brought to this state by, of all people, motherfucking Jonny Boy. It would be beautiful were it not so pathetic.

She catches Pickens by the collar as he tries to slink back out into the rain. He mumbles something incoherent, and she tosses him into the room.

"Jonny Boy," she calls, but the fat man doesn't respond. He brings his fist down into Holzmann's face. She doesn't want him to kill the old man. He could still be useful.

"Jonny Boy!" she shouts again, crossing the room to pull him off Holzmann.

Jonny Boy turns, snarling. Spattered across his skin, visible through the gaps of the balaclava, are flecks of red. He looks ready to turn his wrath on her, to strike her with the same fury that Holzmann just felt. Instead, his eyes narrow, and he deflates, like a toddler finally accepting that the adults will not indulge his tantrum. She snatches the shotgun off the ground. The barrel is cool to the touch. Jonny Boy never fired the thing.

"Where's Vic?" she asks. Jonny Boy looks to the ruins of the nearby door.

"Herr Wright," Holzmann whispers. "You will suffer for this."

"You shut your fucking mouth." Cass raises the shotgun to aim at the old man.

He pulls himself away from the wall, whatever panic he was feeling driven off. He stands straight. A slow trickle of blood highlights the wrinkles that cobweb his face.

"And you must be Cassiopeia," he says. "You, my dear, are on the verge of a grave mistake from which there can be no recovery."

Cass will deal with that bullshit in a minute. She still hasn't gotten an answer from Jonny Boy.

"Where is Vic?" she asks again. He continues to stare at the ruined door. She takes a few steps toward it, keeping Holzmann on the business end of the shotgun. She can smell the mingling of blood and powder now, the stench of human offal.

What's beyond the door doesn't make sense. For all her talk, she's never actually seen a dead body, not even someone who passed peacefully in their sleep, like Vic's grandma. She had always imagined that people would behave a certain way in death. They would hold themselves in a particular manner—leaning against a wall or falling to their knees in a final moment of prayer—before they expire, their head lolling to the side as they slip into a gentle repose.

This room is not gentle. The bodies are not in repose.

It takes time for the details of the room to resolve. For the swirling images to solidify, the fragmentary horrors to coalesce from a hundred tiny details into a singular reality. There are only three bodies in the room. Two look like Holzmann's guards. They wear suits. Their hair is neatly trimmed. The third had perhaps been on a break, or at the end of his shift. He wears a black tracksuit, and a balaclava conceals his face. He is roughly Vic's size and build.

She steps away from the room and its viscera.

"Where is Vic?" she asks for the third time.

Jonny Boy stares at her. "They shot him," he says. His voice rasps in his throat. "Vic is dead."

That doesn't make sense. Vic can't be dead. She just saw him five minutes ago.

"I will give you one final opportunity." Holzmann is still talking. The son of a bitch sounds almost bored. How the fuck can he be so calm? She's supposed to be in fucking charge here. "One chance to save your lives. Give me the gun."

At some point while she was looking into the other room, Jonny Boy must have found a rifle, because he now has one in his hand, and he is about to give it to Holzmann.

"You shut your fucking mouth," she screams at the old man, pointing her shotgun at him once more—she must have let her aim fall away from him, though she has no memory of it—and taking a step closer. "What the fuck are you doing, Jonny Boy?"

Jonny Boy looks from her to the gun in his hand.

"You will not escape me, Herr Wright," Holzmann says. There is an emptiness to his expression that terrifies her. He no longer cares what happens in this room. He has seen how this ends, and now he is merely relaying those facts. "No matter how far you run, I will find you, and I will deliver to you terrible suffering."

"Shut your fucking mouth and turn around." She should kill him, but he might still have value as a hostage. "Pickens, get over here. Grab the safe."

"You don't know what you're doing." Holzmann ignores the weapon aimed at him. "You cannot open that safe."

"I've got the fucking key," she says.

"But not the skill to apply it," he replies gently.

Fuck. The fucking bastard is right.

Looking at this safe, she wouldn't have the first fucking clue how to get it open. She'd been hoping there would be a spot that the weird metal ball would fit in, but it looks to her like any other safe in the world, except for the cluster of holes drilled through the front. There's a dial with a bunch of numbers and a big gray handle, but no clear way to use the key to get it open.

"I'll figure it out," she says, reaching for the handle.

"No," Pickens shouts. "It's trapped. You make one mistake and the safe will destroy itself."

"But give me the key," Holzmann says, "and we will open it together. I've heard good things about your crew, Cassiopeia, and the fact that you were able to get in here tonight speaks volumes to your skills. I'll pay you double what I had offered to Herr Sands. A hundred thousand dollars, plus future employment. There's fifty on the table right over there." He points toward the paper bag.

Keeping her gun trained on Holzmann, Cass grabs the bag. There are five thick bundles of hundred-dollar bills inside.

"Fuck that," she says. "Pickens, you seem to know a lot. You know how to open the safe?"

The man says nothing, but his expression is answer enough.

"Right," she says, waving her gun at him. "You carry the safe. Holzmann here is gonna lead us out."

"Cass," Jonny Boy mewls from beside her. "I don't like this, Cass."

"Just shut the fuck up, and do your fucking job," she says. "Pickens, grab the safe and walk. And you"—this to Holzmann—"anything happens to us, you catch nine double-aught pellets with your head. Jonny Boy, get your shit together, hold that fucking gun straight, and cover our back."

"Will the rain damage anything?" Holzmann asks Pickens.

He thinks for a moment before he responds. "No, the inner core is still intact. The water shouldn't get anywhere that matters. I'll need my gear, though," he says to Cass, pointing to a duffel bag on the workbench.

"Bring what you need," she says. "But you're carrying it."

"We should get Vic," Jonny Boy says. He keeps glancing at the ruined door, though he seems unable to take a step toward it.

"No," Cass says. "We need to get the fuck out of here."

With Pickens carrying the duffel over his shoulder and the safe under his arm, Cass follows Holzmann out into the yard, around the side of the house, and through the front gate once more. Holzmann says nothing more as they march to the van.

"You're being awful quiet," Cass says.

Holzmann shrugs. "You have a gun on me."

"That didn't stop you saying anything before."

Despite the warmth of the summer storm, the gaze that he fixes her with chills her. She has spent her life being ignored and dismissed as a woman or a freak, but she gets the sense, as Holzmann looks at her now, that he truly sees her, that he is judging the full weight of her value.

"You will fail, Cassiopeia Mullen," he says, forcing her to lean in to hear him. "You will err in this foolhardy ploy, and when you do, I will kill you. In the meantime, I am content to remain near, to ensure that your idiocy does not cost me more than the hassle of cleaning up whatever mess you left at my home."

She should have let him stay quiet.

CHAPTER 23

Peter Van Horn, 5:20 P.M.

The crash of thunder jolts him awake. It is dark and pouring rain, and Peter Van Horn has no idea where he is. It returns to him slowly. Tracking Barrett, tracking the old man. He is still parked by the house in Elkhorn. He was supposed to go back to the station. They should have called him. He could have explained.

He takes his phone out, but the screen stays black. The battery is dead.

He grabs the keys·off the center console, fumbling them in the dark. Maybe he can still make it back to the station in time to talk to Sarge. To make them all understand that none of this is his fault.

Movement outside his car draws his attention. People, obscured by dark and rain, come out of the gate of the old man's house. They head away from him. In the strobe of a lightning bolt, he catches the shape of a gun.

What the hell is going on?

This isn't his problem. All that he invites by carrying on is further questions into his own conduct.

He still has his service weapon. Leaving his keys in the ignition, he draws his gun and slides out of the car. He shuts the door quietly behind him, not that anyone could hear it over the rain and thunder. Staying in a low crouch, he runs along the side of the road, following after the figures. He sees one of them, too far away to make out any detail beyond their black clothing, getting into the driver's seat of a white panel van. The van drives away, and Peter is left alone in the rain.

He saw them leaving the old man's house with a gun, though. Someone inside might need help. He should call for backup. He knows he should.

The figures left the gate ajar. Peter opens it with the muzzle of his gun, both leading with the weapon and trying to avoid touching anything directly. He pushes his hair back. Perhaps the wet will keep it in place.

There is a small guardhouse, but he can't see inside. He hurries past toward the house in the center of the lot. The front door is cracked. Light from inside seeps out.

"Hello?" Peter calls as he mounts the steps to the porch. "Is anybody home? This is the Omaha PD."

He gets no response from inside, but the front door has been kicked in. He should call this in. A crime has been committed, the scene is not secure, and he is here without backup. Protocol is to call it in and move off the premises, establish a perimeter, and wait for detectives to arrive.

The front door just barely hangs on its frame, and the hinges groan in protest as Peter nudges it aside and steps into the mansion's foyer.

Holy shit.

Peter isn't one for obscenity, but it feels appropriate now. Nothing else can convey what lies before him. A man in a suit slumps on the ground in the back of the room. He might have been one of the guards that Peter saw earlier. He isn't, but he's dressed the same.

Peter knows he's dead. Living bodies don't look like that. They don't lie that still. He spots a gun on the ground near the corpse. Another door drifts open beyond the dead man, beckoning Peter on to further horrors inside.

Peter can feel that coil tightening across his chest again. Whatever is going on, he should not be here. He doesn't know how this is going to spin against him, but he does know, as surely as he has ever known anything, that this does not end well for him if he is ever linked to this house.

He goes through the last few minutes in his mind. He was careful not to touch anything. There should be no trace that he was ever here. He holsters his gun and walks away. Back down the driveway that bends lazily across the yard. Past the darkened guardhouse—better to not look inside.

He wants to run. More than anything, he wants to break into a sprint and put as much distance between himself and that house—that body— as he possibly can. But there might be people watching. A neighbor looking out a window. He must stay calm.

He gets back to the street, back to his car, and opens the door with trembling hands. The key is still in the ignition. His fingers slip off it at first, but he gets it to turn, and the engine comes stuttering to life. He needs to get home.

Nobody knows he was there. He touched nothing. He left no trace. There were no witnesses. Tomorrow he will go in to work like nothing happened. He will explain to Sergeant Nowicki that he was distraught over the morning's meeting, and he left early. He must have failed to clock out due to the mental duress. Sarge will insist on an official write-up. Professional Oversight will be displeased. He might lose his job. He might lose everything to the bank. But there is somebody out there who wants to do worse. Someone is trying to destroy him. And Peter will not let them put that body on him.

There is no way he can be placed in that house. He left no trace. There won't even be cell records that he was nearby since his phone was dead. He can do this. He just needs to say nothing. Keep his head down and get through it.

That's what he tells himself as he lies in bed, still soaked through from the rain. The adrenaline crash takes him, and his whole body begins to shake. Maybe this is shock, he thinks. He wonders that he can observe his body's reaction, the tremors, the elevated heart rate, the hyperventilation, with such detachment.

He does not experience the things his body is going through. It's as though he were in the chair beside the bed, watching himself undergo this trauma but not participating.

He left no trace, he tells himself.

And he is almost correct.

If he had stopped on the porch, it would have been true. If he had opened the door, but gone no further, then that would have been the end of it. He could have gone in to the station, taken his lumps, and gotten on with his life. But he hadn't stopped at the porch. He entered the house, and as he stepped inside, he stepped into view of a camera, mounted to the ceiling, recording everything that happens in that room. Everyone who enters Holzmann's headquarters.

CHAPTER 24

Cass Mullen, 5:23 P.M.

Cass keeps her speed low as she navigates the suburban streets. They can't risk getting pulled over for running a stop sign.

"Hey, Cass," Jonny Boy says from the back. He's on the storage box, holding the rifle loosely on Holzmann and Pickens, who are on the futon, flanking the safe. "What are we gonna do?"

"We're gonna be rich," she says.

Jonny Boy looks at her through the rearview mirror. "What are we gonna do about Vic?" He pulls the balaclava off, and his face is pink. Rainwater mixed with blood. Vic's blood.

Fuck. For all her complaints, Vic was always there for her. He always had her back. He might have been an idiot, but he was her idiot. And now he's dead.

Holzmann has rattled her. Left her questioning herself. She could have just sold him the key. Stuck to the plan she had this morning. Get it from Barrett, cut out Richard, and set herself up with the biggest game in town. It was a good plan. But she'd gotten it in her head to go after more.

Fuck that, and fuck regrets. She'd never be happy working under Holzmann. Don't think she hadn't noticed that Jonny Boy was "Herr Wright" while she was just "Cassiopeia." Misogynist fuck. She has his key. She has his safe. She has him. He may be the most feared man in Omaha, but she just took down his whole operation with nothing but two dumb fucks.

"We're gonna honor him," she says, meeting Jonny Boy's eye in the mirror. "Every day we're sipping our piña coladas, living the good life, being the baddest motherfuckers around, we'll toast to him."

"He's dead, Cass," Jonny Boy says, as though she didn't fucking know that already. "They shot him, and he died, and I watched him—I watched it happen."

"Yeah. That happened. But we got a job to do, so man the fuck up, and let's find out what he did it all for." She grabs the key from the glove box and tosses it back to Jonny Boy.

He—miracle of miracles—catches it out of the air in his left hand, keeping his right on the rifle. He considers the lump of metal, trying to figure out how to make it work. "What do I do with it?" he asks, waving it around in front of the safe.

"Just open it," Cass says.

Jonny Boy grabs the handle of the safe, but Holzmann puts his hand on top of Jonny Boy's. "Do not force it," he says.

Jonny Boy pulls his hand back. "Don't touch me."

"If you force the handle," Holzmann continues, "then it will destroy the egg inside. You must use the key to open it."

"And how do we do that?" Cass asks. She squints through the dark outside, trying to make out the writing on a street sign. She doesn't want to use the GPS on her phone and leave a digital trace of her presence on these streets. Pickens starts to laugh. He has been compliant so far, but, as his laughter intensifies, she grows concerned.

"What's so funny?" Jonny Boy asks, but the man just keeps laughing. Jonny Boy swings the gun to aim at him, which only causes the laughter to redouble.

Cass turns her focus back to Holzmann. "What's the egg? You said the safe will destroy the egg. What is it?"

Holzmann's eyes flick to hers, and he smiles but says nothing.

Jonny Boy jabs the rifle at Pickens. "Why are you laughing?"

"The key," the man gasps. "Look at it."

Jonny Boy had been holding the key in his left hand. When he raised the gun, he used that hand to grab the forestock, cracking the key into it. Now that it's been pointed out to him, Jonny Boy sees it. In its mirrored skin. A chip. The tin emulsion that the aluminum was bonded to has broken off, revealing the inert plastic beneath.

"What does it mean?" Jonny Boy asks, staring at the gouge in the metal.

Pickens swallows down the trailing end of his nervous laugh. "It's a fake," he says. "That isn't the key."

That doesn't make sense, not after everything they did to get here. "It can't be fake," Cass says, turning in her seat to look for herself.

Holzmann, having decided that he will get no better distraction than this, lunges forward. His shoulder collides with Jonny Boy's gut, but, unable to find purchase on his rain- and blood-slicked clothing, he bounces off the man's prodigious girth.

Cass flinches at his sudden movement, pulling the wheel slightly to the right from her twisted position. At the same time, the back right tire passes over a pothole, and the back of the vehicle begins to drift.

Jonny Boy, spinning to face Holzmann and feeling the seat beneath him move, instinctively grabs for something. His left hand closes around the fake broken key as his right squeezes the trigger of the rifle.

The bullet passes harmlessly over Holzmann and impacts the rear of the van, deforming the latch that holds the doors closed. As Holzmann tumbles into them—having been thrown fully off his feet by the van's sickening lurch to the side—the doors fall open, and he teeters on the precipice.

Cass turns back to the road. She needs to get control of the van before she can sort out the clusterfuck unfolding in the rear. She spins the wheel left, into the drift, and the tires bite into the asphalt once more. The back of the vehicle fishtails as it realigns with their direction of travel.

The rifle's roar deafened her, so she can't hear what's going on behind her. She glances in the mirror, but all she sees are the doors flapping in the rain.

"Jesus, fuck!" Cass shouts. She brings the van to a stop in the middle of the street. "What the fuck is happening back there?"

Jonny Boy looks out the open rear of the van into the dark beyond before pulling the doors closed once more. Face ashen, he turns back to Cass.

"Holzmann's gone," he says.

Fuck.

Cass slams the van into reverse, hoping to find the old man laid out on the pavement, but the same cover the dark and rain gave her earlier makes it impossible to see the street, and someone's coming out of a nearby store to check on what happened.

Fuck. Fuck. Fuck.

Holzmann is gone. The key is fake. Vic is dead.

But they have the safe, and they have Pickens, now curled protectively around it, and Pickens seems to know more about it than they do.

As she puts the van back into drive, she glances in the mirror at the man and the safe.

"So tell me about this egg," she says.

121

CHAPTER 25

Henry Holzmann, 5:29 P.M.

Henry Holzmann picks himself up off the asphalt. His trousers are ripped at the left hip and the right knee, where he bounced as he rolled from the van. He makes an effort to straighten his jacket and restore order to the tuck of his shirt, but the whole outfit will need to be replaced.

He considers going after the van. Cassiopeia and her fat idiot of a lackey have his safe and his safecracker, but he is unarmed and injured from his fall. For several months now, a pain has been growing in his left leg. He has practiced, in the late hours of the night, walking with a cane in preparation for the day when that would become necessary. That day, it would seem, has come early.

A cane offers many advantages if you look past the implicit acknowledgment of weakness. As a gestural tool, it provides a powerful emphasis. It gives the hands an occupation. In material and decoration, it can convey status and origin. It is a weapon.

Holzmann has a number of canes prepared, and they wait for him back at his office. He does not relish the idea, but one must accept one's situation if one is to overcome it. There is no strength to be gained in pretending he is anything other than that which he is: an old man. But those canes are of no use to him now.

He is not far from his headquarters, but he is far enough that walking back is out of the question. There is every possibility that, given the gunfire, the police will be converging there soon, and he has no desire to be there when that occurs.

He will lose the money that was stored there. And the drugs. But that is of no concern. He kept no records in that estate, and what he had there is but a fraction of his operation. Those things can all be replaced. All that matters now is the safe.

He misses the days of pay phones. They offered both anonymity and convenience that cell phones cannot match. If pay phones were still as ubiquitous as they were thirty years ago, he would have been able to reach his people immediately. Even if he carried a phone on him—and he does not, why would he burden himself with a microphone and tracking device?—it would have likely been rendered inoperable by his fall from the van.

"Sir, are you all right?" a young woman behind him calls out.

A pretty girl, the hair in her ponytail curling in the rain, runs toward him with an umbrella. She wears an apron full of pockets bearing the logo of the florist's shop on the street corner. As she catches sight of his disarray, her mouth falls open.

"You're hurt," she cries. "Oh my god, did that car hit you?"

"No, my dear." He gives his jacket sleeves a final tug, situating the cloth as best he can. "I just took a bit of a tumble on the curb. I seem to have misplaced myself in this weather." He gives her as gentle of a smile as he can muster and allows her to take his elbow. She smells of pollen and cut flowers, an odor of life that can only be acquired through killing. As she moves the umbrella to cover him, he pushes it back.

"You are too kind, madam, but please, keep yourself dry. My attire is already a lost cause, but yours need not be sacrificed."

She gives him a strange look, but he keeps his grip on the umbrella firm. She relents and helps him shuffle toward the florist shop.

"What are you doing out in this?" she asks him.

"I was on a walk," he says. She holds the shop door open for him. "I must have lost track of time, and then the storm snuck up on me."

"You wait here. I've got towels and a first aid kit in the back. Do you need an ambulance? Did you hit your head?"

"Oh no, nothing like that," he says. "If I might borrow your phone to call my son, I don't want to impose on you any more than I already have."

She insists on at least cleaning the minor scrapes on his face, and as she fusses over him—"I've a deft hand at this," she says, using a pair of tweezers to pull tiny scraps of rock out of his skin. "Scratched myself raw on plenty of thorns before"—he calls Benny.

Cassiopeia must be dealt with, obviously. His safe and his man, Herr Pickens, must be recovered. He has also learned that Barrett Rye is something more than the bystander he pretended to be. If he had the time, he would like to investigate further, but the operation is in danger, and the man is a threat. He needs to be eliminated.

"Benny, this is your father," he says, when his lieutenant answers the phone.

"Boss?" Benny says in confusion. "What's going on? Cass wasn't at her place."

"I know. I'm at a flower shop with a nice young woman." Holzmann smiles at the girl as she applies an antibiotic cream to his face. "Cassiopeia just dropped by the house for a visit. I went for a walk and am now stuck out in the rain."

"Oh shit," Benny says. "Do you need help?"

"No, no. You have to go pick up that thing from Rye."

"I do?" Benny asks.

"Yes. He has what we need. Send your brother Lang to get me."

"And what about Richard Sands, sir? We found him at Cass's place. He's tied up in the trunk of my car now."

The young woman finally stops pawing at Holzmann and steps away. She whistles a tune Holzmann does not recognize as she packs away the medical supplies in the back.

"Have him verify that Rye gives you the real thing," Holzmann says. "Then eliminate them both." He tells Benny where the flower shop is, then hangs up as the girl returns.

"You've got quite the family, it sounds like," she says, putting the phone back behind the counter.

"Yes," he replies. "I am very blessed."

While he waits, the first sirens sound through the night. The gunshots were reported, it would seem. The headquarters must be abandoned. He has overcome worse before, though. Cassiopeia lost a third of her strength. Richard Sands is already off the table, and soon enough the enigma that is Barrett Rye will be as well. The goal of war, Clausewitz reminds him, is quite simple: the utter destruction of your enemy.

"I wonder what all that's about," the girl muses, looking off toward the sound. Holzmann does not respond.

When his man Lang pulls up with a sedan outside, Holzmann excuses himself, glad to escape the girl's kind ministrations. Lang maintains a farm for him to the west of the city. It is a quiet and secure location from which he can plan his next steps.

By the time they arrive, he knows what he needs to do. He is pleased to see that there are two men on the porch that runs the circumference of the farmhouse. This is getting out of control. He needs to win this war, and at present, his forces are at risk of getting swamped and rolled up. This is why a good commander does not commit everything to the first engagement. You hold your strongest pieces in reserve, waiting until the enemy is deployed and the battle is joined to direct them where they are needed most.

CHAPTER 26

Barrett Rye, 6:12 P.M.

I see the car pull into the alley behind my building about an hour after the rain begins. Benny, the guard who walked me to Holzmann at the coffee stand, is driving with the other man I'd seen in the park in the passenger seat. So something has happened, and now they are coming back. Interesting. Cassiopeia—I'd overheard her name when Holzmann called me from the park—and her boys had done something. She works quickly.

That the car is parked but nobody is coming up to see me does not bode well. I knew this might happen, that Holzmann might take my actions poorly and try to take the key by force. I had hoped I wouldn't need to, but I am willing to demonstrate that this is the far more costly option.

My preparations don't take long, but it's nearly midnight before Benny makes his move. My hallway camera notifies me of his approach. He holds a flashlight in one hand and his gun—already drawn—in the other. He is alone. If I were him, I'd send my partner to cover the fire escape and trap my target in the middle. I need to handle him quickly. I dim the light of my monitor so it doesn't give me away.

My front door creaks satisfyingly when he knocks on it, swinging open on poorly maintained hinges. He hadn't expected that, that I'd leave the door not only unlocked but unlatched. I know I'm giving up an advantage. I'm telling him I know he is there, and in doing so throwing away the element of surprise.

I want to give him a chance, though, to reconsider and turn away. I want him to understand that this can still end peacefully. He is the one taking the aggressive move. Whatever comes next is on his head, not mine.

His light sweeps across the open space of my living room. The kitchen, the couch, the desk, and, finally, the bedroom. He can see my bed, but I am not there. My hiding place is almost childish in its simplicity.

I let the man close the door behind himself before I speak. "You have my money?"

He tracks my voice to the couch. He can't see me, but there's only so much floor space behind it where I could be.

He doesn't announce himself. He doesn't tell me to surrender. He just shoots. So that's the kind of night it's going to be.

I gave him a chance.

He fires five times in rapid succession. The pistol is suppressed, but it is still shockingly loud in the confined space. Like the blows of a jackhammer. But, given the weather, perhaps my neighbors could still look the other way and pretend it was only a lightning strike. Or five.

"There's a new offer on the table," he says. "Give me the key and I let you live." It's a bit rich after he already opened fire. I could be bleeding out on the floor, or already dead. But now he makes the offer. How generous.

He steps carefully in the dark, his back pressed to the wall, keeping his distance from the couch while circling to see behind it.

"Thanks," I say. His light comes around the corner, landing on the speaker sitting on the couch cushions. I'm not there. Never was. I was in my coat closet with a microphone and a blanket over my head to dampen the sound.

Now I've moved. Now I'm behind him.

"But I'll pass."

He turns at the sound of my voice, but he's let me get too close. The hearing protection he is wearing—he knew he was going to fire that gun—muffled my footsteps. I catch his right wrist, the wrist of his gun hand, with my left, isolating it up and away from us. Controlling the gun is my first priority. My second is to end this fight quickly.

I slip my leg behind him and hook his knee, knocking his support out from underneath him and pulling his hip against my own. Then I kick his leg back as my right arm locks across his neck and drives his torso away from me.

Given my size, Benny has no chance to defend himself. Before he even fully absorbs my presence, he is in the air, rolling backward across my hip and toward the ground with his legs flung out in front of him. It is a supremely disorienting takedown.

At a different time in my life, I would have tried to take his gun for myself—or would already have one of my own. He forfeited his rights when he came into my home and tried to kill me. But I'm trying to be better. I'm trying to leave that behind. I don't want to kill this man, but I also can't assume he's alone. I need to eliminate his threat as quickly as I can.

As we fall, I keep control of his wrist, trapping his arm across my body, and wrap a leg around his torso. I hear his head slam into the ground, the back of his skull making first contact. That might be enough to take him out right there, but I need to be sure. You don't fuck around when guns are involved. With my leg holding his chest down, I pull his arm up even further and stretch my back, using my hips as leverage to hyperextend his shoulder, which is trapped between my thighs. I can feel the joint pop and the cartilage tear as the bone rips free from the socket. The gun falls to the ground behind my head. I drop his arm and sweep the gun away as I jump to my feet.

The whole thing takes me less than five seconds.

I glance at my security monitors, visible through the now open door of the closet, but the hallway is still empty, and it is too dark outside to see anyone who might be in the alley. If Benny's compatriot is out there, at least that same darkness has kept me safe, preventing him from firing through the window and risking hitting Benny.

As Benny's flashlight, dropped at the start of the fight, rolls across the ground, though, the beam crosses me, exposing my position to anybody outside. I've just enough time to dive away as a clap of thunder, accompanied by the shattering of my window, heralds another gunshot. Keeping low and to the shadows, I dash toward the wall and this second attacker, reaching cover just as he pokes his gun through the now open gap where my window used to be.

I let him start climbing through before I make my move. Again I try to grab his wrist to control the gun, but it slips through my fingers, and my hand closes around the weapon's barrel instead. I catch his knee with my other hand and drive him back toward my desk.

He hits the solid furniture, my own weight adding force to the impact, and then tumbles to the ground. His finger, already against the trigger, twitches and the gun fires. The slide tears at the skin of my palm, and the heat of the contained explosion burns me. That slide is engineered to use the force of the gunshot to eject the spent shell and load a new one into the chamber. With my hand wrapped around it—though it hurts like hell—I've interrupted that mechanism and jammed the pistol.

I slip a hand underneath his arm and pin his shoulder and wrist with my body. I feel him start to fight me, but he is a hair too late to escape the lock. With my arm beneath his, I have all the leverage I need to torque his elbow up and away, even as his wrist and shoulder remain stuck to the ground. There is a moment of resistance, and then a sickening crack as his elbow shatters.

I rip the gun from his enervated fingers and come once again to my feet as he starts to crawl away from me, dragging himself across the ground with his good arm. A quick glance out the window confirms the fire escape is empty. Benny has started to regain his senses, but there is no fight left in either of them. I find the magazine release and drop it clear.

"You don't know who you're fucking with," Benny says. His partner stops trying to crawl away.

"Neither do you," I say.

I don't like hurting people. I can feel the bile rising. The sound of that elbow snapping echoes in counterpoint to the ringing tinnitus. But just because I don't like hurting people doesn't mean I'm not damned fucking good at it. There's a reason Scarpello valued me, and I can be a scary motherfucker when I need to be.

"Holzmann isn't an enemy you want," Benny says. I have to give him credit: he is remarkably cogent for someone who just had his shoulder ripped out of its socket.

"He chose this, not me," I say as I retrieve the second gun and unload it as well. "Tell your boss if he wants to deal, we can deal. But my price just went up. Now get the fuck out of my house."

I watch from the broken window as they stumble out to their car. The trunk stands open in the rain. There is a brief discussion between them, and they both check the alley. They've lost something, but before they can start a search, Benny catches sight of me. Getting away from me must be worth more than finding whatever was in their trunk, because he slams it closed, and they drive away. No sooner have they turned onto the street than I see their missing quarry hop from behind a dumpster. His flight is halting with both his wrists and ankles tied.

CHAPTER 27

Barrett Rye, 11:50 P.M.

B y the time I get outside, he has stopped trying to run and begun scraping the cord binding him against a wall. So far, the nylon seems to be doing more damage to the brick than the other way around.

"You need a hand?" I ask him.

He looks up at me, and his face falls.

"Oh, you've got to be fucking kidding me," he says.

I haven't seen Richard Sands since I took the key off him behind Brock's gambling den. The intervening day has not been kind to him.

He objects, at first, but I cut him free and convince him I truly mean him no further harm. He follows me back to my apartment, and I get him a glass of hot water with lemon, then leave him alone to shower. As I hang his clothes up to dry in my bedroom, a cell phone tumbles from his pocket. It's gotten a bit wet, so I wrap it in paper towels to dry, then set about restoring order to my place. It gives me a chance to think.

Holzmann sending men to kill me means that this is working. He's getting worried. He's getting desperate. It means Cassiopeia and her team were successful. That I was right to send them, to plant that idea in her head. But how successful? Where should my next move be? To know that, I need information. I need Richard to finish his shower.

I track down the bullets that were fired through my couch. There are some nasty gouges where they ricocheted off the floor, but the wall caught all five. The last one—from the gun that went off in my hand as the second man climbed through the window—is lodged in my front door. My hand is burned, but it will recover. I wipe down and strip the two guns, then toss them in a bag to dispose of tomorrow. I've finished sweeping up the broken glass and begun stapling a sheet of plastic over the window when I hear the shower turn off.

Richard comes out of the bathroom with a towel wrapped around himself. His torso is spotted with bruises and his left eye is partially closed with swelling. By morning it'll all be sour and purple.

"There's Tylenol and aspirin in the bathroom," I tell him.

"I already found them," he says.

I nod, then go back to my work. I'm desperate to ask questions, but that will only put him on the defensive.

"You're fucking dead," he says. "You know that, right?"

I continue repairing the window, letting the chunk of the stapler accentuate my blasé attitude. "You don't scare me," I say.

"I shouldn't. The guy you stole from should."

"I thought I stole from you."

"You can't be this fucking dense, can you?" he asks. Nothing pisses people off or convinces them I'm dumb as a brick quite like aggressive literalism delivered with a completely dry affect. "At least tell me you still have the key."

I nod, and he relaxes a fraction of a degree. "Thank god for that," he says. He's slowed his speech and is talking as he would to a child. "That key belongs to a very scary man named Henry Holzmann."

"Yeah," I say. "He was gonna buy it from me."

"That ship has fucking sailed."

I look at him blankly and let him explain himself. He gestures to the apartment. The broken window. The bullet holes in the couch. The wreckage of my desk.

"It looks like his people made his position clear," he says.

"I beat them," I say.

"Sure," he replies. "You beat Benny and Wade. But Holzmann has more than just those two, and he's pissed as hell. I heard them talking when I was tied up in their trunk. Holzmann got attacked earlier tonight and lost the safe that my key opens."

"That's not my fault," I say. It is, of course, my fault, but that doesn't matter here. If Cassiopeia managed to get the safe, that changes the whole situation. I need to talk to her, and I'm hoping that Richard can help with that.

"The way he sees it, this started when you stole that key," Richard says. "If you didn't do that, none of the rest of this would have happened."

"You lost the key," I say. "Why isn't he pissed at you?"

Richard gestures at the bruises across his body. "He fucking is. But I can still turn this around. Give me the key. Let me take it to him. I'll smooth the whole thing over."

I nod, chewing on my lip as though I'm really considering the option. I can see the hope start to bloom in Richard's eye.

"Who attacked him?" I ask.

"What?" Richard is thrown by the sudden change in topic.

"You said someone attacked him. Someone else has the safe."

"They're nobody," he says, then stops. He's starting to clam up. I might have moved too fast. OK. I'll feed him a little information—let him think I know this already—then he's not taking any risks by letting the rest go.

"Cassiopeia?" I ask.

"It's just Cass," he corrects me.

"OK. If Cass has the safe, and we have the key, why don't we go to her? That's where the payday is, right?"

"We can't do that," Richard says, adopting the plural *we* I planted. "Even Cass is smart enough to know she needs to hide after attacking Holzmann. She'll have gone to ground."

"Do you know where she'd be?" I ask. "If we can get to her before he does . . ." I trail off, letting Richard complete the thought. He wants to give in, but as he takes a breath to tell me, he winces at the bruise in his ribs. And I lose him.

"No," he says. "She'll fuck up, and Holzmann will find her. And then he'll find us. Holzmann is the horse to back here, trust me."

He's the best line I have to Cass, but until he feels safe, he won't tell me anything. I need to give him time. His monsters won't be quite as scary in the light of day.

"Let me think about it," I say.

He frowns. He doesn't want to wait, but he doesn't really have a choice.

I don't expect Holzmann to make another move tonight, but I still make sure all my alarms are set and move a weight rack to block the broken window. I let Richard take the bed and fold myself up on the couch. It's not comfortable, but Richard will either have to go past me or through the alarmed bedroom window if he wants to get away in the night.

Sleep is slow to come. I keep worrying a finger in one of the bullet holes in the cushion. It's only now that I let myself think of how close

I came to death, and I'm surprised by how little it bothers me. What worries me more is how easily I broke those two men.

I dream of Mickey turning away from Laia's gun to face me. He wanted my face to be the last thing he saw. I am not paralyzed in the dream. I can move. I can stop Laia and save Mickey. But I'm not fast enough. Never fast enough. Time and again I live through the moment. Mickey turns. I reach out to stop her. Three piddling firecrackers.

Mickey dies in my arms, and I watch as the realization enters his eyes.

CHAPTER 28

An Interjection

'm not a good person. You don't get to do the things I've done and still lay claim to that word. The world will always fuck people over. I can't fix that. I only hoped to stop adding to the pain.

But the world had other plans, and Mickey died. Scarpello was going to kill me, too. I had to get him his money. Maybe if I came back with enough, he'd not only forgive my transgressions but let me go entirely. Maybe I could still make good on the promises Mickey and I made, still find that life we talked of. Without him it would never hold the light it had once offered, but it would be something.

This was supposed to be a card trick. Some sleight of hand, a bit of misdirection, then a flourish and a reveal. People don't get hurt in a card trick. When the magician's assistant climbs into the box and the spinning blade comes down, she isn't really sawed in half. The threat gives the show its frisson, but the danger is never real. What sort of monster would see that? What sort of madman would put it on?

But this was never going to be a magic trick. It began with a murder. How could I ask you to sit there and be entertained at these frivolities?

Who would care that I transformed a handkerchief into a dove on a stage littered with corpses?

My whole life I wanted to be a magician, but the world had other ideas. It's time I came to terms with that. I am not a magician. I am a fighter. I am fighting for my life, and the threat is a hell of a lot closer than I think.

CHAPTER 29

Three Months Ago

T his game is dumb."

Mickey looked across his coffee table at me, then back down at the Go board and the mess of white and black stones, far more white than black.

"No," he said. "This game is hard. Make your move."

"Why?" I asked. "You've already won. You've made your point."

The game had started well enough. There were small skirmishes in the corners as we built our forces out, each trying to establish a stronghold from which to envelop the other. But as Mickey moved my focus from one location to the next, I realized that soon the fight in his right corner would grow into a stone he had placed seemingly at random on his third turn. Then he would flank my line and turn it back.

"I'm not trying to make a point," he said. "We're playing a game, and the game's not done. Play a stone."

I could have abandoned that fight and moved elsewhere, trying to build a new beachhead while he mopped up my forces. But everywhere I looked he already had a formation nearby, ready to pounce on any nascent deployment I attempted before it could build up the strength to survive and fight back.

"We're not playing a game," I said, but I played a stone. "You're just humiliating me."

"If you want to get good at Go—" Mickey began, dropping a stone right where I wanted to be in four turns. It looked isolated and weak, but it was closer to his reinforcements than mine.

"Lose your first hundred games as quickly as possible," I finished the aphorism for him. "I've already lost this game. You beat me. I concede. Why are we still doing this?"

I would have felt bad laying the guilt on so thick, but he knew he was pissing me off. He didn't have to be an ass to beat me. All of our time together these days was spent either playing Go or planning how to get a little bit more money from Scarpello.

The stress of it all was getting to him. Mickey wasn't a liar. He had no innate talent for this work. He was just a kid who was good with numbers whose parents fell on hard times. Mickey had been in the eleventh grade when things got really desperate for them. In every STEM course his school offered he was top of his class, but his parents knew that while the banks thought they were a bad investment, financial aid boards would see their middle-class lifestyle and their house in the suburbs and decide that they could definitely pay full tuition. They didn't want to let Mickey know how dire the situation was, so they went to Scarpello instead.

They'd kept up the façade for two years, just barely staying ahead of the payments, but then everything collapsed in 2008, and Scarpello sent people calling to collect. That crew—I wasn't a part of it—saw there was no way Mickey's parents would ever get out of the hole they'd dug for themselves, so Scarpello reached out with an alternative.

He could beat the hell out of Mickey's folks. He could threaten them with increasingly severe punishments and extract a few more pennies from that already-wrung rag, and when the last drop of blood had been twisted from them, he could kill them. Or Mickey could come work for him. Scarpello would pay for the rest of his education, but he would switch from a civil engineering program to financial analysis.

The criminal world was changing. While there would always be some need for men like me, that need was shrinking. The real money wasn't on the street. Diversification, they called it. Scarpello wanted to diversify, and he wanted to start by investing in Mickey.

"If you want to stop, we can," he said. I had hurt him. Playing this stupid game was how he dealt with stress. And I was making him feel like shit for trying to teach it to me.

"No," I said. "I do want to learn." I could see he didn't believe me.

I played a stone next to his. It was just as isolated, but I hoped it wasn't exactly where he had anticipated I was going. He looked at it. He frowned. And then he smiled.

"I'm sorry if I'm being a bitch," he said.

"Maybe just a little," I teased him, trying to inject some levity. Trying to assuage my wounded pride. It was the wrong thing to say.

"I mean it," he said, choosing his words carefully. "This game is hard. People have been playing it for two thousand years, and the strategy is still developing. I know it feels like I'm being shitty to you, but I know you. I could tell you how to play until I'm blue in the face, but you'll learn a hundred times faster by just playing the game, making your mistakes, and then figuring out how to fix them. That move here"—he pointed to the stone I just played—"is the best you've ever made. If I hadn't been pushing you, you'd never have found that.

"I'm not trying to prove anything by beating you at a game I've been playing for years. I'm being a bitch because you can do better than this, but you've got to get your teeth knocked in a couple hundred times to learn how. You're the cleverest person I've ever met, and the fact that other people can't see that is a fucking tragedy, but please don't ever think I don't know how smart you are."

Well, fuck. That might've been the nicest thing anyone had ever said to me. I wanted to say something to acknowledge what it meant to hear him say that, but I didn't know what could, so instead I played my next stone. I guess it was the right thing to do, because Mickey's smile returned. Then he looked back at the game board.

"You motherfucker," he said. While he had been making his incredibly sweet and lovely and touching speech, I had been slightly repositioning our stones. What had been an unassailable sea of white had been weakened in a few key places, and black had launched a half dozen surprise counterassaults at critical junctures. Even with my mediocre understanding I knew enough to see that within ten plays I would recapture vast swaths of territory and turn the tide of the game. I gave him my best idiot grin.

"Make your move," I said.

"Oh, I intend to." He came to his feet, stepping around the board to climb on to the couch, straddling my lap. When he kissed me, all thoughts of stones and strategy fled.

We made the most of what time we had. I couldn't stay the night. He had an early morning. Scarpello had been talking about promoting Mickey up the chain, moving him out of direct collections and into the second tier of laundering. Mickey would be spending the next week or so touring the cash businesses that Scarpello used to legitimize his income.

"How much longer are we going to do this?" I asked as I was getting ready to leave. He was still in bed. He would take a shower after I left. "The stress is making you miserable." We'd had this conversation before.

"Soon," he said. "I just want to make sure we have enough."

"We have enough to get away," I said. I wanted to tell him that every day I worked for Scarpello I felt a little bit more of myself ground away to nothing. That every time I hurt someone, it cost me. But I couldn't lay more weight on his narrow shoulders.

"Sure," he said. "And how long do we survive once we have? I want to make sure we never have to do anything like this again."

I didn't want to agree, but I didn't want to argue with him, either. I wouldn't be able to see him for a week. I wasn't going to leave on a fight.

"We're safe," he continued. "Scarpello has no idea what we're doing. After this trip, I'll have access to five times as much money, and I'll have that many more places to hide it."

"This wasn't supposed to be about the money."

"It isn't," he said, and I did my best to believe him. "But after everything we've given that man, after everything he's taken from us, don't we deserve more than just scraping by? I can do this. I can set us up for the rest of our lives."

Mickey sat up, and the sheet fell off his torso. He was skinny. Not unhealthy, but skinny. His ribs pressed lightly against his chest, and he felt so fragile when I held him in my arms. I wanted to pick him up and run from all of this. To tell him I didn't care about how we lived. As long as we were together, I'd be happy. I'd keep him safe. But he was right. Wherever we wound up, we would need money. We were so close, but we needed more. And we deserved more.

"You're right," I said.

"Of course I am. Come here."

I sat on the bed, and I leaned into him. He held my head against his chest, and I listened to his heart beating as he ran his fingers up and down my spine. As long as I had this to come back to, I could do anything. If I had to go out and grind away a little bit more of my humanity, then I would. And when I returned here, he would salve the burns and bind the bleeding wounds, and this incredible man would keep me whole.

We couldn't let anyone know we were together. Not because we were men—-the old guard who would have cared about that was rapidly dying off—but because we didn't want to draw attention. The lack of a connection between us was our strongest protection. You can't form a conspiracy with someone you don't know.

So while he was gone I pretended that everything was fine, and I wasn't missing the man that I loved, and I hadn't decided to leave this all behind. If anyone noticed that I wasn't performing up to par, they didn't say anything. I guess that's a benefit to being a big scary bruiser: you've got to really fuck up before somebody is willing to confront you.

I bought a Go board for myself and spent my nights going through a book of famous matches, trying to understand why the masters had done what they did. It was almost three weeks before I saw Mickey again, and I hadn't made any progress at all.

He was breathless with nerves, nearly vibrating as he opened the door to his apartment and I slipped inside. I pulled him to me, smelling him, feeling his body against mine. I thought he was excited to see me, and he was, but not in the way that I had expected. I leaned down to kiss him, and he responded, but he didn't meet my urgency.

"What's wrong?" I asked him, ready for him to say that he had found someone else, that he had finally realized I was the idiot that everyone thought I was. He smiled his crooked smile.

"I figured it out," he said. He had this infuriating way of making enigmatic statements that pretended to say a huge amount while providing no useful information. Then he would pause, forcing me to ask follow-up questions, which he acted slightly put-upon to answer, as though I should have been able to understand on my own.

"Figured what out?"

"How to do it. How to get enough money that we can go away and never have to worry about someone coming after us or how we're going to pay for anything ever again. So tell me, love, are you ready to be stupid fucking rich?"

SUNDAY

CHAPTER 30

Peter Van Horn, 7:02 A.M.

Two consecutive nights of poor sleep have not done Peter any favors.

His eyes burn as he rolls out of bed. He's not normally a coffee drinker. Beyond never developing a taste for it, the caffeine gives him anxiety. But he needs to be able to think, so he stops for coffee on his way to the station. The spring in his chest is tighter than ever, and he has no appetite, but he knows he will need something to settle his stomach when the bitter drink hits it. He buys a scone and fights half the dry pastry down.

When he walks into the station, he can feel the caffeine starting to work. The background hum of the station is a buzzing roar. The bullpen feels overfilled, but agoraphobia frequently accompanies Peter's anxiety, so he pushes it aside, marveling briefly at his ability to do so. Perhaps the exhaustion is hitting his neuroses as strongly as it is his consciousness.

His movements feel at once both frenetic and restrained, as if he were sprinting through neck-deep water. His muscles vibrate against his bones, pulling furiously in all directions but moving him nowhere. The mass of officers bounces around him in the bullpen like the unbound atoms of a gas. Sergeant Nowicki is across the room, studying a clipboard.

Peter can't fix this problem. So he will do what he should have done already and throw himself on the mercy of the system. It might not give the result he wants, but it is still his best chance. Yielding to Owen's demands was not his critical error. It was failing to report to Sarge quickly enough. By the time he could tell his story, his enemies had already poisoned the water. He must not allow them to deliver a second, fatal dose.

He should have gone straight to the sergeant last night. He had done nothing wrong, aside from leaving the station to track down Barrett, and if he can get in front of this, he might have a chance to save himself.

"Sergeant," he says.

"Van Horn." Sarge doesn't glance up from his assignment roster. "Find a corner and take a seat."

"Sir, I need to speak with you." Peter tries to fill his voice with urgency but gets only desperation.

"Look around you, Peter. Does it look like I have time?"

With it pointed out to him now, Peter takes in the bullpen. What he had thought was caffeine jitters is actual chaos. The place is swarming. Every workstation is occupied. A small army of officers is setting up something in the briefing room.

"What's going on, sir?" Peter asks.

"You're the luckiest son of a bitch on the force is what," Sarge says, dropping the roster and grabbing Peter by the elbow to walk him toward the break room. "Because while everyone else is going to spend the next week running off-the-books OT, you get to sit your ass here and perform the critical task of ensuring the coffeepot doesn't run dry while Professional Oversight takes their sweet time getting to your investigation."

"Please, sir," Peter says. He hates talking back to authority. "There's something I have to tell you."

Sarge pushes Peter into the break room and stands in the door, blocking his escape.

"Peter," he says. "There was a shooting war last night within a hundred yards of a city councilman's home, and I need to make sure that your fifty-three colleagues don't make fucking fools of themselves as we organize our response, so unless you are planning on telling me that you were the dumb motherfucker who shot up Elkhorn, whatever you have to say can wait. Am I clear?"

They already found it. Should he still say something? Has he missed his chance?

If he had not been so tired the night before, then Peter might have planned for what to do in this situation. But he has no plan, and he's never been one for improvising.

Instead, he conjures in his mind a coin. He pictures the face and the obverse, and he lays it onto his thumb, and he flicks it into the air, and he watches as it spins, waiting for it to fall, for him to catch it, for it to reveal heads or tails to tell him how to act.

But it does not fall. It hangs there, flashing in the light as it flips over and over and offers him no guidance.

"Right," says Sarge. "That's what I thought." And he wades back into the sea of the bullpen.

Peter looks around the break room. The coffeepot is empty.

So that's it. Here he is, once again, sitting and waiting for the world to decide what it wants to do with him. Another day will pass. Another day where he is alive, and his family is dead, and he does nothing to justify his continued existence.

He rests his head on the cracked plastic of the table and listens to the coffeemaker hiss. Other people are doing work. They are looking into a horrific crime. They see a problem, and they are going out to fix it, each in their own small way, and he is here.

CHAPTER 31

Barrett Rye, 8:14 A.M.

The pounding on my door wakes me. My alarms are buzzing, but I must have slept through them. It takes me three heartbeats to remember where I am, to escape the miasma of my dream. Richard is in the bedroom staring at me. Good. He's still here at least.

I silence the alarms and glance at the monitors. Two police officers stand at my apartment door. They stopped pounding when they heard my alarm go quiet.

"Barrett Rye," one of them yells. "Open up. We can hear you in there."

"We're fucked," Richard whispers, moving from the bedroom to stand beside me. "Those two work for him. Owen and Conrad." He taps the monitor, pointing to each in turn.

"Don't worry," I say. "I'll handle them."

"Like you did Benny and Wade?"

I push Richard back into the bedroom. "Stay in there and keep quiet. I'll get rid of them. Then we can find Cass, OK?"

Richard doesn't look convinced, but I don't have the time to secure his support. I close him in the bedroom, then go to greet the police.

I keep one shoulder blocking the door, hoping to make it clear that they are not welcome.

The one who Richard called Owen smiles at me. It is a charming smile, I must admit. Both men look to be in their forties. Owen, a bit taller, is handsome in a suburban barbecue dad kind of way. He's got a bit of a gut but healthy muscle underneath it. His face bears all the hallmarks of symmetrical attractiveness, but with enough weathering to keep him approachable. The other, Conrad, has nothing warm or handsome about him. He scowls at the world through narrowed eyes with his too-hairy arms crossed tightly over his chest.

"You must be Barrett," Owen says, all neighborly conviviality. "Do you mind if we come in?"

You should never talk to the cops—especially when actively committing crimes—but I guess the message I sent Holzmann last night wasn't strong enough. I'll need to bloody his nose a bit more before he believes that I mean business.

I shut the coat closet, hiding my security monitors, then let the front door swing open.

Conrad frowns as he walks past. "Nice place you got here," he says, tapping a stack of weight plates with his toe. "I love the vibe." I suspect he doesn't.

"Forgive my partner," Owen says as he follows Conrad in.

I give him a blank smile. "OK." I shrug.

I say nothing more. Silence hangs across the room. Owen and Conrad are here to intimidate me, and when people are scared, they talk. They search for the words that will end the threat. I need these two frustrated. I refuse to give them what they want.

Owen breaks first, snorting out a small laugh. "I'm glad we could sort that out," he says. Charming. Defusing.

"What happened there?" Conrad points to the plastic-covered window. He picks at it, pulling a few of the staples free from the wall.

I take a moment to respond, as though struggling to remember. "A bird," I say, before quieting again, looking between the two with placid emptiness.

"You should get it repaired," he says. "Like Giuliani said, shit like this encourages more crime. If people can't even respect themselves enough to fix up their homes, who knows what they're capable of." He gives the plastic a heavier tug, ripping it. He's not getting the reaction he needs so he is escalating. Good.

"What do you do, Barrett?" Owen asks, trying to get me talking. Conrad is moving toward the bedroom door. Toward Richard.

"I'm a trainer," I say, stringing three words together for the first time since they walked in. "You two looking to work out?"

Conrad looks at me. Away from the bedroom.

"Maybe," Owen says. "There's always room for improvement." He jiggles his belly with a smile. The polite thing would be to laugh with him or offer some reassuring words. I stare.

Conrad huffs and resumes his meander, coming to a stop at my couch. He sticks a finger into one of the bullet holes. "What about this? Another bird?"

I shrug. "Found it like that."

The cops' decision to change course happens silently. If they can't intimidate through implication, then they will have to be more direct. They've placed themselves on opposite sides of the room with me between them. Conrad's hand falls to his telescoping baton, and he shows me his teeth. I wouldn't call it a smile.

He is brought up short by a noise from the bedroom. A metallic clang. His hand moves from his baton to his firearm.

"Is there somebody in there?" Owen asks.

"Just my neighbor out for a smoke," I say, willing it to be true. For it not to be the alternative: Richard fleeing. To quiet the alarm, I had to disable the sensors on the bedroom windows. I need to find Cass, and Richard is my only lead on her.

Conrad opens the door and steps through. I'm trying to think of a way to justify Richard's presence, hoping he's still present for me to justify, when Conrad calls back: "All clear." He holsters his weapon.

"Did I do something wrong, officers?" I ask. I need to find Richard, but I can't until I deal with these two. And they've stepped away from the precipice. We're back to talking.

"A mutual friend asked us to come by and pick something up," Owen says.

"What?" I keep my expression blank and uncomprehending, building up their frustration again. Reminding them why they were ready to move to violence.

"You have something that our friend wants," he says, slowing his speech and overenunciating the words, but I still don't respond. "A European gentleman."

"Holzmann?" I ask innocently.

Owen glowers at me, trying to convey the importance of these words, but knowing I have as much chance of understanding as the cinder block wall behind me.

"Our friend appreciates discretion," he says.

"Ohhh," I say with exaggerated comprehension. "Tell our friend"—I wink heavily at the word—"that the package is at the post office. Cash on delivery."

"What the fuck does that mean?" Conrad asks. He has circled behind me. I glance over my shoulder, and he smiles that empty smile.

"Can I be straight with you two?" I ask. "I have no idea what's going on. I won this thing in a game of cards. Holzma—" I catch myself and start again. "Our mutual friend was going to buy it. Or I thought he was, but then someone else took it, and—"

I don't defend myself when Conrad moves. This is the cost to be rid of these two. Accepting that it's necessary doesn't make it hurt any less, though, when Conrad's baton slams into the back of my right knee. My leg buckles and I fall. Even on my knees I'm still a hair taller than him, but the next swing will be at the back of my skull.

"Is he fucking with us?" Conrad asks. I get the feeling he's not expecting an answer. "I think he's fucking with us."

"What my partner is saying," Owen says, "is that you don't need to understand what's happening. Your comprehension is not necessary for your compliance. All that you need to know is that shit rolls downhill. Some bitch stole from our friend last night, which has made him upset. That's a problem for me and my partner, which makes it a problem for you, because you, you dumb motherfucker, are at the very fucking bottom of the hill." So much for him being the friendly one.

"I should call Holzmann," I say.

"Don't," says Owen. "He's pissed enough at you already."

"If he's sending us after you, then you know you done fucked up bad." Conrad pokes the side of my head with the tip of his baton. "So let's quit dicking around, and you just give us what we want."

Right. That's enough. Now to get rid of them.

"Fuck off," I say.

"Is he resisting?" Owen asks with overt theatricality. "It looks like he is resisting and poses a clear and present danger to your safety and/or the safety of others."

"I believe he is," says Conrad. I hear his gun slide free of its holster once more.

"Wait," I say, falling back to sit on my heels.

"You gonna give us what we want?" Owen asks.

"In the closet, by the door," I say.

Owen opens the door, and it takes him a moment to absorb what he's seeing.

"What the fuck is this?" he asks. He steps aside to give Conrad a good view of the screens mounted there and the image of all three of us, viewed through the little lens hanging from my ceiling.

"If anything happens to me, that video goes to the *World-Herald*," I say.

"He's bluffing," Conrad says.

I am, of course. The recording is real, but I have no dead man's switch. These two can't be sure of that, though.

"Let's just bring him in."

"No. We'll leave, and then he'll do the right thing." Conrad leans down to whisper in my ear. "Isn't that right? I don't want to have to find you down some cameraless alley."

I do my best to look appropriately chastened. Conrad kicks my bruised knee on his way past me and out the door.

CHAPTER 32

Barrett Rye, 8:22 A.M.

wait until they drive away, then rush to pick up Richard's trail. I head toward the river. There's always people there. It's the safest place to flee to. Richard has a head start of several minutes, though. I've no chance of actually tracking him down, but I still have to try.

I've done everything I set out to do, except for the single most important part. I made chaos, but I haven't managed it. Richard will lead Holzmann to Cass and to the safe. I'll still have the key, but it will be giving the man a win. It will be an easing of the pressure when that pressure has to be constant and unrelenting.

So I run to the river. Maybe I'll get lucky. I run the length of the park that celebrates where Lewis and Clark crossed on their journey west. It confirms what I already know. He's gone.

Walking back, I pass an honest-to-god newsstand, what must be the last in the city. It has mostly shifted to selling snacks and drinks but still has some shelf space dedicated to periodicals. The morning's headline catches my breath in my throat.

"Just terrible, isn't it?" the proprietor says, seeing me looking at the paper. "That kinda thing isn't supposed to happen here."

I mutely buy a copy and step away.

MASSACRE IN ELKHORN! the headline reads. *Five dead in mass shooting.* Below the fold, there is a picture of a body being wheeled out of a gated estate. Four of the deceased are named in the article, but not this one. He is just "a victim." I know him, though. I just saw him yesterday.

Vic Velasquez is dead.

More bodies.

Too many bodies.

There weren't supposed to be any.

Vic is dead, alongside Daryl Buckner, Arnold Parziale, Lyle Wynn, and Cole Foote, the men who he killed on his way out. None of them were good people, but what right does that give me to end their lives?

I put the idea in Cass Mullen's head to steal the safe, to sow disorder so that I might come away with a bit more money. It was perfectly executed. Just a sentence. A few words. A nudge. And she did exactly what I wanted her to do. Now I have not only gotten Mickey killed, but laid five more out as well.

I don't carry the blame for their deaths alone—we all made our choices, after all—but I do carry a part of it. My victory, if I can even reach it when it is still anything but assured, will be tainted by the deaths and suffering that made it possible.

Enough people have died for this stupid fucking quest of mine. I wanted to stop hurting people. I thought I could do something other than cause pain. Because Mickey convinced me—sweet fucking Mickey who loved me and I couldn't even look in the eye as he died for me—that I could be more.

Mickey was the smartest person I've ever met. The rest of the world might think I'm good for nothing but pounding faces and breaking bones, but Mickey saw something else, and I was so desperate that I believed him. He loved me; surely that was proof that I could be more. It turns out Mickey might have been a genius, but he was a miserable judge of character.

There was a French magician, M. Robert-Houdin, in the 1800s who could grow a living tree from a sprinkling of ash. I thought that could be me. I could transform the destruction of my existence into something beautiful. Instead, I've done—this.

"Are you all right, dude?" A trio of joggers, faces flush in the morning wind, have paused to look up at me. I don't know how long I've been staring at the river. "You look lost," their leader says. "Can we help you find something?"

I wave them off and turn back to the city. I need to end this. If I go straight to Holzmann, though, he is still going to go after Cass. More people will be hurt. I have to get to her first. I've sown this chaos. Now I need to fix it. But I still don't know how. Not until my phone buzzes in my pocket.

That is curious. My land line is publicly listed, but I haven't given my cell number to anybody since I got it on my arrival in Omaha. Still, I've got a fair guess who's texting me. The message is simple:

Bring it to me. NOW.

That doesn't give me the plan, though. It just reminds me of something I forgot. Richard isn't my only lead on Cass. When he left, he left something behind.

It's still there when I get home, wrapped in paper towels on my counter. Richard's cell phone. He couldn't retrieve it in his flight, not with the cops in my living room. It's a new-looking Android, which should be fine after a night in the rain, but the screen is cracked and starting to chip away at the corners. The damage looks recent, the result, no doubt, of Richard's treatment by Holzmann's men. I hope the waterproofing wasn't too badly compromised, and I press the power button.

Nothing. The phone is still and dead and lifeless.

But maybe—

I find a charger and plug it in.

And then it chimes, and the screen lights up. It's locked, of course, but I smile as I see the glowing circle with the wavy spiral at the bottom of the display. I don't have time to brute-force my way through a password, but this phone can be unlocked with a fingerprint, and Richard left a clean one on the monitors in my closet, where he pointed out the two cops. I lift the print and make a mold of it from the same plastic resin I used for my fake keys, then transfer it to sticky tack from my posters. The phone accepts my fake. I open Richard's contacts and scroll down, and there she is. Cass Mullen.

CHAPTER 33

Cass Mullen, 9:06 A.M.

Everything will look better in the morning. That's what they say. Well, Cass has made it to morning, and things aren't looking any fucking better. Vic is still dead. Holzmann is still searching for her. And Jonny Boy hasn't moved once from the bed where he collapsed after they got back to Vic's place.

Just about the only positives are that she still has the safe and she still has the guy who can open it. While Jonny Boy was weeping in what used to be Vic's room, Cass tied up Pickens in the spare bedroom and interrogated him. The technical details of the safe flew over her head, and she didn't want to reveal her ignorance with follow-ups, so she only has a basic understanding, but that's enough.

To get it open, they'll need the key—the real key—that Barrett has. Pickens doesn't know what's in the safe beyond the fact that Holzmann called it an egg. He doesn't need to know more, though, and neither does Cass. Holzmann offered her six figures for the key. Whatever is in there is valuable, and Cass is going to get it.

There's just one problem. It was apparent the night before, and it remains just as insurmountable today. She doesn't have the key, and she has no idea how to change that. They can go back to Barrett's apartment and try to shake him down again, but that would mean leaving Pickens alone, and she knows better than to trust her ability to restrain somebody who picks locks for a living.

If Vic were still around, then she could leave him in charge and take Jonny Boy back to Barrett's, but, of course, he's not. She could get what she needs out of Barrett on her own regardless of his size—guns are, after all, nature's great equalizer—but Jonny Boy can't guard Pickens. He's too soft. Pickens would be untied and on the road ten minutes after she left, and then she'd be fucked again. And she sure as shit isn't going to send Jonny Boy off to try to take on the giant.

She throws open the door to Vic's room. Jonny Boy lies in the bed, on top of the blankets, and looks up at her with watery eyes.

"All right," she says. "That's enough fucking moping. Get out of bed. We've got work to do."

Jonny Boy watches her, his lip quavering. "I shoulda done something," he says. "I just keep thinking about it. He cleared the first two rooms, and then we—we heard people in the next one, and we went in, and they just—they shot him, and I shoulda done something."

Of course Jonny Boy would make this about him. His grief. His pain.

"Yeah," she says. "You fucking should have. You were supposed to be watching out for him. Now get the fuck out of bed and help me fix this nightmare."

A rattle from the other room draws her wrath away. Pickens is awake. With a final glare at Jonny Boy, who is now openly crying again, she leaves to make sure the fucking locksmith isn't escaping.

He's not. He's just in the corner of the room doing something to the safe. She tied him to the radiator with a bike lock, and he's stretched the chain to its full length. He steps back and looks away as she barrels through the door.

"The fuck are you up to?" she asks, her hand drifting to the Hellcat at her waist.

His eyes lock onto the gun, and he slides further from the safe, slowly raising his hands and showing his open palms.

"I was just checking it over," he says. "It shouldn't get thrown around like it did."

"And is it OK?"

Pickens shrugs. "I think so?"

This amateur hour shit is going to make her sick.

"Right," she says. "Good."

And then Jonny Boy's fucking phone rings.

The sheer, overwhelming stupidity—though why she'd expect anything else is a mystery at this point—is nearly too much for her. "Don't fucking move," she says, then rushes back through the living room.

Jonny Boy is sitting on the edge of the bed, his phone to his ear. "Yeah," he says. "That's me. Who is this? Why do you have Richard's phone?"

"Jesus, fuck, Jonny Boy," she yells at him. "Get the fuck off your phone!"

Jonny Boy's face pales. "It's him," he says. "Barrett. He wants to make a deal."

That catches Cass up short. It would appear she has just a bit of luck left in the tank. She snatches the phone out of Jonny Boy's limp hand. "That key you gave me was fucking fake," she says into it.

She can hear him breathe a few times on the other end of the call, processing the rapid change.

"Yeah," he says eventually. "Sorry. I was gonna sell the real one to Holzmann. Then he tried to have me killed."

"Fuck Holzmann," she says. Jonny Boy winces on the bed below her, rubbing the scabs on his knuckles from where he hit the old man. "That old bitch doesn't scare me."

"Me neither," Barrett says. "He pisses me off. Had me shot at. I don't like getting shot at."

"I don't blame you," she says. "I'd be mad as fuck if somebody took a shot at me. Went back on a deal like that. Fuck him."

"Yeah," Barrett says, and then he just breathes into the phone some more.

"You wanna get back at him?" Cass asks.

"How?"

"Sell me the key."

Barrett thinks that over. "He was gonna give me fifty Gs for it."

"You give me the key, the real fucking key, and the money is all yours."

"You actually have the money this time?"

She looks through the door at the paper lunch bag she took from Holzmann's. "Yeah," she says. "I got the cash last night."

"The key's no good without the safe," Barrett points out.

"I've got it fucking handled," she says. "I've got the safe and someone to open it. All I need's the key. It'll be the easiest fifty thousand you ever made."

She tells him where Vic's place is, and he says he'll be there soon. Once she's off the phone, she pops out the SIM card and breaks it in half, then smashes the phone itself. Jonny Boy lets out a pained groan but doesn't otherwise object.

"They can track this shit, Jonny Boy," she tells him. "You gotta be more careful."

Jonny Boy leaves the bedroom, but he doesn't get further than the couch before he collapses again and points toward Pickens. "Do we have to keep him tied up? It's really not a good look."

Cass glances at Pickens, the Black man she is keeping in chains. Fuck.

"It's OK," Pickens calls over. "I mean, if you want to untie me that's cool, but I get it."

"See?" Cass says. "Everything's kosher." Jonny Boy doesn't seem convinced. "There any fucking food in this house?" she asks to distract him.

"No," he says. "I checked while you were sleeping."

"There's a Hy-Vee down the street," she says. "Go get us some breakfast, and get the fuck back here before Barrett shows up, OK?"

Jonny Boy lumbers to his feet, his expression brightening at the prospect of food. He gets as far as the door before he digs in his pockets. "This is all I've got," he says, holding up a ten-dollar bill.

"Then take some fucking more," she says, waving at the bag with fifty thousand dollars.

"Aren't we giving that to Barrett?"

She rolls her eyes. "Sure. We wouldn't want to short him. My wallet's in the van. Take what you need. We can afford it."

Once he's gone, she thinks about saying something to Pickens but decides she doesn't really want to deal with small talk right now. Instead, she sweeps up the remains of Jonny Boy's phone.

Barrett called from Richard Sands's number. She idly wonders what that could mean but doesn't give it too much consideration. If the big guy shows up with him in tow, then she'll deal with it. Richard is a fucking coward. She only has to worry about Barrett, and that idiot thinks he's walking into a friendly trade, while she'll be the one with the guns. Jonny Boy won't like it, but he'll fall in line. He always does.

CHAPTER 34

Richard Sands, 9:35 A.M.

Richard doesn't like to bet big on anything less than a sure thing, but right now he needs to do something drastic to get back into Holzmann's good graces. So, less than twelve hours after escaping from him, Richard, using a phone in the back of a dive bar, calls Benny to surrender. Except now he can offer what he couldn't before: the location of both the key and the safe.

Benny says he's in the hospital, but he'll send someone out to grab Richard and bring him to Holzmann. The driver says very little as they leave the city for the soy fields of Nebraska. Holzmann, he says, has temporarily relocated, but he doesn't explain further. The car takes a dirt road to a modest farmhouse built atop a low hill, rising like a pustule from the perfect flatness of the Nebraska plains. The driver tells Richard that Holzmann is waiting around back.

Richard, wishing he had a chance to get a change of clothes, circles the house, keeping himself to a casual saunter. Holzmann, currently in a conversation with the farmhouse's owner, Lang, looks up at Richard's approach. The wind forces them to stand close, bending their heads together to be heard.

"Explain to me why I should not have you killed right now for your failures," Holzmann demands.

Richard laughs, searching for levity, but when neither Holzmann nor Lang respond, he swallows and sets to pleading for his life. He wraps the words in his best salesman's patter, starting from the assumption that Holzmann will need him now that Cass has the safe and Rye has muddied the waters with his fake key. Richard has made mistakes, but nobody else knows where Cass is or what the real key looks like.

Holzmann listens to him patiently, and when Richard seems to be done making his case, he responds: "I can find Cassiopeia without you. My locksmith can identify the fakes."

Richard points out that he could have fled, but instead came here to share what information he could. He wants to do what's right.

Holzmann considers this too, and only when he is again sure that Richard has finished does he speak: "Schopenhauer says that the basis for morality—for doing what is right—is compassion. For an action to have moral worth, for it to be 'the right thing,' it must consider the suffering of another. And so I ask you, Herr Sands, why do you not consider my suffering?"

Richard starts to object, to say that he does, but Holzmann holds up a finger to silence him.

"You do not, Herr Sands. You know where my safe is. You know where my key is. I am suffering without these things. Please, Herr Sands, show compassion."

Richard swallows, hesitant to give up his only leverage, but he wants to show that he is a team player. So he explains how Rye wants to sell Cass the key and how Cass's crew has a house in Saddle Creek they use as a hideout.

"Thank you, Richard," Holzmann says.

Richard barely has time to recognize that Holzmann called him by his first name before Lang fires a bullet through the side of his head. While the ringing in their ears subsides, Lang starts unfolding the heavy plastic bag that he will use to store Richard's body. Holzmann has a use for it.

"Schopenhauer was a Pole," Holzmann says, once he can hear his own voice again. "His weakness corrupted the fatherland." He looks down at the pathetic corpse. So much trouble because this coward had to play a card game. But it was Holzmann who assigned him the task, and it is ultimately at his feet that the responsibility falls. "Call in our reserves," he says to Lang. "We are going to Saddle Creek."

Lang wipes his bloody hands on his slacks. "Why don't we just buy off Cass and this Rye guy? It'll be cheaper and easier."

Holzmann frowns, a sour feeling rising in his gut. "No," he says. "To abandon our intentions is to accept defeat. Make the call. I will pay what is necessary."

CHAPTER 35

Owen Oster, 10:07 A.M.

Owen hates being upset, but he is already in a bad mood, and being in a bad mood puts him in a worse mood. Life is short, and he only gets the one, so to waste any of it feeling upset is a terrible thing. But some days the world conspires against him.

He had gone to bed last night flush with the feeling of money in his pocket and a beautiful woman beside him. This was how things were supposed to work in Owen's life.

He liked being a police officer. He liked the respect it earned him. He liked being one of the good guys. He liked being able to crack a couple skulls every once in a while. The side opportunities it afforded him allowed him a life of comfort and ease, and even in his forties he could still bring home a stunning piece of ass for the night.

And then Holzmann had woken him up and ordered him to get the key after they'd already brought him the safe. He negotiated double pay for the last-minute work, but the disrespect of it rankled him.

Conrad said they should take the money and shut up. Owen had trusted Conrad to watch out for him since high school, and Conrad had never led him astray. Owen had wanted to go to UNL and play for the Huskers, maybe even turn pro after college, but Conrad convinced him to join the force instead. Conrad had said he knew Owen could make it, but was worried about his own chances—never mind that it was Conrad, not Owen, who'd made the All-State team. The whole thing with Holzmann was Conrad's doing, too. Owen was the pretty face and the winning smile, and he was fine following Conrad behind the scenes. That didn't mean he had to enjoy accepting Holzmann's disrespect.

But he'd done it, and they'd gone after the key, and then that giant fucker sent them off with their tails between their legs. The guy was too dumb to know not to talk about Holzmann directly, but smart enough to have a camera set up to watch them.

Owen had spent his morning getting shit on by people who were beneath him.

And now he and Conrad are getting called in to work—on their day off—which means something big has happened and the department needs to look like it's on top of things. So instead of the relaxing afternoon he was looking forward to, he's going to get an afternoon of menial make-work so the brass can look good.

He's hoping to talk with Sarge about getting onto one of the better assignments, but Captain Dumetz is already running a briefing when he and Conrad make it into the station.

"Oh shit," Conrad says. Behind Dumetz, a crime board has been put together.

The board is filled with pictures of a massacre. They were taken in and around a house, once fancy, now covered in blood and bullets. It's a house Owen has seen before, but only in fleeting glances through the gate. He and Conrad never go onto the property.

". . . where they found"—Dumetz is in the middle of his briefing, pointing to pictures of bagged drugs next to the pictures of the bodies—"almost half a million dollars' worth of cocaine, heroin, MDMA, marijuana, ketamine, GHB, and assorted other compounds, along with a smaller amount of currency. These men"—Dumetz points to a cluster of photographs of corpses—"are known associates of Henry Holzmann, and the house is believed to be his as well. We are still trying to identify the final body. Elkhorn is outside our usual range of operations, but command is worried that this could be the opening salvo in a larger war."

Owen feels like he's going to be sick. The last thing that he and Conrad need right now is additional scrutiny on Holzmann. The Kraut fucker could have at least given them a heads-up that they were walking into this. The brass was content to ignore Holzmann—and by extension, Owen and Conrad—so long as he kept violent crime contained to the North Omaha street gangs he supplies. A gunfight among the seven-figure homes of Elkhorn will require a response.

Owen's phone vibrates in his pocket, but he's in no mood to deal with anyone right now, so he lets it go to voicemail. A moment later Conrad's phone starts to buzz. If someone is calling them both, it can only be Holzmann. He'll deal with it later.

After the briefing lets out and Sarge gives them all their assignments—he and Conrad will be following up on leads generated by the tip line—Conrad pulls him aside.

"That motherfucker fucked us," Conrad says. "There's no fucking way this doesn't blow up in our faces."

"He tried calling us," Owen says.

"He's gonna want us to clean up this fucking mess for him."

"So what do we do?"

"Let me think," Conrad says.

While he does that, Owen takes a stroll to the break room to grab coffee for them both. Peter Van Horn is there, taking a nap on one of the tables. There were rumors going around yesterday, but it looks like the kid is going to be OK. Owen's glad he won't be screwed by what they did. Petey is a bit weird, but he might actually make a good cop someday.

When he gets back with the coffee, Conrad seems to have worked through whatever it is that he needed to.

"Don't call him back yet," Conrad says. "Let him stew. If he wants us to save his ass, we're gonna be damn well paid for it."

This is why Owen loves Conrad. Even when the line breaks and the pocket is collapsing, Conrad will spot a way out and clear it for him.

CHAPTER 36

Barrett Rye, 10:23 A.M.

The address Cass gave me is in a pleasant enough middle-class neighborhood. I take the bus most of the way there after disposing of the broken-down pistols. The streets are wide, but all the streets in this city are wide. There are a few trees around, plenty of grass and green space, but there are as many windows with bars as not. This house is protected by a stone wall, about six feet high. It's low enough that I can see over but most folks can't without jumping.

I circle through the alley behind it to scope out the house, a small, post-war ranch home in need of a new roof and a power wash. The lawn is dead, and the small pool is filled with green murk. A towel sits on one of the four half-collapsed patio chairs. The windows are open, and I hear an argument inside. I recognize Cass's voice.

"Christ, Jonny Boy," she's saying. "Why the fuck would you know that?"

"We talked about it," Jonny Boy says. His voice is thick from crying. "The last time he got arrested, there was a guy who died in there. They burn everyone and just dump the ashes in a big grave out back if nobody claims them."

"So what's your fucking plan? You roll up to the police, be like, 'Hey, that guy you found last night in the rich dude's house with all the bodies? Yeah, can we go bury him?' How the fuck do you think that's gonna end?"

"I'm just worried about him," Jonny Boy says.

"Just fucking once, Jonny Boy, I wish you'd worry about me." I can hear Cass pacing. "Worry about the son of a bitch you beat the shit out of and robbed last night."

"We're safe here, right? We just gotta wait for the key, then we all get paid, and we're out of here?"

"Yes, because I set it up. I got us the safe. I got Barrett to come here with the key. What the fuck have you done?"

I've heard enough. There's a gate leading to the yard from the alley, but I take the long way around to the front. Cass cracks the front door as I approach, looking at me over the wall. Tucked into her waistband is a small gun. Her eyes are bloodshot. She doesn't look like she slept all night.

"Did anyone follow you?" she asks.

I switched buses four times on my way here, and with my circling around the alley, I would have spotted a tail. I don't need to tell her all that, though. She gets a shrug.

With a cautious glance down the street, she waves me into the house. The entry opens up on a living space with a kitchen further inside, and doors head off in either direction to what I assume are the bedrooms, two small ones to the right and a master to the left. There are some blankets thrown over the plastic cover on the couch, and a thick layer of dust coats the shelves. There are spider webs in the corners of the room, and one of the ceiling lights is out.

Jonny Boy comes to his feet as I enter. He was sitting at a small table near one of the bedroom doors. An impressive-looking shotgun rests against the wall, and he reaches for it, but any threat is undercut as a glob of egg salad falls from the sandwich in his other hand. He has only a blink to decide whether he wants to grab the gun or the food. He abandons the gun, swiping out to catch the egg salad, but is too late. It falls to the dusty ground with a pitiful splat.

"Jesus fuck, Jonny Boy," Cass says from behind me as she closes the door. "Have some fucking self-respect."

Jonny Boy shrinks into himself and puts the sandwich down next to a beat-up paper lunch bag. I move away from the front door, trying to put space between myself and Cass. I run a finger along the wallpaper, tracing a crack. From behind the door by Jonny Boy somebody coughs. Cass said they had somebody to open the safe. He must be back there.

Jonny Boy looks from me to his dripping lunch on the table. "I owe you a sandwich," he says.

This is who I sent against Holzmann. I didn't have the most respect for Cass and her crew when they showed up at my place yesterday, but they had seemed more competent than this. But they're just children. They weren't ready for what I made them do.

"I'm sorry I hit you," I say.

"Me too," Jonny Boy says. "We're all on the same side now, though. I got some peanut butter in the kitchen. You want that? It's not as good as turkey, but it's something."

"Jonny Boy," Cass interrupts. "We're here to do fucking business, not discuss sandwiches."

I keep watching Jonny Boy. His eyes are red and swollen from crying, and every time Cass speaks, he flinches a little. I dealt out plenty of pain on Scarpello's behalf, but I've never had to watch it ramify and cascade across a person's life. I'd always been able to walk away.

"You know what," I say. "Some peanut butter sounds real fucking nice right now."

Jonny Boy's expression lightens. It's not a full smile, but it's something. Just a little bit of, not happiness, but slightly less sadness. He takes a step toward the kitchen.

"I got some bananas," he says. "You want me to cut one of those up in there? They're fresh. I just bought them this morning."

"Stay the fuck there, Jonny Boy," Cass snaps at him. "We're not playing pimp my fucking sandwich over here. And you," she says to me. "Do you have the fucking key?"

I reach into my jacket and pull out the key. The real key. Cass grabs for it, but I step back, maintaining distance. With her at the door and Jonny Boy behind me, I can't stay far away from them both. Jonny Boy seems the less likely to make a sudden move, so I retreat toward him and the door I heard the cough from.

"And it's the real fucking key this time?" she asks. She takes another step forward.

"Yeah," I say. "But are you sure you want this? I heard about what happened to your friend. I don't know what this key is, but it can't be worth dying over, right?"

"I don't want to fuck with Holzmann," Jonny Boy says.

Maybe it's my guilt, but there is something in Jonny Boy that calls to me. I know what it's like to realize that every choice you've made was wrong, and the people you care about are paying for it. I want to reach out and tell him that he didn't make these choices. That his friend is dead because of me.

"You should have thought of that," Cass says, "before you beat the shit out of the guy and almost shot his fucking head off." She lays a hand on the grip of her pistol and looks over my shoulder at Jonny Boy, signaling something to him.

"Oh, right," he says. "This is for you." He offers me the beat-up lunch bag. "It's the fifty thousand. Plus what we took from your place."

"No, you fuck," Cass says. "Not the money. Pick up the fucking gun."

Jonny Boy and I both look at Cass with dumb surprise. I'm not shocked as she draws the pistol from her waistband, but Jonny Boy genuinely seems to be. Still, he reaches reluctantly for the shotgun.

"You want me to shoot him?" he asks.

"If he doesn't hand over the key, then yes, I want you to fucking shoot him."

I put the key behind my back and turn it to the door. They can't get behind me if my back is to the wall. Someone moves in there. There is a rustling of cloth and clatter of metal. Hopefully they'll stay where they are.

"I don't want to shoot anybody," Jonny Boy says. He picked up the shotgun, but he's not aiming it at me. "I don't like this anymore, Cass. This isn't what was supposed to happen. Vic wasn't—"

"Jonny Boy, you fat motherfucker," Cass interrupts him. "All you have to do is not fall apart long enough to get the key, and we're out, but apparently even that is too fucking much for you."

Cass takes another step toward me—or maybe toward Jonny Boy. She is nearly within my reach.

I want to intervene, but I don't know how to stop what I've put in motion. Everything I do makes things worse. The pot is already boiling, and I'm just adding more heat.

There's over fifty thousand dollars in a brown paper bag on the table. It won't get me away from Scarpello, but it will keep me alive. Mickey thought I could be more, and that got him killed. It got Vic and Daryl and Arnold and Lyle and Cole killed, too. Maybe the best I can do for these people is take the fifty thousand and go back to Scarpello. Just disappear.

Outside, a couple car doors open and close. Other people going about their day, dealing with their own dramas and tragedies. Their own crises that they're trying to address with just as much urgency. They are as unaware of what's happening here as I am of what's going on in their lives, and we will have as much effect on each other. Whoever is in the room behind me coughs twice more.

Cass is less than five feet away from me now. She's still looking at Jonny Boy, still making sure that he puts his gun on me, and she's let herself get within my reach. I've been shifting my weight away from her, onto my back foot. When I move, I explode out, pushing off at a slight angle to Cass as I slap out with my hand.

I catch the side of the little pistol with my palm, swinging it away and closing my fingers around it as my momentum carries me forward. The metal is warm where it lay against her body. I tuck a shoulder and slam into her chest as I twist with my hand, breaking the gun free. She stumbles away, and I flip the gun in my grip, raising it to aim at her.

I only hit her hard enough to create distance, but her face flushes red with anger.

"Fucking shoot him!" she screams at Jonny Boy.

I hold my other hand out to Jonny Boy, hoping to forestall him, hoping that I read him right. My palm is out, fingers up—the universal sign for stop—but for my pinky, which curls around the key. If I'm wrong, then he shoots me here, and that's the end.

I roll my hand over, palm up, and uncoil my pinky, releasing the key. Offering it to him.

"Just give me the money," I say. "And the key is yours."

I keep Cass in my peripheral vision, but I don't think she's going to make a move. I focus on Jonny Boy. The shotgun wavers. His finger is still outside the trigger guard.

180

"I don't want to hurt anyone," I say. "I just need the money, and you'll never see me again."

"Shoot him," Cass says. Jonny Boy doesn't move. There're people out on the street, shuffling around. Voices filter through the open windows.

"I'm just going to leave this here," I say as I put the key down on the table and reach for the bag. "And I'll take this, and I guess I'll take a rain check on that sandwich, OK?"

Jonny Boy nods. I grab the bag and start to back toward the front door. Cass yells obscenities that aren't worth repeating, alternating her vitriol between me and Jonny Boy, but she doesn't move, and Jonny Boy lets the shotgun fall to his side.

"I'm sorry about Vic," I say as I reach the door. "He seemed like a good guy." I have no idea what kind of guy he was, but Jonny Boy seems to appreciate the sentiment.

With my back still to the door, I open it and step through. There are three new cars on the street, two big black SUVs and a little two-door Honda. The Honda looks familiar, but I can't quite place it. The SUVs are definitely Holzmann's, but I don't see his men anywhere, which can only mean that they are pressed up against the wall, waiting to come in.

As if that was the signal, the gate flies inward, and an armed man steps into the yard.

I've got the money. My continued presence in Omaha will only make things worse. I should just leave. Run. Get away from this house, away from Holzmann's ambush, and never look back. Abandon Cass and Jonny Boy to their fate. I need nothing more from them. That's what I should do.

Instead, I go back inside and slam the door shut.

"Holzmann is here," I say.

Cass snatches the shotgun from Jonny Boy's hands. "Let's fucking end this," she says.

Something splashes into the pool in the backyard.

I can still run.

"No," I say. "There's too many of them. You two get out of here. I'll buy you time."

Cass narrows her eyes. She's never been given anything in her life that didn't come with a cost.

"Cassiopeia!" Holzmann calls from the yard. "Herr Wright, we have business to attend to."

I toss the bag of cash to Jonny Boy. "Just go," I say. I drag the couch over to barricade the front door.

"Why?" Jonny Boy looks at me.

I can't tell him the real reason. Because I'm an idiot. Because I feel guilty. Because I can't escape this world, but maybe he can. Cass wouldn't accept that. I need to give them something else.

"Whatever's in that safe, I want a part of it," I say. Greed she can understand. This isn't noble self-sacrifice. This is calculated risk. And it's not entirely a lie. I do want more money. I can still get more money.

"I heard them out back," Cass says. "We'll go out the bedroom windows and over the fence." She grabs Jonny Boy and leads him into the room I had been in front of. I see the safe and a man chained to a radiator before the door closes again.

Holzmann's men bang on the front door.

Maybe I can keep them tied up here long enough. Maybe I can keep their focus on me and give Jonny Boy enough time to get away.

I pop in some earplugs—don't leave home without them—and let out my biggest, scariest war cry as Holzmann's men pound the door and the wood starts to splinter. The little pistol I took off Cass holds twelve rounds.

I fire them all.

CHAPTER 37

Jonny Boy Wright, 10:36 A.M.

Jonny Boy is exhausted.

Vic is dead, Holzmann wants to kill him, and he and Cass betrayed Barrett, the only person who has been nice to him. Jonny Boy is ready to lie down on the ground and let it all end. He's led a miserable life in which he couldn't even be a criminal right.

He deserves all the hatred that's heaped upon him. Maybe if he hadn't been such a coward, Vic would still be alive. Maybe if he'd stood up to Cass, and they hadn't turned on Richard, none of this would have happened. But he is a coward. He'll never stand up to Cass. When everyone else abandoned him, she was there. She's only hard on him to make him stronger. If he doesn't want to be yelled at, he should be less of a little bitch.

Cass pulls Jonny Boy into the spare bedroom. This is where he and Vic would stay up all night playing video games. The tiny twenty-four-inch TV is still in the corner, though the Xbox is long gone. The lockpicker tries to make himself small in the corner of the room. Jonny Boy goes to the window, keeping himself low. Cass thinks Holzmann already has people back there, but it looks clear.

"How long'll it take you to open the safe?" Cass asks. She swings the shotgun—when did she take the shotgun from him?—to aim at the man. His once crisp shirt is covered in sweat stains, and the collar hangs limply open.

"Thirty minutes," he says. "If I have the key. What's going on?"

Cass ignores his question and holds up the key she got from Barrett. "Is this the real one?"

Jonny Boy has never been great at reading people, but even he can see the recognition in the man's eyes.

"Right," Cass says. "Stand back, Jonny Boy." She pockets the key and turns to aim the shotgun at the safe.

"No!" The lockpicker cries, throwing himself toward her. The bike chain pulls him up short. "Even with the key, you can't shoot it open. The force will trigger the mechanism and destroy what's inside."

"Fuck!" Cass shouts. A loud crash signals the arrival of Holzmann's men at the front of the house.

"Come on," Jonny Boy says to Cass. "Let's just go." He opens the window and works his body through the gap.

"Fine," Cass says. "But we're coming back for that." She waves at the safe before following him through the window.

Barrett's scream comes from inside the house, and the gunfire begins. Jonny Boy drags himself over the wall and through the neighbor's yard. He and Cass make it to the end of the alley without running into any of Holzmann's men. Gasping for breath, Jonny Boy slows to a walk, but he keeps moving until they have several twisting blocks between themselves and the house. They betrayed Barrett, and then he came back to help them, buying them time to escape. Jonny Boy doesn't want to think about what happened to him.

Cass makes them walk several miles before they get on a bus. Jonny Boy's feet and legs are burning. His back is a column of agony. His knees barely bend as he sits, and he doesn't think he will ever be able to stand again. He feels bad for whoever has to clean the pool of sweat forming beneath him.

"What are we gonna do about Vic?" he asks.

"Not this again," Cass groans.

Vic has no family left. His dad was never there, and his mom stopped taking his visits after she had the bad luck to get a third possession conviction down in Kansas, winning her a twenty-five-year sentence.

"He'd want to be with his abuela."

"Let's worry about what the fuck is gonna happen to us first. Goddamn."

"Sure," he says. He doesn't see why they can't do both, but he doesn't want to make Cass mad. He watches the passing houses. Each one has a family. If any of them died, there'd be people there to go to the morgue and claim the body. There would be a funeral. It would be nice. Who would do that for Vic if they're on the run?

"I can't fucking deal with you right now," Cass says as the bus approaches a stop. "I'm gonna stay at Aunt Marta's tonight. Find somewhere else to lay low. Come by tomorrow, and we'll figure out what we're gonna do about this shit show."

Jonny Boy leans his head against the vibrating glass of the window. He hurts too much to keep moving or to keep fighting.

"Come on, man," Cass says, punching his shoulder as she rises to her feet. "We got this, yeah? We gotta see it through. For Vic."

She's right. Vic is counting on them. He waves to her as she walks away, and she rolls her eyes. He wishes he could be a better friend to her. Vic always knew how to make her happy. He could help her forget everything that was stacked against her.

Jonny Boy rides the bus in circles. He sits on that hard chair as the houses and trees go by. People sit down, and they leave, and the sweat dries off his skin.

CHAPTER 38

Owen Oster, 11:48 A.M.

The third time Holzmann tries to call them, Conrad and Owen head to a quiet corner of the motor pool to answer it.

"How are we playing this?" Owen asks, his thumb hovering over the glowing green circle on the phone.

"Tear the fucker a new one," Conrad says. "He's gonna ask us to clean up his mess. Make him pay."

Owen nods and answers the call.

"I have another task for you," Holzmann says as soon as the line is connected.

"What the fuck did you do?" Owen says in a whispered shout. An officer across the lot glances his way but quickly moves on.

"Excuse me?" Holzmann asks. He is not used to being spoken to in such a way.

"No," Owen says. "You don't get to be indignant here."

He can hear Holzmann take a centering breath. "Herr Oster," he says. "Of what do you speak?"

"I speak," Owen spits out the plosive syllables with as much derision as he can muster, "of the five fucking bodies found on your property last night. Multiple homicides in Elkhorn? Fuck, man. What the fuck happened?" With each "fuck" he can hear Holzmann hiss in displeasure.

"Nothing I am not prepared for," Holzmann says, as though that's a sufficient answer.

"That's not fucking good enough. They got your stash. They got your money—"

"They got nothing I was not prepared to give them. You do not need to concern yourself with this any further."

"I'll concern myself with whatever the fuck I want. You don't seem to be grasping the severity of the clusterfuck we find ourselves in here. The entire fucking OPD is on this. There's rumors the FBI might get involved."

"Send the pictures," Holzmann says, and it takes Owen a moment to realize that Holzmann is ignoring him to carry on some other conversation.

Owen can't make out anything further as Holzmann covers the receiver. He can only hear muffled voices and background static. After a brief exchange, Holzmann returns to the call.

"It is resolved," he says. "Now I need you to find—"

"No," Owen interrupts him. "You don't get it. It's our asses hanging out in the breeze here, so until this goes away, we're done. No contact. No work. Nothing." Owen looks to Conrad, wanting to make sure he hasn't pushed things too far, and Conrad gives him a thumbs-up. An operation doesn't take a hit like Holzmann's did last night only to shrug and move on. The fucker is going to need eyes on the inside, and he'll pay what he has to to get them.

"I need you to find Cassiopeia Mullen," Holzmann says, as though Owen had not spoken at all. "She has my key."

This isn't what Holzmann is supposed to be asking them for. He's supposed to need help getting the police off his back. He's supposed to be desperate to avoid scrutiny, especially if there is a war brewing. Instead, he's still going on about this fucking key. Owen looks to Conrad, unsure how to continue, and Conrad waves his finger in a circle, the signal to keep going.

"Fuck you, Henry," Owen says.

"All action," responds Holzmann enigmatically, meeting Owen's vitriol with bullshit sagacity, "takes place in a kind of twilight, which, like a fog, tends to make things appear grotesque and larger than they really are."

"What the fuck does that mean?"

Holzmann clears his throat. The college lecturer prepares to deliver his wisdom to the seminar. "It means that you do not have the full picture of what is happening, and your ignorance is making monsters out of already vanquished foes. The investigation into these murders will deepen, but its lens will not fall on you. You and your partner shall be spared this professional scrutiny if—and this *if* is quite important, Herr Oster—you find me Cassiopeia Mullen."

Conrad mouths *fuck him* to Owen. Nobody fucking threatens them.

"Fuck off," Owen says, ready to hang up.

"The key opens a safe," Holzmann says. "In the safe is an object of such great value as to make all else seem nothing by comparison. But without this object, my problems grow tiresome, and when my problems are tiresome, your problems are insurmountable. Find me Cassiopeia, and I will make your concerns disappear amidst a shower of wealth. Fail me, and, well—" He trails off. "Do not fail."

The line goes dead. Holzmann hung up on him. "Well fuck you too," Owen says, sliding the phone back into his pocket.

"Something is going on here," Conrad says. "This isn't how Holzmann works. He's careful and deliberate, and he's always treated us well."

It's true. Holzmann has been an ideal partner. Until this week.

"What do you think is happening?" Owen asks.

"I don't know." Conrad grimaces. "And I don't like it."

"What he said about not needing to worry about blowback, do you think that's true? Can he really keep this under control?"

"Maybe." Conrad leads them back into the station. "I'm sure he has a plan. Whether we're protected, though?" Conrad shrugs. "Let's hope he's got our back, but assume we're on our own."

"He's gotta know that if we go down, we're taking him with us."

"All I know is he thinks he's better than us, and he's keeping us in the dark. That's not how you treat a partner, and if he won't respect us, it's time we stopped respecting him."

In a way, Owen always knew this would happen. At the end of the day, Holzmann is a criminal—he's a civilized criminal, but he's a criminal nonetheless—and Conrad has a point. There can be no relationship where there is no respect.

For the time being, the two have nothing to do. The tip line hasn't been set up yet, so there are no tips for them to follow. Owen grabs a workstation and logs in as Melissa Fulli. There's no reason they can't get started tracking down Cassiopeia Mullen, just in case.

She's got a couple arrests for larceny. Two for assault that she pled down. A juvie file, though that's under seal. She's a person of interest in a string of home break-ins in Leavenworth and Old Market. She appears to be just another garden-variety petty criminal.

"Hey," Owen says, getting Conrad's attention. One of Mullen's known associates stands out to him. "Is this guy"—Owen points from the screen to the board in the briefing room—"that guy?"

"Son of a bitch." The not-yet-identified body from the Elkhorn massacre is Mullen's friend, Victor Velasquez. He has his own file, twice the length of Mullen's. His fingerprints are in the system. His body will be IDed by the end of the day.

"Should we tell someone?" Owen asks. Sergeant Nowicki is across the bullpen. They'd win a lot of goodwill bringing this to him.

"No," Conrad says. "We need to stay as far away from this as we can."

"And if Holzmann isn't bullshitting us? If he really can keep us clean, but only if we track down Mullen for him?"

They can track down this girl, that's not hard, but they're going to leave a trail behind if they do. When the ID on Velasquez's body comes back, that's going to lead the main investigation to Mullen. Questions will come up about why they were looking into her. Questions they can't answer.

But if they don't track her down, they're burning Holzmann. The last two days notwithstanding, he hasn't lied to them once. If he can protect them, but only if they find Mullen, they need to do so, and fast.

"All right, people," Sarge calls across the bullpen. "Tip line is up, get ready for every fucking crackpot in the city to come forward."

Conrad smiles. "I've got an idea."

CHAPTER 39

Owen Oster, 12:56 P.M.

They have to camp out in the file room for an hour, doing their best to dodge Sarge and avoid getting put on some bullshit lead while staying close enough that when their own anonymous tip makes its way through the system, Conrad is within earshot.

Jesse Taylor gets assigned to it. Owen doesn't know him personally—they usually work different shifts—but he's never heard anything about the guy, which is a good sign. You only hear about the really good or really bad ones. Owen catches up with him on the far side of the pen.

"Taylor," he says, leaning against the workstation wall and giving his best smile. "How's it going?"

Taylor blinks up at Owen, trying to place him, trying to decide how to react.

"Fine," he says, opting for the noncommittal route.

"Hey, listen," Owen says, grabbing a chair from the adjoining station. "I got a favor to ask. Nothing big." He looks around the pen to ensure they aren't being eavesdropped on before leaning back in. "That

191

girl Nowicki just put you on, my partner liked her for a break-in last year. We did some of the best damn police work you've ever seen, and then the detectives went and fucked it up, lost chain of custody on this necklace we tracked back to her and, well, you know. It's a break-in. Nobody looked that hard. But he was so fucking proud of his work, and to see it just thrown out like that—he's still pissed. So here's the thing. You mind if we look into this one? My partner would really like to have a word with her."

"Just to be clear," Taylor says, "you're asking if you can do my work for me?"

Owen nods.

"And this is me doing you a favor?"

Owen nods again.

"So you want nothing in return?"

Owen shakes his head. Taylor doesn't have to think too hard.

Twenty minutes later Owen is back in the database, this time logged in as himself, and noting down known addresses for Cassiopeia Mullen and her associates. Conrad is on the phone setting up flags on her cell and credit cards. It isn't, in the strictest sense of the term, legal for him to be requesting those things without a warrant or probable cause, and any evidence derived from those flags would be thrown out of court. But they're not planning on developing any evidence.

Silence washes across the bullpen as two people walk in. The two are cops, or at least they wear badges, though nobody in the room would claim brotherhood with them. A man and a woman, unremarkable in professional navy suits. The woman is pudgy from decades behind a desk. The man needs more sun. Owen doesn't know them, but he doesn't need to. Professional Oversight has a look to them. A way of carrying themselves. A way of sucking all the joy and life out of a room full of police. They scan the room, catch sight of Owen and Conrad, and start toward them.

So this is how it ends. A brilliant fucking finale to the two shittiest days of his life. All Owen wanted was a quiet life of comfort. He'd done his work. He was a good guy. That should have been enough for the world, but it was full of liars and cheats who wanted to take advantage of him. And at the end of the day, was what he'd done so fucking bad? Sure, he and Conrad had broken the law, but only to help shitty criminals hurt each other more.

Owen won't run or cower or hide. He's a fucking man, and he'll take the world's bullshit on the chin. He and Conrad come to their feet, standing tall and proud in the face of gross injustice. The detectives walk toward them.

And then they pass. The woman casts a curious glance Owen's way, and then he is forgotten. They continue across the room, stopping at Sarge's desk for a moment of quiet conversation. His shoulders slump, and he presses his fingers into his forehead. He leads the two across the pen and into the break room, then comes back out, alone, and closes the door.

"Break room's closed," he calls to the pen. At the collective groan and scattering of boos, he raises his hands. "None of you lazy fucks should be taking breaks anyways." He waves away a few more shouts and heads to the shift commander's office.

"Fuck," Owen says, sitting down once more and letting out a held breath.

"I'm fucking done with this," Conrad says. Sweat prickles his forehead. "I can't take this fucking stress."

"I've been trying to tell you to do some meditation."

"Nah, man. It's all too much."

"So what?" Owen asks. "You want to go straight?"

"Fuck no, but I'm done working for Holzmann."

"With Holzmann," Owen corrects him.

Conrad frowns, then continues, "He wants to get into this safe badly enough that he's burning every bridge he has to get it. Whatever's in there is worth more to him than the network he spent his life building. We know what the safe looks like. We're tracking the key now. And we know the guy who can open it."

"So what are you saying?" Owen asks.

"I'm saying I think it's time we hung up our dirty badges and went into business for ourselves."

CHAPTER 40

Peter Van Horn, 1:19 P.M.

Sergeant Nowicki's voice wakes Peter from his nap. "There's your guy," he says. "The fuck do you people think he did, gets you out here in one day?"

"Thank you, Sergeant," a woman replies, the dismissal clear in her voice. "We'll take it from here."

"Just stay out of my people's way. We've got real police work to do."

"Close the door on your way out, please." A man this time. Peter doesn't recognize either of their voices. He cracks one eye.

They're police. That much is obvious. They wear the same neutral suits that detectives always wear. Plus, they've got badges around their necks. The badges are the big giveaway. They both look to be in their fifties. Maybe forties? Peter has never been good at judging ages. The man, with the tired air of a civil servant, gives the door a tug, making sure the latch caught. The woman looks down at Peter and smiles. She reminds him of his mother. She has the same calm about her. She has seen the worst the world can throw at her and survived. She pulls out the chair next to his and sits.

"Peter Van Horn?" she asks, extending her hand. Peter takes it. Her shake isn't overtly feminine, but neither does she go out of her way to prove her strength. "I'm Chloe Rutherford. This is Ethan Pruitt. Do you mind if we join you?"

Peter can't help but notice that she already has.

"Go ahead," he says. As Ethan sits across from him, Peter gets a better view of their badges, which identify them as being a part of the Professional Oversight division.

"Thanks, Peter," Ethan says. "Do you mind if we call you Peter, or would you prefer Officer Van Horn?"

"Peter is fine." These two seem nice enough. If his life is going to be ruined—to the extent that a life he doesn't like and didn't want can be ruined—it might as well be by nice people.

"Great," says Ethan, smiling across at him. "Hopefully this won't take too much of your time. We just have a couple things we want to clear up."

"We know how people look at us," Chloe says, picking up right as Ethan stops. "We know what they say. We're traitors, right? The worst of the worst?" She smiles as she says it, and Peter just shrugs.

"Odd as it might seem, though," Ethan continues, "we're actually on the same side. All of us here at this table want the same thing. We want to find the truth about what happened and put this whole mess behind us so you can get back to what really matters."

"Putting the real criminals away," Chloe finishes for him. "So we appreciate your candor here, Peter. It means a lot to us."

"Yeah," Peter says. "Sure. I've been trying to tell people all along what's happened, but nobody wants to listen."

Chloe folds her hands in her lap. "That's what we're here for, Peter. We're here to listen. So why don't you just start at the beginning?"

As she looks in his eyes, keeping his gaze on her, Ethan pulls a pad from his briefcase to take notes. It'll be a relief to tell someone, but the coil hasn't let go of his chest. The dread is still there. The absolute confidence that disaster is looming, just around the corner, and no matter what he does, it will come for him.

"Right," he says. "So two nights ago I was moonlighting at a U-Store-It."

Once Peter starts talking, it's hard to stop, and the events of the night come pouring out. The disagreement with Owen, the implied offer of questionable money, Owen's missing car in the parking lot. He tries to include as much detail as he can. You never know what might be important. As Peter is about to launch into a description of the meeting with Dumetz and Owen lying on the phone, Ethan puts his pen down and clears his throat.

"Is something wrong?" Peter asks.

Ethan frowns and starts flipping through his briefcase. "No, Peter," he says. "This is all great. We were hoping, though—ah, here we go." His fingers close on a thick piece of glossy paper. A picture. Peter doesn't know what it shows, but, at the same time, he does. Not the details of it. The details don't matter. But the gist.

He was going to tell them. He was. He's not trying to hide anything. He doesn't know how they got it—he left no trace—but that doesn't matter. He was going to tell them, but now it looks like he was lying. It looks like he was hiding. Because he didn't get to tell. They already knew. He left no trace, but they knew. Ethan turns the paper over and lays it flat on the table so everyone can see.

"We were hoping—" Ethan is saying, but Peter can't hear him. Can't hear anything over the roaring in his ears and the screaming in his chest and he can't breathe. His body locks. This can't be happening. He's not a bad person. He might not be a great cop, but he's not bad. It all keeps going sideways, and he can't get out.

His arms won't move. He grips the side of the table and he can feel the pain in his fingers as the tendons strain and the hiss of the coffeemaker at the end of a brew cycle scratches at his ears and he needs to get out of this room.

He doesn't know how, but he knows that this will end with him in a box. A jail cell or a coffin. Like his family. His brother. He was so weak at the end, gasping for breath, but he always fought. Always strained to pull air into traitorous, dying lungs. And here's Peter, the one who lived, the one whose body isn't actively destroying itself, and what is he doing? He can't even make his chest rise. Can't pull in air, though nothing is broken in his body except for him.

He stares at the picture and he can't breathe and the room narrows to just him and the image.

"We were hoping that you might tell us—" Ethan is still saying. How long does it take him to speak one sentence? How long for the executioner's axe to fall?

The room isn't narrowing. The room is just as painfully small as it has always been. These were the last moments of freedom that Peter had, and he spent them sleeping on a plastic table, brewing eleven pots of coffee. He can feel something in his finger pop as his hand strains against the table. There is just him and the picture and he can't breathe and the box is closing in on him.

His arms are pinned to his sides. This is what death is like. This is what his brother and parents went through. What awaits him. He is paralyzed and he can't breathe and there is just him and the doom walking toward him. Coming up out of the table. Out of the picture. There is nothing but the picture.

"We were hoping you might tell us about this," Ethan finishes saying. The blow is delivered. The axe lands.

Peter looks at the picture, and there, on the table, is him, in black and white, standing in a room, and he is standing there in a ready crouch with his arms out straight, and in his hand is a gun, his gun, his gun is in his hand, and his gun is pointing at a body on the ground and he is standing there with his gun, and there is nothing but him and the picture of him and neither of them are moving, and he can't breathe.

"Peter?" Chloe is beside him, and she is reaching out, but he can't turn to look at her because she isn't there. It is just him and the picture and the growing blackness.

◆

"Peter?" Chloe says.

Peter is lying on the ground. There is a bag over his mouth, recycling his breath back to him, and something cool on his head, doing its best to contain the pain behind his brow. His eyes slowly open. His head is pounding, and it takes him a moment to place himself.

"Welcome back," Chloe says. "You scared us for a second there." She is kneeling beside him, holding the paper bag to his mouth.

Now he remembers.

He was going to tell these two everything. They had been so nice, and it would be such a relief to unburden himself, to lay it all in someone else's lap.

And then he had a panic attack.

But lying here now, on the ground with a damp cloth pressed to the spike driving through his head, Peter knows that he can't tell them anything.

"How's your head?" Chloe asks. "You hit it pretty hard on your way down."

Ethan and Chloe are not his friends. They do not want the truth. They want to turn a red case black. They want to say that Peter is a bad cop, but the rot stops with him.

"Do you feel up to keep going?" Ethan asks him from across the room. "We'd really like to get this ironed out quickly."

Ethan and Chloe are here to lay the wrongs of the entire department on his back and drive him into the forest to be eaten by wolves, so that the rest of their people might continue their pristine, sin-free lives.

"I think," Peter says, bringing himself up to a sitting position, "that we should get my union rep in here."

"Are you sure about that, Peter?" Ethan asks. "Right now, we're just having a friendly talk. Three police all looking for the truth together. If the union gets involved, this whole thing gets a lot more—" He pauses, searching for the right word, or at least pretending to. "Official."

Chloe puts herself between Peter and the door. She's not trapping him, but he will have to walk around her to get out.

"Peter, please think about this," she says. "We know you have debts. And we both started off on a beat as well. We know how hard it can be to get by on what the department pays you, and that's without family obligations. If someone is trying to take advantage of you, we can help. Whatever hole you think you're in, I don't care how deep, there's a way out of it, but that way is through us."

Peter has no friends. There is nobody left on this earth who loves him. If he is going to get out, then he needs to do what he should have done from the very beginning.

Peter Van Horn doesn't like questions. They nag at him. Like mosquito bites, they sit just this side of painful. They grab at his focus, blemishes on the smooth surface of his existence. There are too many questions now.

"I'm done talking," Peter says.

He is going to get answers.

CHAPTER 41

Jonny Boy Wright, 2:46 P.M.

E nd of the line," the bus driver calls, making his way down the aisle. "Everybody off." Besides Jonny Boy, there're two homeless people and one confused old Mexican woman who got on the wrong bus. She pleads with the driver in Spanish, but he gestures to the back door and herds her out.

Jonny Boy steps onto the curb and is struck by two things. The first is hunger. It has been hours since he ate that egg salad sandwich, and though he can still taste the metallic bite of the chives, all sense of satiety has long since fled. The second is that he has absolutely no idea where he is. Looking around, he recognizes none of the buildings. The street names of the nearest intersection are completely foreign to him. He could head east until he hits the Missouri, then follow it to more familiar territory, but his feet still hurt, and the hours on the bus left the knots in his back more tightly clenched than before.

One of the homeless people, a man whose age is beyond determination, must have noticed Jonny Boy's confused desperation, because he comes up beside him and says: "You need a place to stay?"

"Yeah," says Jonny Boy. "I guess I do."

The man smiles with rotting teeth and puts a hand on Jonny Boy's elbow. "Your first night on the streets?"

Jonny Boy nods and starts walking with the man.

"You were smart to get away from the city. There's nothing good for us there."

Jonny Boy lets the man lead him to a stand of trees on the side of a hill. There's a chain-link fence, but one of the posts has fallen, and they clamber over the twisted metal. Once among the trees, the hill crests and falls away into a shallow bowl in which six people have set up tents and sleeping bags. The camp is hidden from the street, and they've worked to keep it clean. There's a cooking fire in the center and clotheslines filled with blankets, still damp from last night's deluge. A small pile of dried goods and bottled water sits under a tarp. The camp's residents watch Jonny Boy approach down the shallow bank. They are wary, but not hostile.

"You're safe here," the man tells him. "We all pull our own weight, and we look out for each other. But you try anything, we'll do what needs doing." He eyes the bruises and scrapes across Jonny Boy's face and knuckles.

"You don't have to worry about me," Jonny Boy says, tucking his hands into his pockets. "I don't want to hurt anyone."

"Good. I'm Eli, by the way."

Eli introduces Jonny Boy around the camp, but Jonny Boy is too tired and overwhelmed to process the names. Of the six others, four look younger than he is, and two must still be minors. They get work when they can and dumpster dive when they can't, doing their best to stay away from people and the threat they pose. The two older women go into the city each morning to collect empty cans and scrap to sell at the recycling plant. Eli usually maintains the camp but had a meeting with his social worker today. Nobody asks Jonny Boy what he's doing on the streets, nor do they offer their own stories.

Jonny Boy tries to be sociable, to meet this welcome with kindness, but he is exhausted. His legs burn, his back aches, and the dull throbs of a dozen small bruises press at his patience. It is only once he settles into a quiet peace, though, sheltering beneath a still-damp blanket on a pile of leaves, that the true pain begins to grow.

He hasn't let himself acknowledge it. He said the words. He even fought with Cass about it, but he's not truly felt it. It hasn't been real. He had known Vic for fifteen years, since Vic and his mom followed his abuela up to the States. His English hadn't been great, but that first day Vic traded a cold tamale for Jonny Boy's Lunchable, and they'd been friends since.

He is saved from his grief by the rising pain in his gut.

"Umm, excuse me," he says quietly, and Eli looks over at him from his own shady spot, waiting out the last of the afternoon's heat. "Is there any food?"

Eli glances at the small pile of cans, then back at Jonny Boy. At his stomach. At the folds of fat on his cheeks. At the rolls beneath his chin where his neck should be. Jonny Boy's face flushes with shame. He fumbles in his pockets, coming out with a crumpled ten-dollar bill.

"Or anywhere I could get some?"

Eli relaxes and directs him to a convenience store near the bus stop. Jonny Boy's feet and back still hurt, but the pain grounds him. It keeps his mind on the present moment. Keeps his thoughts from wandering.

The air in the convenience store is a blessed relief. The wave of crisp chill makes him aware of how hot he's been. He relishes it until a glare from the cashier gets him moving again. He grabs a pack of Advil and a big bottle of water from the refrigerator, and is about to order a hotdog when he spots a case of premade food: sandwiches of every kind, cut in half and sealed into triangular boxes. Roast beef, ham, tuna, turkey, on white bread or wheat, for a buck fifty each.

This is all he ever wanted. Cass wants money and status and respect, and she deserves all those things, but he never cared. They'd be nice, but they're not for him. He's just a dumb, fat fuck with no prospects and no purpose. But food has always understood him, and he has always understood it. He doesn't need anything fancy. Some carbs and fat and protein are enough to bring him joy. Cass eats to sustain herself, and Vic ate to build his body, but for Jonny Boy, eating is as close to a sacrament as he can get.

He grabs a turkey sandwich and a ham and is heading to the register when a thought occurs to him. He still has Cass's credit card that he'd borrowed this morning to get groceries.

He sweeps up a dozen more sandwiches, as many as can fit in his arms. He dumps them all on the counter, suddenly worried that the cashier might think him suspicious, might wonder why he needs so many. The cashier rings up the food, water, and pills. It comes out to twenty-six something.

Jonny Boy slides the card into the machine, sure that the cashier will see Cassiopeia Mullen printed across the front and refuse the sale. It seems to take the machine longer than normal to run, but the transaction goes through. The cashier puts everything in a bag and promptly goes back to acting as though Jonny Boy never existed.

After climbing back over the fallen fence and down into the camp, he takes the pills, water, and two sandwiches and hands the rest to Eli.

"Thanks for letting me stay," he says.

The man looks into the bag and grins his brown smile. "Bless you," Eli says, adding the bag to the stack of dry goods. A couple of the kids watch Jonny Boy with, if anything, more wariness than they had when he first arrived. Jonny Boy returns to his pile of leaves to eat on his own.

"Don't be offended," Eli says, sitting next to him a few minutes later. "The world hasn't been kind to them."

"I get it," Jonny Boy says. "But you were nice to me, so I just . . ." He trails off, but Eli nods, seeming to understand. "I do have a question, though," Jonny Boy continues, struggling to find the right words. "Do you know what happens when someone dies and they don't have, like, family, or whatever, to come and get the body? Do they still get buried?"

Eli takes a deep breath and closes his eyes. "Are you in trouble?" he asks, and there is a concern in the question not just for Jonny Boy's well-being but for the safety of his little group.

"A friend of mine—" Jonny Boy starts, but he can't finish the sentence. "I can't go to the police to claim him, but I don't know—He'd want to be with his abuela. She's buried in Saddle Creek."

"Does he have other family?" Eli asks. Jonny Boy shakes his head. "They'll try to find family, but if there's nobody, then the city will cremate him."

"He wouldn't want that," Jonny Boy objects.

"The world isn't kind." There isn't much more to say after that.

CHAPTER 42

Peter Van Horn, 3:54 P.M.

The union is worthless. Peter is shuffled between waiting rooms, each with increasingly more anodyne portraits of police, police dogs, and smiling kids, for the better part of an hour before he is able to speak with someone of authority. A woman in a power suit with a tiny shred of lettuce hanging across her front tooth introduces herself as Ally, "like I'll be your ally, but with an *e* sound instead of an *i*." She is appropriately horrified to hear of his predicament, but as soon as Peter mentions his suspicions of Owen and Conrad, the discussion comes to a halt.

"Now, Peter," she tells him. "I understand that you're upset, and I'm upset right alongside you at this absolute atrocity of injustice. But the solution isn't to pass the blame to other, equally innocent officers."

"But don't—" Peter tries to interject.

"You've done the right thing." She powers through his interruption. "Don't say another word to Professional Oversight. We're all on your side here, Peter, and now that we're involved, this whole thing is going to slow way down." She leans over her desk and pitches her voice lower. "Ninety-nine times out of a hundred, we just have to wait them out. The last thing you want to do is stir the water with talk about your fellow officers. You're gonna be fine, Peter. Thanks for coming in today. I'll reach out in a month or two if PO wants to have another interview, but I expect you'll be back on patrol and missing the office before you know it."

She stands and offers him a handshake. There's no chance for follow-up questions.

No matter what Ally says, Peter knows this isn't going to blow over. He doesn't know what he did to offend Owen Oster, but one of their careers is ending.

Sarge has moved Peter onto third shift until this is all cleared up. He'll be in processing and filing, making sure that all the paper generated during the day winds up properly sorted before it disappears into the basement. Sarge says it's to keep Peter out of the public eye and away from Dumetz's ire.

He has a few more hours before he has to be back at the station. He needs sleep—real sleep in a bed in the dark—and a shower and a change of clothes. His hair is greasy enough that it's been hours since he last needed to push it out of his eyes, and he's sure he's grown quite ripe in the summer heat. He can't smell it himself, but that doesn't mean it isn't there.

He had learned something new, though, after his disastrous interview with Ethan and Chloe. He'd caught sight of the board in the briefing room and a picture in the center of it. The old man that Barrett led him to was Henry Holzmann, the owner of the house in Elkhorn, and apparently the king of vice in the city.

Peter doesn't know how, yet, but Owen and Conrad and what had happened at the U-Store-It are all connected to the massacre. If he can bring proof of that to Ethan and Chloe, then he might be able to get out from under this. So Peter cannot go home and rest. He cannot shower. He cannot clean his hair or wash away the stink of the last two days. He has to find proof before Owen destroys him.

◆

Conrad's brother-in-law is easy to track down. He works in the warehouse of a packaging supply wholesaler. Peter looked up all his information before coming to the union hall.

"Hello?" the man says when he answers his cell. Peter is surprised at the smooth tenor of his voice. He'd been expecting something gruff and gravelly like Conrad's.

"Hey, is this Walter?" Peter asks. "I work with Conrad. Do you have a sec?"

There's a pause before Walter answers, and a hesitancy to his response when it comes. "Sure. What's up?"

"Conrad said you went out to a great bar the other night," Peter says. "I was hoping to grab the name from you."

"Yeah," Walter answers, again slowly. "Why don't you just ask him?"

"He's not here?" Peter says, unable to keep the question out of his voice. Great recovery. Ten out of ten.

"Whatever," Walter snorts after another pause. "It was a place called the Nine Ball. Conrad, Owen, and me were there all night, got there just after nine. That it? I gotta get back to work."

"That's it. Thanks," Peter says. Walter had been coached to give Owen and Conrad an alibi.

It's a twenty-minute drive to the Nine Ball, a billiards room on the opposite side of the city from the U-Store-It. It's a long and skinny establishment with seven pool tables running down the side, the bar in the back, and a dozen cocktail tables up front. There's only one game in progress right now, a trio of old men who squint against the light as Peter pushes the door open. Another man stares silently from behind the bar as Peter makes the long walk back to it. A couple of security cameras watch the front door, and a few more cover the staff door in the back.

"How are you doing today, sir?" Peter asks, flashing his badge to the bartender and pulling himself onto a rickety stool. The bartender grunts at him. Not a very cop-friendly place, this. Peter puts on a smile and psychs himself up to lie. "I'm looking into something that happened nearby two nights ago. Do you still have the footage from those cameras?"

The bartender squints toward the door, studying the cameras as though seeing them for the first time. He hacks a ball of phlegm from deep in his throat, spits it into a paper cup, and then looks back to Peter. "Gets wiped every seventy hours," the bartender says.

"Excellent, then you still have it. Would you mind if I had a look?"

"You got a warrant?"

"I don't. I was hoping you might let me see anyways."

"Need a warrant."

Peter anticipated this response and wrote a speech on the drive over. He's seen enough cop shows to know the major points he needs to hit. Now he only needs to deliver it. He channels his best Owen impression, laying on that affected, threatening empathy.

"I could get a warrant, sure," he says. The words feel awkward and artificial in his mouth. This is worse than trying to swear. "The thing is, it'll take me who knows how long to do that, and in the meantime, now that you know that footage is germane to an ongoing investigation, I've got to warn you that it's a felony to destroy it, which means you're going to have to preserve it for as long as it takes me to get my warrant."

"Can't do that," the bartender says with a helpless shrug. "It's an automatic system."

Peter nods his head sympathetically. "Unfortunately, that doesn't matter. It's still destruction of evidence and obstruction of justice. Two felonies, actually."

"Just give the fucking pig what he wants," one of the pool players calls from across the room. "We need more beer here."

"You only want to look?" the bartender asks.

Peter nods. "I'm trying to see if someone came through here." He stops himself before he says more. There's no need to risk giving the man another reason to object.

"Fuck it," the man says. "Let me serve them, then I'll set you up in the office."

Once he's alone with the security footage, Peter copies it to his phone and starts going through to confirm that Owen and Conrad didn't come anywhere near this place two nights ago. If it comes to a trial, the video will be thrown out without a proper chain of custody to establish its origin, but it's better than nothing. It is, at least, a start.

It's evening by the time he's done, and he is exhausted. There's no way he'll be able to keep his eyes open through a whole night of filing, and he can't afford to be caught napping on the job. Ally told him the plan was to slow things down. If he were smart, he would have listened. There was no reason to wear himself out with this.

Except there was. If he'd come here tomorrow, the footage would have been gone. Yes, he's tired. Yes, it will be hard to get through his shift. But he's made it through worse than a sleepless night. If he'd done the smart thing, he'd have been rested and washed, but it would have still been his word against Owen's. Instead, he has his first proof of Owen's lies.

He's going to need more than this, though, before he can go back to Ethan and Chloe. They want to pin this on him and be done with it. Expanding their investigation from one rogue cop to department-spanning corruption is going to take more than a lying brother-in-law and some grainy bar footage. But he is, at least, moving toward something.

Maybe it's time he starts not doing the smart thing a bit more often.

CHAPTER 43

Jonny Boy Wright, 8:09 P.M.

As the sun falls and darkness comes, Eli extinguishes the fire—night fires draw all sorts of unwanted attention—and the camp settles into tents and sleeping bags. Jonny Boy sees one of the kids grab a sandwich, and he smiles at her. She gives a small wave before retreating to safety.

Vic wasn't the most religious of people, but he still called himself a Catholic. When he got drunk enough, he'd talk about the resurrection at the end of days. How the dead would return, and the saved would be brought into the Kingdom of God. This was the only body he'd ever get, Vic said, which is why he took such good care of it. How would he be resurrected if his body was burnt?

Jonny Boy tries not to think about it. He tries not to think about anything. Tomorrow he'll find Cass, and she'll figure something out.

It's still dark when he's woken by someone shaking his shoulder, and the foul odor of Eli's breath overwhelms his senses.

"Police," says the man.

Everything in Jonny Boy's body hurts, but he struggles to his feet. Eli leads him to the crest of the bowl, where he points out a cop fighting his way over the fallen fence. The cop must have heard them, because he looks up, shining his light toward the trees where they are. Jonny Boy and Eli both fall to the ground, but not quickly enough.

"I see you up there, you motherfuckers," the cop yells. "Send Mullen down, and I can be on my fucking way."

"Are you Mullen?" Eli whispers.

"No," Jonny Boy says. "That's Cass. Why would they be looking for her here?"

Eli can only shrug. "You need to leave," he says.

A hand tugs on Jonny Boy's leg, and he turns to see the girl who'd waved to him.

"Follow me," she says. "There's another way out of here."

She takes Jonny Boy to a second gap in the fence. The metal protests as she pulls it out of the way, and the cut edges tear at his clothes, but he makes it through.

No sooner is he out, though, than another voice shouts to him. "OPD," it says. "Get on the fucking ground!"

"Go!" the girl hiss-yells at Jonny Boy, and he takes off running. Agony burns through his shins with each footfall, and it takes all his concentration to keep his prodigious weight upright on the grassy hill, but, one thundering step at a time, he makes it down.

"Stop right fucking there!" the cop shouts as Jonny Boy barrels toward him. But the cop doesn't have a weapon out, and Jonny Boy couldn't stop, even if he wanted to.

It's like hitting cement. The cop plants himself and puts his hands into Jonny Boy's chest and catches the full force of his charge, driving all the air from his lungs. But the cop's feet slide on the grass, and his weight shifts back, and the two, like kaiju battling in the shallows off the coast of Japan, tilt toward the ground.

That ground is almost softer than the cop's block as Jonny Boy hits it and rolls, his forward momentum not quite fully arrested. He gets his feet underneath him again and looks back over his shoulder. The cop glares at him from his hands and knees.

"Do not make me chase you," the cop gasps out. As Jonny Boy starts to run, the cop yells to his partner, "Owen, I fucking need you over here!"

Jonny Boy must have landed poorly in his tumble, because the fire in his legs is sharper. His left ankle screams with every stride, but he finds his way across the grass and back to the street, and he ignores the pain. Up ahead is a commercial area, low buildings where he can lose himself. He just needs to get there.

The leg appears from around the building suddenly. It clips Jonny Boy's left shin. Pain blossoms, and then he is aloft, floating through the air, arms thrown out, mouth open in a voiceless scream.

He was wrong about running into the cop being like hitting cement. Hitting the sidewalk is like hitting cement. His left hand lands first, and his skin abrades away against the rough surface. His left thigh hits next. He already bled off enough energy that this collision will merely bruise his flesh, though the cloth of his pants does give way.

He skids to a halt and looks back. Another cop leans against the wall, looking down at him, as the one he tackled tromps his way toward them, gasping for breath.

"I fucking told you," the gasping cop says, "not to make me chase you. Didn't I fucking say that?"

Jonny Boy pushes himself up onto his elbows, and the cop kicks him in the side for his effort.

"Jesus, Conrad," the cop who tripped him—presumably Owen—says, turning to his partner. "You gotta hit the gym more. You're falling apart in your old age."

"I can still block with the best of them," Conrad says. "I stopped this fat fucker, didn't I?"

"No," Owen says. "You fucking didn't."

"Whatever." Conrad looks down at Jonny Boy, head tilted to the side.

"Now that we've caught him," Owen says, "maybe he can tell us who the fuck he is and why he made us chase him."

Jonny Boy blinks up at the two. They don't know who he is? That's right. They're here for Cass, not for him.

"He's in the book," Conrad says. "This is Jon Wright, aka Jonny Boy, compatriot of one Cassiopeia Mullen."

"You're the one who used her card?" Owen asks Jonny Boy.

Shit. He's a fucking idiot. Of course they were tracking her credit card. How could he have been so stupid?

"You, my friend, are not cut out for this life," Owen says, shaking his head sadly. "But I've got some good news for you." He squats down to be at Jonny Boy's level. "Unless you find some way to make yourself valuable to us, it won't matter what kind of life you're suited to."

Conrad undoes the snap on his holster.

Jonny Boy lies back against the cement, curls his knees into his body, and waits. What an appropriately miserable end to a pointless life. He's going to die here on the side of the road in the dark spot between two dimming streetlights. He'd like to say he tried his best and the cards were stacked against him, but, if he looks at it with clear eyes, he has to admit that he made this bed. It was his own weakness and nothing else that brought him here. At least he and Vic can be burned together. They can discover what awaits the cremated at the resurrection at each other's sides.

No. Vic deserves better than that.

Jonny Boy swallows down the vomit rising in his throat. He's not going to let that happen. Cass will just have to go this one alone. "Fuck it," he says. "I told Cass this was a bad idea. You guys are after the key, right?"

Owen smiles at him. "It's all we ever wanted."

"Can you get my friend a funeral? Make sure he gets buried?"

"No problem," Conrad says.

"Wait," Owen interjects. "Like an actual funeral, or are you asking us to off somebody?"

"No," Jonny Boy says. "He got shot the other night. I want him to get a real funeral, with a headstone and flowers and shit."

"OK. Sure. We can do that," Conrad nods.

"Cass has the key," Jonny Boy says. "And I can take you to her."

The two help Jonny Boy to his feet and take him to where they're parked. He climbs into the back of their Jeep and directs them to Aunt Marta's. She's not really his aunt. She's just an old woman who lived down the street and treated him nice when he was younger. She never had children of her own, so she'd look after the neighborhood kids instead. He feels bad about bringing these two to her place, but she'll understand.

CHAPTER 44

Jonny Boy Wright, 9:17 P.M.

Aunt Marta's house is an old German colonial at the end of a block, and Owen parks them a couple lots down from it. Jonny Boy used to hide in the attic when he was too bruised from school to go home. Aunt Marta would pretend she didn't hear him running in and would putter around the house, loudly announcing all the food she was cooking. Then she'd leave a plate of lasagna or shepherd's pie or roast chicken at the base of the ladder. He never learned to cook himself, but he always wanted to. He wanted to share the comfort she had given him.

"Cass'll be in there," Jonny Boy says, pointing to a second-story window. "That's where the guest room is. Aunt Marta always leaves the door unlocked. She says she trusts us kids."

"All right," Owen says. He gets out of the car, but instead of heading toward the house, he opens Jonny Boy's door. "Lead on, big man. If this is a trap, you're getting three rounds in the back."

Jonny Boy doesn't want to go in. He doesn't want to see Cass's face when she realizes he betrayed her. But Owen has a gun, so he gets out and walks to the house.

His arm is bleeding, and his shins still burn, but he needs to see this through. For Vic. And for Cass. She might hate him when it's all over, but she'll still be alive. And maybe, if he makes it through to the other side, Aunt Marta will teach him how to make her gravy.

He leads the two cops down the street and up to the door. For a moment he can pretend that the cops aren't there, and the guns aren't there, and none of this has happened, and he's nine years old again, and his parents are having another fight. He's run away, and he'll hide in the attic, and everything will be fine.

The front door is unlocked, and the middle hinge squeaks, just like it always does. The house is dark, but Jonny Boy doesn't need lights to navigate it. Off to the left is the dining room table and the kitchen beyond that. The circle of chairs around the fireplace is to the right. Straight ahead is the staircase. Fifteen steps. The fourth and thirteenth will groan beneath his weight, but the rest will be silent. There are little carved birds at the ends of the banisters. At the top of the stairs is Aunt Marta's room, and the hallway turns back on itself there, leading to the guest room above the front door. The attic ladder comes out of the ceiling halfway down that hall.

He is about to tell the cops about the squeaky boards when a light turns on upstairs. There is a muffled shout and then a scream, piercing and wordless.

Jonny Boy is shoved aside as Owen and Conrad shoulder past him, flicking on their flashlights, their guns already drawn, and sprint up the stairs. He doesn't want to go toward the scream. Everything in him tells him he should turn around and run out the door, but he knows that voice. It was Aunt Marta.

Despite the burning in his legs, he rushes up the stairs. Streamers of pain shoot through his joints. By habit he skips the noisy steps. He reaches the landing and sees the door to Aunt Marta's room is open, but the light is coming from behind him. He turns to the guest room, the source of the light, just in time to see Owen and Conrad crash in with shouts of "Hands in the fucking air!" and "Police!"

Dreading what he'll find, knowing only that it will be some fresh, miserable punishment for his failures, Jonny Boy makes his way to the room. Conrad stands in the doorway, his gun raised.

The bed, a simple twin, is perpendicular to the door, near the back wall and beside the two windows on the front of the house. There's a closet to the right and a rocking chair in the corner to the left. Aunt Marta stands beside it, her face as white as her nightgown, and her mouth still agape from her scream. Beside her is Owen, his own gun raised and aimed across the room at a woman who Jonny Boy has never seen before but who has two pistols of her own, one pointed at Owen and the other at Conrad. Conrad's weapon is aimed not at her but at Barrett Rye, who stands beneath one of the windows beside the bed. Barrett's clothes are too small for his massive frame, one hand is bandaged, and his face and body are covered in bruises. At his feet on the ground is Cass, on her back with her arms raised protectively.

CHAPTER 45

Barrett Rye, 10:31 A.M.

A h, fuck.

There's a part of this story I was hoping I could skip.

There're some things I'd rather not go through.

But if this is going to make sense, if you are going to understand how I came to be working with Laia Quintana, the woman who killed Mickey, then I think I'm gonna have to take you through it all.

Fuck.

OK.

We're going to have to back up a bit.

Where was I then?

Right. I'm at Vic's grandma's place, Cass and Jonny Boy just fled through a window, Holzmann is outside, and I've just emptied my clip into the floor, hoping to stall him.

While the men out front hunker down for cover, I slip out the back door, around the pool, and over the fence into one of the neighbor's yards.

Someone peeks through the curtain, their attention piqued by the gunfire, no doubt. They duck back into their house when they see me.

I cross two more yards before I go into the alley. If Holzmann put people there to watch it, then hopefully they will think me just a curious neighbor, investigating the action like the window peeper I just left. It's not like I'm recognizable.

It's all for nothing, though.

The alley is narrow and lined with trash cans and old, broken furniture. There's a car parked at the near end, so I take the long way. It's about two hundred feet to the street. Less than a minute at a leisurely stroll, thirty seconds at a hurried walk. I'm twenty feet from the end when the little Honda I saw out front pulls around, and I realize where I've seen it before. Because she is in the driver's seat.

She's twenty feet away. I could close that distance and overpower her before she gets her seatbelt off. I could turn and run and put three fences between us before she's out of the car with her weapon drawn. People make a big deal about the fight-or-flight response, but there is a third option that isn't talked about, but which is far more common than either of the other two.

If you startle an opossum, it doesn't "play dead" in the sense of putting on a ruse and waiting for the danger to pass. It enters an actual, involuntary state of catatonia. It fully loses consciousness and could no more decide to wake up and flee or turn its teeth on its attacker than it could float away. The choice isn't between fight and flight. The choice is between fight, flight, and freeze.

Twenty feet away is Laia Quintana. She is closer than she's been since the day she put three bullets in Mickey's back, and I do just as much now as I did then: nothing. She stares back at me, seemingly just as dumbfounded at my presence as I am at hers. I have never seen her so vulnerable. The lines of her face are softened by confusion.

Laia recovers before I do, and she steps from the car, keeping a safe distance between us.

"You can't be serious," she says.

"What are you doing here?" I ask. I know the answer. She's taken another job for Scarpello. To finish what she started in that office. To put me in the ground, just like she did Mickey.

The gun is light in my hand, and I have never regretted anything as much as I regret emptying the clip. I know that she didn't give the order to kill him, but it would be something to kill her. A small salve on the still-festering sore of his death.

She laughs, and I hate her for it. The bitch who killed Mickey should have no joy. I want to indulge that anger. I want to let it sweep over me with its burning clarity.

"Scarpello is going to lose his mind," she says.

"I'm getting him his money," I say. "You can just head on back."

"You're the problem that Holzmann needed help with?"

That draws me up short.

"You're working for Holzmann?" I ask.

"You always were a step behind," she says, shaking the confines of the car seat out of her muscles. "I've been wondering what it'd be like to take you down. Figured I'd lost my chance after I did in your boy and you disappeared. But here you are."

I'm not a perfect man. I tried to do better. I truly did. But my self-control has run out. I surrender to the primal urges. The monster that destroyed my family stands before me, and I will not let her escape again. I raise the gun and squeeze the trigger. I don't care that it's empty. She dives to the side, behind a plastic trash bin, but as she hears the quiet click of the firing pin striking air, she plants against the wall and launches back at me.

I'm not worried. I don't say this to be arrogant, but because this is the way of the world. I know her reputation, but, ultimately, I have nearly two feet and over a hundred pounds on her. The simple fact is that weight classes exist for a reason. In a one-on-one, straight-up fight, so long as they know what they're doing, the bigger fighter wins every time. And I know what I'm doing.

But so does she, and she's still charging. It's suicide. No matter how fast or clever she is, she can't win this fight. And she has to know it, which means I've missed something.

A flash of metal in her hands. I'm moving before I process it. When you see a cutting edge, there's only one reasonable response. A gun I can handle. I can control a gun, disable it, get it away. But everything I try to do against a knife would bring me closer to that blade.

A few years ago, some guys down in Brazil had professional fighters spar against untrained volunteers, except they gave the idiots rubber knives. Nine times out of ten, the person with the knife won. And that was when it was wielded by someone who had no idea how to use it.

I just barely slip the blade and shuffle out of her reach. I take my eyes off her for a fraction of a heartbeat, searching the alley for something I can use to my advantage. There's some trash cans, a discarded rake, and a baby stroller with three wheels. In the time it takes me to see that, she steps in, sharp point leading, but with her elbow cocked back, concealing the precise extent of her reach. I don't have time to get out of her way. I push the knife aside, accepting a cut across my palm to save my stomach, and lash out with a low kick, hoping to take her down. If I can get her on the ground, the fight is over, knife or no knife.

But her leg isn't where it should be. I was so focused on the blade, I missed her step to the side. She squares up to my undefended flank and throws two quick jabs before dancing back out of my reach. She's now further into the alley than I am. I could get out. There's nothing between me and the street. I could run.

"You're supposed to be better than this," she taunts me. "Scarpello's best. I've been looking forward to this for years."

She wants me mad. To forget the knife is there. To let my emotions get the better of me and overcommit. To give her an opening.

"Your little bitch fought harder than this," she says. "This is the one thing you're supposed to be good at."

I turn to face her.

I've spent my whole life being told I am nothing but a big, dumb brute. That's all anyone ever let me be, and it's all that she sees when she looks at me. She thinks she's the only one here with a brain. Well fuck her.

She darts at me again, and again I go for the parry, feigning acceptance of another incidental cut to throw an overhand that'll take her off her feet. She ducks the heavy blow, but I'm not trying to land it. I just want to get in close. I get one arm around her, grab her wrist with my bloody hand, and drive her with all my weight into the wall.

I slam her hand into the bricks, hoping to force the knife loose. She brings a knee into my side, but she can't get the leverage to make it hurt, and she doesn't have the mass to force me off her. Three times her hand hits the brick before the knife falls away.

What I should do now is end it. Bring her to the ground and choke her out or smash her head into the cement until she goes to sleep. Holzmann is still around, and I don't know how long I have. But I don't want this to be over. I want her to hurt. She left me helpless on the ground while she killed the only good thing I ever had. I'm not helpless anymore.

I throw her across the alley. She hits the ground with a heavy thud, then rolls to her feet, testing the fingers of her injured hand.

"So we're here to fight after all," she says, but I can see the flicker of worry as she looks past me, timing how long until Holzmann arrives with reinforcements.

I let my anger free. All the pain since Mickey died. Every extra bit of myself that I had to forsake. I let it all loose, and I move forward to attack.

The best she can do is stay out of my way, to hope I let her retrieve the knife, but I give her nothing. Each time my fist strikes flesh, I feel a bit of peace return. A bit of rightness restored to the world.

I leave her no quarter. She ducks many of my blows, and blocks more, catching them on her own hands or forearms. But she is tiring. This will end soon.

She tries to slip outside a punch and pivot around me, but I see it coming. As she moves to my side, I catch her with a back elbow, and she tumbles to the ground. She manages two steps away from me but doesn't come fully to her feet again. She is doubled over, gasping for breath, one hand on her legs, the other in a pile of trash.

I want it to last forever.

I don't enjoy violence. I am good at it, but I have never sought it out. It has always left me feeling less than I was before. But not now. This is righteousness. This is holy vengeance. This is Justice lifting her blindfold and tilting her scales, allowing one perfect moment to slip through into a world of bullshit and pain. The world took everything from me and offers me only this fragment of peace, and I want to live in it forever.

I swing at her with every ounce of loathing and regret that I have.

And she twists with impossible speed. My punch goes wide. Her hand comes up from the ground, and she has a broken brick in it, and all my weight is already moving toward her, and I can't get out of the way, and the brick swings up into my face.

I stumble away. Bitter copper spreads across my tongue. The ground shifts beneath my feet. She rises, far less injured or tired than she let on, and steps around me to pick up her knife.

"This is your problem," she says. I try to follow her and nearly lose my footing as the earth spins in the other direction. "You think you're the smartest person that ever added two and two together to get four."

I step toward her, but my feet are not moving.

"But what you never figured out," she continues, circling me, "is that no matter how big or smart or fast you are—" The floor slips further sideways and falls toward me. I'm looking up at her, and she's standing on the ceiling, and the sky is beneath me.

"There's always someone better."

A solid blow to the head isn't what the movies make it out to be. There's no smash to black until one aspirin later when everything is fine. The human brain doesn't want to lose consciousness, especially not in a crisis. We only do that when the damage we are sustaining is so severe that literally anything would be better than to continue. I can feel the contractions rising up my throat as my body instinctively vomits, emptying my stomach prophylactically.

I hear footsteps and a rhythmic clicking. Holzmann walks toward me. The rapping of his cane drills into my brain with each step.

The common wisdom is that you shouldn't let someone sleep if you suspect they've suffered a concussion. Like in so many other cases, the common wisdom here is wrong. You want to watch for signs of internal bleeding or damage to the skull, but sleeping is fine. Sleeping is good. Sleeping is how we heal.

"Bring him to the farm," Holzmann says. I try to stay awake, but it's a futile effort, and as two sets of hands roll me over to bind my arms behind me, I succumb to the black.

I should have taken the money and run.

CHAPTER 46

Barrett Rye, 12:18 P.M.

I come to in a room that smells of mildew and damp cement. A triangle of shrouded fluorescent tubes overhead gives a soft, diffuse light at odds with the bare walls and gray ceiling. The ground has stopped moving, but the piercing pain in my head remains. I move my jaw in a circle, feeling the muscles of my face stretch and listening to the slight crunch of my jawbone. All seems to be in place, and there is no further pain or popping that might suggest a skull fracture.

Next, I wiggle my fingers and toes. A leather strap holds my head to a metal table, and others immobilize my arms, legs, and chest. An EKG beeps merrily beside me, picking up its pace as consciousness returns.

"Just be still there," a man says from beyond my field of vision. "I'll let the others know you're awake." He stands, metal chair legs scraping against the cement floor, and leaves the room through a heavy door. A slight gust of air washes across me, and I realize I am naked.

I stretch my fingers out to test the straps holding me down. Metal ratchets hold them tight, and small padlocks secure them. My limbs are too long for the table, so the straps lie across my forearms and calves. If

I could get my hands on the lock, I could torque it against the shackle and break myself free, but it is just beyond my reach.

Time passes. Could be a minute. Could be an hour. The door opens, and more footsteps come in. Three people, one of them Holzmann by the tapping of his cane.

"Get him up, Herr Lang," Holzmann says.

An aging soldier walks into my field of view. He reaches under the table, coming close enough that I can smell the sour of the morning's coffee on his breath. He moves mechanically, a tired machine straining a few last revolutions from worn-down springs. This is what awaits me should I return to Scarpello. As he adjusts levers beneath the table, it begins to tilt, raising me up so I can see Holzmann and Laia standing at the door.

"Welcome back, Herr Rye," Holzmann says, leaning on his cane. "Allow me to formally introduce you to Laia Quintana, come all the way from Chicago, just for you."

Laia hasn't told him that we know each other.

"You have caused me a great deal of consternation," he continues. "You will make amends, in time. But you are not ready. If the enemy is to be coerced, you must put him in a situation that is even more unpleasant than the sacrifice you call upon him to make."

From his intonation, I'm guessing that last bit is a quotation, and he waits for me to respond. I don't. He frowns.

"Well," he says. "I shall leave you to get better acquainted. Let us give them some privacy, Lang."

Once they're gone, Laia flashes me a hand signal to stay quiet. She checks the hallway to make sure we are truly alone before securing the door and considering me.

"Your many faults aside," she says, eyes sliding away from my face, "I gotta admit, you are a sight."

"What are you doing here, Laia?" I ask.

She looks away. "I'm sorry," she says. "Holzmann wants to shame you, but that was beneath me." She sounds almost genuine. She takes off her jacket and lays it across me.

I have no idea how to respond to that. She gives a little grunt and moves past me to a sink mounted on the wall. She washes her hands, dries them on a towel, then fills a glass of water.

"For a man on the run, you didn't get far," she says. "You think crossing Iowa is enough to get away from Scarpello?" She holds the water to my mouth and slowly tilts it up, letting me drink. It burns against my throat but tastes heavenly nonetheless. I take three greedy gulps before she pulls the glass away. "Go slow, I don't want you to throw it up again."

"I'm not on the run," I say, eyes still locked on the water. I should be looking for a way out, testing her, finding an angle, but the anger that sustained me in the alley is gone. I just want to drink some more water and go back to sleep. Concussions are a hell of a drug.

"Then why'd you flee Chicago?" she asks.

"I didn't. I told Scarpello I'd pay him. I came here to get the money."

"You should have been clearer, then. He thinks you're trying to get out of your debts." She heads back to the sink and turns it on again. This time she fills not the glass but a large bucket.

"What are you doing, Laia?" I try again.

"Holzmann reached out to him," she says, watching the bucket fill. "They're not allies, per se, more like professional acquaintances. If you catch him in an honest mood, Scarpello will admit he can't stand Holzmann. Says he reeks of desperation. But Holzmann's money spends, so when someone started giving him trouble, Scarpello put him in touch with me." She turns the faucet off and grabs a hand towel.

"So you're his errand girl now?"

"No," she says with a patronizing smile. She has all the power here, and she won't let me get a rise out of her. She's too professional for that. "He feeds me jobs he can't do himself. There's good money in troubleshooting." She pulls a small wedge of rubber out of her pocket. "Now open up."

She's done talking. Time to get to work. She hooks a finger into my mouth and forces it open. I am briefly thankful she washed her hands, but then she jams the rubber between my teeth. She leans down and starts shifting the levers that Lang had manipulated earlier. The table tilts back. The beeping of the EKG accelerates.

"Holzmann thinks that you could be a valuable asset," she says. "He's lost a few men recently. He thinks he can turn you to his own uses and has asked me to do that."

The table angles down toward the floor. I can feel my circulatory system working to keep the blood from pooling in my head, and the pounding of the concussion redoubles. I try to say something but can't form words around the hunk of rubber keeping my jaw open. Laia just pats my forehead and lays the towel across my face.

"It's a waste of time, but he's the client, so he gets what he wants," she says, leaning in close. "So let's just bear down and get through the unpleasantness. Once it's finished, we'll go back to Chicago together."

We like to think that we are strong people. I could endure that, we tell ourselves when we see stories of cowardice. That wouldn't be me. I would be better.

She starts to pour the water. It spreads across my face, pooling in my mouth and nose, and the gag reflex is involuntary. I gasp and retch at the same time. The air is thick with too much moisture. Not enough oxygen. I try to breathe, but my mouth is full of water. I know I won't drown, but my lungs disagree. With each too-wet inhale they send a panicked signal to my brain. I am dying, they scream.

Here's the truth.

We are not strong. We do not endure. We are not better. We are all cowards in the end.

Fear of drowning is hard-coded into us. Has been—deep and pure—ever since that first fish pulled itself out of the primordial ocean. When the water reaches for you and calls you home, the terror is absolute.

I'm sorry about this. I know I'm breaking the rules as narrator here, but I've already been strapped to that table, and I've made it out the other side. I don't want to go through it again. You've gotten the parts that are important. There's nothing left but pain and fear. If Laia would let me talk, I would tell her anything to make it end. That's how torture works. But she doesn't want anything from me. She has a job, and she's going to do it. Best we take her advice and just get through it.

The concussion saves me in the end. My brain can only take so much before it gives in, and the sweet oblivion of sleep sets me free.

CHAPTER 47

Barrett Rye, 3:06 P.M.

When I wake up, Laia is gone. I've got an IV in my elbow, and the EKG has been joined by a pulse oximeter on my finger and an automatic blood pressure cuff on my arm. It's almost the complete basic hospital suite.

I wiggle my extremities again to make sure everything is still working and do a quick inventory of my injuries and pains. The cut on my palm was stitched and bandaged while I was out. Other than that, the headache, continued dizziness, bruises along my sides, forearms, and hands from the scuffles with Laia and Cass's crew, some shallow cuts and abrasions on my arms and legs from the restraints, and a tension in my right shoulder that I can't quite place the source of, I'm perfectly hale.

I can hear a regular beep from the medical monitor behind me, and a slow breath beyond that suggests I'm not alone in the room. My table has been reset to a flat position. Laia took her jacket, and I am once more naked.

I stay quiet as I slowly bring mucus up from my throat into my mouth. Then I breathe through my teeth, letting the saliva bubble through the narrow gaps, mixing with the thickening mucus and forming a slimy foam. It takes about ten minutes to fill my mouth.

I start rattling my restraints in escalating convulsions. I hear my guard stir and knock his chair over. It's Lang, the older man from before. As he looks down at me, I roll my eyes back and open my mouth, releasing the foam to ooze across my lips.

Lang considers me but doesn't move to help. I continue convulsing, opening up a few of the scabs on my arms. He wordlessly rolls the monitor around, showing me the perfect tranquility my vitals reveal.

So that didn't work.

"You done?" he asks, arching an eyebrow down at me.

I shrug. "Can't blame me for trying."

He leaves.

"I gotta piss," I call after him.

He looks back at me. "You're tied to that table until the boss tells me otherwise."

It is surprisingly hard to pee at inappropriate times. Years of training your body not to release are not quickly overridden, and there is a difference between letting go when you need to and actively forcing your bladder to evacuate. All I'm saying is it's tough. Go ahead and try.

I manage. It's not a pleasant experience, peeing all over your own chest. It gets Lang's attention, though.

"Jesus, fuck, man!" he cries. He starts filling the bucket to clean me off.

With the monitor in front of me, the EKG leads now cross my body rather than pooling behind me. As soon as Lang's back is turned, I use the slight flexibility offered by my free wrists to stretch my fingers out and clasp the wire. When Lang tosses the bucket of water over me, I start coughing and convulsing again.

"You already tried that," he says.

Then I pull the EKG wire free and lie suddenly still as the machine lets loose a shrill alarm. I palm the wire end, and Lang doesn't seem to notice it, his attention focused instead on the sudden appearance of a flat line where my heartbeat used to be. He curses and rushes to my side, reaching for my neck to find a pulse before remembering that neck just got drenched in piss.

I have only a few seconds while he vacillates as to whether or not he should touch me. I twist a loop into the end of the wire and—ever so carefully—hook it over the padlock holding my wrist secure and draw the lock the last few millimeters to my waiting fingers. With it in hand, I twist. The hardened steel shank doesn't break, but the rest of the lock isn't as sturdy and the body of it crumbles.

Lang's eyes go wide as he realizes my arm is free, but I move faster than he can react. I grab his head. My thumb goes under his jaw, digging into the muscles of his neck and squeezing into the carotid sinus as my fingers wrap around the side of his face, pulling him into the pressure of my thumb. He fights hard, but I've caught him by surprise. It takes ten seconds for him to lose consciousness and fall to the ground.

I have to move fast now. With blood flow restored, he will wake up quickly. He'll be confused when he comes back—oxygen starvation does that to a brain—but I still need to hurry. I make short work of the remaining locks and am glad to be free, but I've also destroyed the only restraining device at hand.

Lang is still unconscious, so I yank the IV from my arm—a glance at the bag tells me they've been giving me acetaminophen and magnesium as well as saline; how kind—and use the plastic tubing to tie him to the table. His eyes are fluttering open as I run from the room.

Through the door is an unremarkable basement. There's a furnace, a bunch of tools on shelves, and some boxes stacked along the walls. Rough wood stairs climb to the building above, and a storm door leads outside. I grab a hammer and head up the stairs.

They take me to the thoroughly modern kitchen of a modest farmhouse. Marble countertop rings the large room with a butcher's block island at its center. Through the window above the sink, I see a wide green lawn and soy fields in the distance. An open door behind me leads to a hallway. A low murmur of voices filters from upstairs, and another door—currently closed—heads off in a perpendicular direction. I'm not alone in this kitchen, though. Standing on the other side of the island, one hand holding a bowl of soup and the other reaching for a weapon beneath the counter, is Jim Pickens.

He puts the soup down slowly, but he doesn't raise his gun. He takes in the battered state of my face and body. "Are you OK?" he asks in a whisper.

"Laia is here," I tell him, matching his quiet tone. "If she tells Holzmann who I am—that I've been playing him from the start—" I don't need to finish the thought. I'm only alive because Holzmann thinks he can use me.

"I know." Pickens grabs my arm and pushes me toward the closed door. "There's cars out front. They keep the keys in them."

"What are we going to do about her?" I ask. "She could ruin everything." A crash comes from the basement, and Lang screams out a warning.

Pickens leads me to a rustic living room, starkly at odds with the clean minimalism of the kitchen. "I can handle her," he says. "You need to get out of here."

The living room takes us to a hallway running the length of the house. A back door, the kitchen, and stairs leading up lie at the far end of it, and the front door is right next to us along with a door to the home's other wing.

"Are you sure?" I ask. Pickens is a man of many talents, but this has never been one of them. We're out of time, though. Lang's warning roused the people upstairs.

"I've got this," Pickens says. "I can do like you taught me. You just keep yourself safe." He's right. I need to be gone. One thing has to happen first, though. He knows it, too.

"I should try to stop you," he says, and I nod. "Try not to make it hurt too much." He braces himself.

"You ready?" I ask. Before he can respond, I punch him in the face. Hard enough to draw blood, but not so hard as to risk breaking a bone. He collapses to the ground with a shocked grunt, and I run.

So, yeah. I might have left one other thing out.

CHAPTER 48

Two Months Ago

You're sure this is a good idea?" I asked Mickey. I'd asked him a dozen times already, but I couldn't help myself. I didn't like not having all the information.

He knew it stressed me out, and he'd be lying if he told me he didn't take some pleasure in it. It wasn't often that he got to do the big reveal, and he was relishing the opportunity to draw out my suspense.

"Yes, love," he said, pulling himself against me and running a hand down my back in a familiar gesture that just toed the line between comforting and patronizing.

The sun had set about thirty minutes ago, and most of the shops on this commercial strip were already closed for the night. It had been two days since Mickey got back from his three-week trip, and he still hadn't told me his plan to make us "stupid rich."

"We won't have to do this anymore," he said when I pressed him. "No more lying. No more stealing. And no needing to look over our shoulders. We can have the lives we were always supposed to."

Mickey was losing weight. I hadn't noticed before, or maybe I'd just chosen to look the other way, but after three weeks apart, it was apparent. He couldn't sustain this, and we both knew it. We needed a way out.

I had offered to step up what I was doing. There was no reason we couldn't expand, start taking more. I could even run a couple small-time jobs on the side. That might be safer than stealing from Scarpello directly. But Mickey said this new job would be enough, so I let him have his secrets. I'd endured two days of gentle teasing and done my best to keep my own anxieties in check, and now we were here, on this random street about ten miles south of downtown Chicago.

"At least tell me who we're meeting," I said.

"Do you trust me?" he asked.

"Of course."

"Good. Then trust me."

With that, he pulled me into a locksmith's shop. The door was open, even though the store was dark, with just the light from the back office illuminating the floor. The front was small, barely enough space for a couple of people, the counter, and some racks of key blanks. The walls were lined with door handles and cylinder locks.

"We're closed," the proprietor called from the back. Mickey threw the bolt on the front door, locking it behind us.

"Yeah," he said. "I know."

A man in a wrinkled white shirt with the collar open and his sleeves rolled up came out from the back. He was a little younger than Mickey, and he wiped sweat from his brow as he took me in. I let him stare. I was used to it.

"You weren't lying about him, were you, Mick?" he observed, after a moment.

"Quit gawking, Jim," Mickey said. "Jim, this is Barrett Rye. Barrett, Jim Pickens."

"Right," said Pickens, collecting himself quickly. He thrust a hand out to shake mine. "Should we talk in the back?"

The back wasn't much more spacious than the front, but it felt more private. Pickens, Mickey explained to me, was one of his accounts. Pickens had fallen behind on his insurance premium. It was stupid, he knew, and he shouldn't have let it happen, but it did, and he had the misfortune of being hit by burglars in the two weeks he was without coverage. Locksmith's tools are expensive, and no bank wanted to extend him the capital he'd need to get up and running again, so he'd been forced to go to Scarpello for help. Again, stupid, but he hadn't had a choice.

He was up on his payments, had been for two years running, but he was only covering the interest. Without an influx of cash from somewhere, he'd never get out from under the principal, which, Mickey pointed out, was the intent from Scarpello's point of view. So he'd started taking jobs of questionable legality. He risked his license every time he didn't verify ownership before opening a lock, but the money was too good to turn away. And then he'd been approached by someone from out of state.

"How much do you know about Omaha?" he asked me.

"Warren Buffett lives there?" was the most I could come up with. I honestly don't think I'd considered the city once in my entire life.

"Along with a host of lesser millionaires," Pickens said. "Money like that doesn't exist in isolation. I was asked to open a safe that belonged to some old manufacturing magnate, but the job didn't feel right. The guy hiring me is mostly known for selling girls and shipping drugs, not moving stolen goods, and he was working extra hard to keep the thing quiet. So I told Mickey about it."

"You kick a good lead Scarpello's way, and he'll let some of your debt go," Mickey explained. "I looked into it. That's where I was the last few weeks, and I think I've finally gotten everything figured out. There's a lot of money at stake here, and no one that matters has any idea that it's happening. Scarpello has no clue, and this guy out in Omaha is a nobody."

"If we go out there," Pickens continued, "we're talking about millions of dollars for each of us. If you can keep me safe and Mickey can cover our tracks, I can do the rest. But we're going to need all of us."

"Think about it," Mickey said. "In a week, we can be free."

Four days later, Mickey was dead. Our plan of stealing the Fabergé egg died with him.

It didn't make sense. None of it made sense. So I buried myself in work, and for a time I was the mindless brute everyone thought I was. I wish I could say I lived the cliché and lost myself in a bottle, but I didn't. I lost myself in blood. It's not a time in my life I want to dwell on.

A month later, Jim Pickens knocked on my door at four in the morning.

"I'm so sorry," he said. "I just heard what happened. I thought you guys had backed out, but then, I just found out, and—I'm sorry."

I didn't have it in me to get rid of him. He looked so sad and pathetic in the hallway of my apartment building, so I opened the door and let him in.

"What are you doing here?" I asked him. I moved over to the small table where my mail lived to offer him a chair. He stayed by the door.

"The guy out in Omaha hit a snag," he said. "He needs a special key to get into the safe, and he still hasn't tracked one down. We can still do this."

"No," I said. "We can't. Not without—not without a money guy."

"We don't need him."

"Yes, we fucking do!" I screamed. I'd been living in anger for the last month. I'd been steeping in it. Anger was all I had left. The chair

I had offered was in the air, and then Pickens was crumpled on the ground, hands covering his face, blood leaking out from between his fingers. The chair was broken beside him.

He left, and I didn't get back to sleep.

By the time the sun came up, I had my plan. It took me five days to work up the courage to go see Pickens and put it into motion. It was a hell of a lot uglier than Mickey's plan, but it could work. We could do it with just the two of us.

Like I said, this story doesn't end with me getting the egg. Without Mickey, Pickens and I wouldn't be able to hide the money. But with Pickens applying pressure from the inside, and me making trouble on the outside, we could still get paid enough to get him out of debt and buy my life back. It wasn't much. It wasn't what we'd hoped for, but it was something.

At least, that was the plan. As Holzmann would gleefully remind us, it was a Prussian, Helmuth von Moltke, who coined the phrase "no plan survives contact with the enemy."

CHAPTER 49

Jim Pickens, 3:15 P.M.

Pickens can count on two hands the number of times he's been punched. Maybe it gets easier with time, like running or cheap tequila. The more you do, the less each one hurts. If that's the case, he hasn't reached that point yet, and he has no desire to try. As Barrett's fist hits his face, his vision flashes red, and his legs go out from under him.

A door slams, and footsteps race down the stairs behind him. He gestures limply toward the front as one of Holzmann's men runs past. A hand grabs Pickens beneath his arm and pulls him to his feet. Holzmann's grip is strong, and even though they're the same height, Pickens feels small beneath the man's gaze.

He tried to avoid just this situation. He's been here for days longer than he should have, and Holzmann refuses to let him leave the farmhouse. He has spent most of his time upstairs in one of the bedrooms, slowly making his way through the small library of history books that Holzmann maintains here. It isn't his preferred genre, but it has been a way to pass the time and keep to himself.

Pickens is not a natural liar. He is a locksmith. He loves the puzzle of a well-made lock. The challenge of a particularly tricky keyway or a novel cylinder construction. He likes to take apart machines and see how they fit together. He doesn't like worrying that he'll say the wrong thing and get himself killed.

Holzmann stares into him. Why the hell did he say he could run interference with Laia? He can't even cover for himself. It all seemed so obvious in the moment. Barrett needed to escape, and if they got caught together, then it would all be over, so to get rid of Barrett, he said that he could handle Laia. He's ten seconds into that mission, and it is already falling apart.

"You are not supposed to have a gun," Holzmann says.

Pickens had forgotten he was holding the weapon. He drops it, and as it clatters to the ground, he winces and wonders if dropping a gun can make it fire. The gun falls still, though.

"It was out on the counter, and when Barrett ran past, I thought I could stop him, but he hit me, and—" Pickens forces himself to stop talking. Stop volunteering information. Answer the question asked, and no more.

Holzmann studies him a moment more before responding. "This is all right. I did not hire you for your weapons expertise. There are others for that." Holzmann bends over to retrieve the gun. He leans heavily on his cane and winces as his hip stretches. "Come, let us watch them work."

Laia stands on the wraparound porch. She has a rifle slung across the crook of her elbow and leans against one of the beams holding up the roof. One of Holzmann's men is beside her with his own sidearm drawn, but Laia waves the man down.

"Put that away," she says. "We won't need it. Isn't that right, Barrett?"

Barrett stands in the driveway. He is still naked. Pickens doesn't know why that should surprise him. The man was naked less than a minute ago, but there is something about the nudity being outside that makes it more shocking.

There are three cars, but Barrett can't reach them before Laia could put a round in him, and there are at least two hundred yards of open grass before the fields of crops offer anything tall enough to hide within.

"What do you want?" Barrett asks Holzmann.

"Only what you took from me, Herr Rye." Holzmann hands the pistol off to his man and walks down the steps to the driveway, carefully placing his cane so it doesn't slip between the wooden slats.

"Well, I don't have it," Barrett says, gesturing to his own naked body. "But I think you already knew that."

"Not just the key," Holzmann says, planting his cane and leaning on it with both hands. "This is not all you have taken. You have also taken my time and my men, and this trouble has taken my reputation as well. You have taken advantage of my trust and goodwill. You aided Cassiopeia Mullen in attacking me. Her associate, Herr Wright, laid his hands upon me, and yet he lives. You have taken much from me, but you will return it."

Pickens needs to get out. They took their shot. Now they need to accept it wasn't enough. Barrett is standing naked as a jaybird in Holzmann's yard with a gun pointed at him and as many options as he has clothes. He made a good run of it and kept this whole thing going longer than Pickens would have thought possible, but it's all about to come crashing down, and when it does, Pickens will be crushed right alongside him.

Barrett stares down Holzmann. He's a proud man, and he doesn't like to admit that he's been beaten, but the time has come, and as Pickens sees his shoulders hunch and the fight leave him, he knows that he's made the right decision. If Barrett had gotten away, maybe it could have been different. But he hasn't, and it's not. It's time they both saw to their own survival.

Barrett speaks quietly with Holzmann for a moment. Pickens can't hear the words, but he doesn't need to. They are negotiating Barrett's acquiescence. They shake hands, and Holzmann turns back to the farmhouse with a tight smile. It is the most joy that Pickens has ever seen the man express.

"Herr Lang, please find something that our friend can wear. He can hardly do his work in this state." Holzmann isn't relaxed. The very word is anathema to the man. But he is at ease. He is back in control, and for the first time since Richard failed to deliver the key, all is right with his world. "Miss Quintana, I must commend you on your excellent work so far. Would you kindly accompany Herr Rye as he retrieves my stolen goods?"

Once Lang returns with a too-small set of clothes—Barrett's had been cut off him when he was brought in—Laia leads the man to her car, a compact two-door. He looks at the passenger seat in disbelief but, after sliding it back as far as it can go, does manage to fold himself through the door. The car dips low on its shocks as it takes his weight.

Pickens returns to the house and his quiet room upstairs. There are still a couple of hours until nightfall, and he wants to be rested when he leaves. Despite the scale of Holzmann's operation, Omaha's high-end vice market requires very little enforcement power. With the losses he's suffered, Holzmann has been understaffed at this farmhouse. Once the sun is down, Pickens should be able to slip out, grab a car, and get away.

He has just begun reading an account of William of Orange's religious reforms in England—a sure way to get himself to sleep for a few hours—when there is a knock. Without waiting, Holzmann enters the room and offers a bag of ice to Pickens.

"For your face," he says. "I do not want the swelling to obstruct your vision. I will need you operating at full capacity."

Pickens holds the ice gingerly against his bruised cheek. Holzmann, rather than leaving, pulls the chair out from the small desk and sits down. Pickens closes his book and sets it aside.

"Is there something I can help you with, sir?" he asks.

Holzmann points at the book. "Are you enjoying this?"

"Sure," he says carefully. "I'm not really a history reader, but it's fine, I guess."

"I think it is fascinating, how many problems faced the English and the French because of their convoluted rules of ascendancy," Holzmann muses. "Think of the wars and revolutions that they could have avoided with a clearer method for establishing who was in control instead of their absurd systems of marriages and cousins. How much better the system in Prussia was. There we chose our ruler. You Americans think you invented democracy, but we have always elected our kings, going as far back as the days of the Romans."

Pickens remains quiet. He's dealt with enough weird old white guys to know when to let their pontifications go uninterrupted.

"It is vitally important for both a people collectively and a person individually to know to whom they owe allegiance," Holzmann continues. "There can be no ambiguity and no room for disagreement or confusion in the chain of command. This is what I have always believed, and so, Herr Pickens, I ask you: Who do you follow?"

"I follow you, sir," Pickens says.

Holzmann's face remains unreadable. "No, I think you do not." He raises a hand to forestall Pickens's objection. "But this is acceptable. You are a mercenary, and you do not, in truth, follow me. You are not my man. You belong to the purse. Still, while you are under my employ, I must ask for, if not your allegiance, then at the very least your obedience."

"Of course, sir," Pickens says. He only needs to get through a few more hours.

"Good. So tell me, please, about Barrett." Holzmann crosses one leg over the other and lays his cane across his lap. There is a slight quirk to his mouth, an open invitation to speak.

"What do you mean?" asks Pickens. In the last two days he has been hit, kidnapped, and tied up. Yet he never felt danger like he does at this moment, looking into the pitiless eyes of the man sitting across from him. He feels not like a hunted animal, at risk of falling into a snare, but like one who already stepped into the noose, though he cannot see it.

"Barrett Rye," Holzmann says again. "Tell me who he is."

The rope is tightening. The trap has been released.

Pickens is glad for the ice pack. He holds it to his face. The cold slows his breathing, and he hides behind it for a moment. Give up nothing, Barrett would say. If Holzmann knew what was happening, then Pickens would already be dead. The man is fishing.

"He's just a guy," Pickens says, hoping his voice will stay steady. He wants to say more. He almost says more. But he stops himself.

"How do you know him?" Holzmann presses. Again, Pickens remains silent. "Your obedience, Herr Pickens. This is all that I ask. You know this man. Tell me how."

"I—" Pickens starts, but Holzmann interrupts.

"Think carefully before you lie to me. You had not met him. You did not know he was brought here. Yet you identified him easily as he escaped from you."

Pickens knew this would happen. He'd kept it up for so long, only to fall apart in the end. It was such a stupid mistake, too. Every instinct tells him to come clean. To cut his losses and tell Holzmann the truth. But he saw what that earned the hapless thief, Richard. No. He has to push on. Holzmann doesn't know everything. He's still fishing.

"We're both from Chicago," Pickens says. "I've seen him around there, but I didn't know him."

"And why did you not tell me this before?" Holzmann asks.

"That was the first time I'd seen him," Pickens says. "We run in different circles. The name didn't mean anything until I saw him, then I remembered who he was."

Holzmann studies Pickens for a long moment, weighing his fate. Then he nods acceptance of the lie, and it comes clear to Pickens. He understands how the tumblers of the man's mind align. Holzmann doesn't think that Pickens betrayed him. Pickens is just a locksmith. Just a Black boy. He's not capable of the cleverness necessary to outsmart a brilliant mind like Holzmann's. That's not why he was mad.

He was mad because there was information he didn't have. He was blindsided by the fact that Barrett Rye was a player, and in that, Pickens sees how to keep his promise and eliminate two threats with four simple words.

"Laia didn't tell you?"

CHAPTER 50

Barrett Rye, 3:52 P.M.

I hate small cars. You'd think it was the legroom, right? That's what most people assume the problem is, but they're wrong. Sure, it sucks having to fold my knees to my chest, but the real indignity is the head space. The roof of the car is roughly where my shoulders want to be. To fit, I have to slide down in the seat. I wind up in a fetal position, all but on my back with my feet on the dash. God help me if we get in a wreck. Best-case scenario the airbag snaps my legs.

I sit in ignominious silence, watching the soy roll past, trying to ignore the growing pain in my spine—just one more ache to add to the list—and the rising nausea, whether from motion sickness or the concussion remains anyone's guess.

I need to get Pickens out, and while I know he said he would handle Laia, this is well outside his usual field. Much as it sickens me, I'm going to need her help to pull this off. I'd rather grab the wheel and drive us into oncoming traffic, but I think Mickey would want me to do it this way. So what do I know about Laia Quintana?

She's a mercenary, and a damned good one at that. She's professional. She won't do an ounce of work beyond what she is paid to do, but neither will she go back on a contract once she's accepted it. I wish I knew more about what drove her, but money is always a good guess, and thankfully, that's the one thing I can offer right now. So the question then becomes how to tease out the cracks in her relationship with Holzmann. I'm so wrapped up in this puzzle that I don't pay attention to our travel until the car starts accelerating onto 680.

"Wait, where are we going? I need to get downtown," I say, twisting so I can see Laia. She has unholstered her gun and casually holds it in her left hand as she steers with her right. If I want to make a grab for it, I'll have to reach all the way across her.

"There's been a change of plans," she says. "I'm taking you back to Chicago."

"What about Holzmann's key?" I ask. "He hired you to get it back, right? You can't get it back without me."

She sighs. "Don't be an idiot. Of course I can get it back without you. You think Cass Mullen can hide from me? Holzmann will be pissed at the delay, but I'll get him what he paid for, and I'm not risking you slipping away again."

"I'm gonna get Scarpello's money," I say. "I'll pay him back ten times over."

"No, you won't." She checks over her shoulder to merge into traffic. "He's gone public with his grievances. He can't back down now."

"I can still make this work. Just give me a chance." I know I sound desperate, but I'll trade my pride for my life.

"You've had enough of those already."

"Please, Laia. I don't know what I did to offend you, but I'm sorry. I can make it right. Just—don't take me back to Chicago. Not yet."

"Barrett," she says. "It's not about you. It never was. You keep thinking this is personal, but it's just work."

"I thought you'd been looking forward to this?" I point out. "Taking down Scarpello's favorite, proving you're better than me."

"I just needed you pissed off, ya big dolt. How else am I supposed to beat you in a fight?"

"If it's professional, then let me make a professional appeal," I say, trying another approach. "You have no idea how much money is in play here."

"Not about that either," she says. She doesn't sound frustrated or upset with my pleading. If anything, she sounds bored. She's giving me nothing to work with. "It's the principle of the thing. You stole from Scarpello, and when he showed you mercy, you jumped ship."

"Does he know I'm here yet?" I ask. "That you're bringing me in?"

"No. I don't make a promise until I know I can deliver, and I didn't have you in hand."

"OK," I say, letting the desperation creep into my voice again. It's not hard to fake. If she doesn't buy this, then I am well and truly fucked. I have no more backups. "Just give me one day."

If she hasn't told Scarpello she has me, then it doesn't cost her anything to give me twenty-four more hours. She is silent for a moment, pondering. Or maybe she's just paying attention to the freeway. She slips into traffic between two eighteen-wheelers, and sighs.

"No," she says. Just one word. That's it.

"Then just tonight," I offer. "I'll get you the money, and you can do whatever you want with it. Keep it. Take it to Scarpello. I don't care. Just—please don't take me back."

"You're not listening to me."

"And if I fuck up, you've still got me, right?" I rush over her objections. If she can't vocalize them, they aren't real. "I won't leave your sight. Just until morning. Just give me a chance to get this money."

She glances over, eyebrow raised. "It doesn't matter if you come back with a million dollars," she says. "You're worth more to him as an example."

She gave me a number. That's all I need.

"And what if I came back with ten million?" I ask.

She snorts out a laugh. "Sure, you tell me how you're gonna make ten million dollars in a night, and then we'll talk."

I wait a moment before I respond. She's not taking me seriously.

"You're right," I say. "I'm not going to get ten million." I sit back into my chair, trying to get as comfortable as I can, and wait for her to return her attention to the road. "I'm getting ten million for Scarpello and another ten for you."

At first, she thinks it's desperation, but I've spent the last few miles teaching her what I sound like when I'm desperate. That was me at the end of my rope, throwing out garbage to buy another few minutes of life. This is something else entirely. It takes time to sink in, and I don't press it. I've got her on my line. I'm just waiting for her to realize it.

She turns her blinker on and takes the next exit. She doesn't say a word until we're off the freeway and in the shade of some trees in a church parking lot.

"Tell me more," she says.

So I do. I tell her about the rich old man, Maxwell Novak, and his art collection. I tell her about the safe in the safe and the key and the Fabergé egg. I tell her how Holzmann approached Pickens and he told Mickey. I tell her my plan to steal the key and recruit Cass and Jonny Boy to help me get the safe away from Holzmann.

Laia isn't one for betrayals, so I tell her I was going to pay them half a million, more than fair compensation, while I made off with the lion's share. It was going to be a peace offering to Scarpello. Then she showed up and threw the whole plan into disarray. I could take on Holzmann and his boonie soldiers, but not with her supporting him.

She listens attentively as I lay it all out, asking only a few questions as we go. And when I'm done, Laia sits back in her chair and lets out a slow breath.

"Jesus," she whispers. "All these years you've been Scarpello's pet boogeyman, and you've had a brain of your own the whole time?"

I shrug. Of everyone I thought I'd reveal this part of myself to, Laia Quintana is about as low on the list as you can get, but I need her now more than I need to keep my secrets. And it's nice to be recognized, even if it is by your enemy.

"I guess I never wanted anything more," I say. I need her to trust me. That means opening up, just a little. "Or at least, never thought I could have it. Not until I met Mickey."

"You really loved him?" she asks.

"He was the first person who saw me as more than just this," I say, giving her a biceps flex. It's a bit absurd, having a heartfelt confession while folded in half in a tiny car seat, and the strangeness of the moment hits us both. Laia laughs, and I do too, and for a moment she seems almost human. I nearly forget that she's the one who pulled the trigger.

"I thought he was just a pretty face taking advantage of you," she says. "I told Scarpello to give you a chance, you know? Told him that in my professional opinion you got blinded by good dick and shouldn't be held to the same level of account. I'm not trying to win brownie points or anything. I'm just saying—you had me fooled."

I get out of the car to stretch while she looks up the nearest public library. I need a computer. The key—the real key—isn't the only thing I'd left with Cass.

In 1965 Gordon Moore, a semiconductor scientist, predicted that the size of a microchip would be cut in half every two years. Forty years later he confessed that this had been wild extrapolation and unreliable guesswork, but Moore's law—as the maxim came to be known—had proved remarkably accurate. Modern computer chips have become so small, it is no longer manufacturing concerns that limit the size of our devices but the laws of physics. The wires are so close that they interfere with each other at a subatomic level. The upshot is you can fit a tiny computer and battery onto a wafer smaller than a fingernail, and I had planted one of those on Cass.

That chip has been searching every thirty minutes for nearby Wi-Fi and cellular signals to check back in with a central server and announce its location. At the library, that server tells me that Cass—or at least her shirt—spent the last few hours in a townhouse owned by a woman named Marta Sepovim.

The sun is setting by the time we arrive, and we decide to wait until full dark to make our move. This gives Laia time to lay out her terms. Holzmann hired her to recover the key. Once she does that, her duty is complete. I will wait nearby while she relieves Holzmann of the egg. If I run, she will find me and kill me slowly. Once she has the egg, I will be free to leave. I won't be out from under Scarpello's bounty, but at least Laia won't pursue it. At this point, it's the best offer I'm going to get.

Laia and I break into an abandoned apartment down the street to wait. That should draw less attention than me folded into the front seat of her car. I try to get some sleep on the dusty floor.

CHAPTER 51

Barrett Rye, 9:15 P.M.

A fter not nearly enough time, Laia is shaking me awake. The sun is down. The house lights are off. Cass must have gone to sleep early, exhausted by the day.

The front door of the townhouse is unlocked, either an omen of good fortune or the bait of a trap, and the hinge needs oil. We sweep the bottom floor, finding little but chintzy furniture and framed pictures of a woman with a variety of smiling children. I'm surprised there are no Hummel figurines, though there is a set of presidential commemorative plates—from both parties, running all the way back to Nixon—hanging above the kitchen door.

Two of the stairs creak as we make our way up to the bedrooms. Laia has drawn one of her pistols, and I lead the way unarmed. She had more guns in the car, but denied me use of them.

An old woman sleeps in the bedroom at the top of the steps. I spot a cat on the bed beside her and go still, but the cat doesn't move. It doesn't even breathe. The thing is stuffed. It's a good piece of work. Creepy as hell, but extraordinarily lifelike.

We turn to the other bedroom at the end of the hall. There, asleep beneath an open window, is Cass. There's no sign of Jonny Boy. On the table beside the bed sits the key. Laia waves for me to get it while she stays at the door. I creep past Cass, keeping my weight spread lest I find another squeaky floorboard and wake her.

Even asleep Cass looks angry. Her brow creases, and her eyes move beneath her lids. Whatever she is dreaming does not look pleasant. I'm here for a reason, though, and I reach for the key.

A motor draws my attention back to the window as headlights shine through it from the street below. And that light is enough to set Cass stirring. She rolls over in bed, away from the window and toward me. Her eyes flutter open. Her pupils narrow in the light. Before she can scream, I clamp a hand over her mouth.

She bites into my finger, and I feel blood flow. She throws herself backward and away from me, tangling in the sheets and tumbling out of the bed. I snatch for her, but not quickly enough, as she scuttles across the floor.

Laia throws on the lights, and I shield my eyes at the sudden brightness, giving Cass a moment more to get away from me. She stops her flight when she sees the gun Laia aims at her.

"Someone is downstairs," Laia whispers to me, and we both look to the door to see the old woman standing there in her dressing gown. She opens her mouth and lets out a piercing shriek of terror.

Cass uses the distraction to dive past me and toward the window, but I grab the back of her collar and throw her onto the bed. I snatch the key up off the table and am turning to the door when the bright LED of a flashlight catches me in the face, and a man from the hallway screams, "Hands in the fucking air!" and another shouts, "Police!"

Laia draws her second pistol to cover the cops—Owen and Conrad—as they push into the room. Trying to aim two guns at once is absurd, but if anyone can do it, it's her.

Owen and Conrad shout at Laia to drop her guns, but she's not paying them any attention.

That's when Jonny Boy runs to the door, and you're all caught up again.

I meet Jonny Boy's eye. The man is panicking. His whole world is falling apart because I wanted to change mine. He's just lost one of the only two friends he has in this world, and now the other one—miserable piece of shit though she may be—is in a room full of guns and pissed off people. Maybe I'll never be who Mickey thought I was, but my failings don't have to be Jonny Boy's.

Nobody else has seen him. Laia's attention is split between the cops, they both have their backs to the door, Marta is huddled in the corner, and Cass is still glaring at me. I don't know how this ends, but he doesn't need to be here for it. I give him a wave with my fingers. A gentle shooing. He slinks away from the door and into the darkness of the hallway beyond.

"Put your fucking guns down!" Conrad yells at Laia, and, surprisingly, she complies. She doesn't lower them completely, but she at least directs them slightly toward the ground.

"We're on the same team," she says, keeping her voice level. "We're all working for Holzmann."

"He didn't tell us about you," Conrad replies, but he, too, lowers his gun a few degrees.

"He wouldn't have." Laia lets disdain creep into her voice. "The arrogant bastard doesn't think anyone needs to know anything. And that's how we wind up here, pointing guns at friends."

"That does sound like him," Owen says. "All that bullshit he was talking about fog and monsters."

"And what about the big fucker?" Conrad asks, gesturing toward me. "He supposed to be on our side now, too?"

"He's Holzmann's new trained bear," Laia says.

The problem with cease-fires is they are still a long way from peace. You can ease tensions all you like, but you put three heavily armed, paranoid, and pissed off people in a room together, and it doesn't take much to set them off. All you need is a twitch or a word or a flash of nerves. Or the growl of an engine coming to life on the street outside.

It is the most banal of sounds. A starter spins the pistons, pulling in oxygen, as a spark flashes through a spray of gasoline. The fury of an explosion contained in a cylinder the size of a fist. We hear it so often it fades into the background. But here, in this room and at this moment, it courses through the delicate, transitory silence.

I let my legs go limp and fall as the first gunshot rebounds through the room. Cass hits the floor next to me, her eyes wide.

"Do you have a gun?" she asks, shouting through the ringing that deafens us both. I shake my head, and she curses. I need to get away, and I can't have the key when I do. If I have it, Laia has it, and there's one more thing I need to do before that happens.

I don't want to give you the wrong impression. I'm not pursuing some master stratagem. This train jumped the tracks long ago and has been barreling through a forest ever since. All I'm trying to do is keep the fucker from crashing into the very next tree and hoping I can bring it to a stop before I entirely lose control. I guess that would be the train tipping over? Fuck, this metaphor is bad. Let's pretend it was better. I can find a more appropriate one when there aren't guns going off all around me. I put the key into Cass's hand.

"Our deal still stands," I shout at her. "I know where the safe is. I'll find you."

I point toward the window and hold up three fingers. She doesn't understand. I lower a finger. Two left. A countdown. She nods. At one, I grab the frame of the twin bed we're hiding behind. Laia has driven the two cops out into the hallway, and they now fire blindly through the door. She has taken cover around the corner inside the room.

When my last finger falls, I heave, lifting the entire bed and throwing it toward the door. As it tumbles through the air, scattering sheets and pillows haphazardly, Cass jumps through the open window.

In the blizzard of linens, the gunfire has lapsed, and as the bed crashes into the wall, I vault over the debris and through the door. I get past the two cops, too stunned to react, and sprint down the hall. This passage runs parallel to the stairs, which descend in the opposite direction, and I jump over the railing to the stairs below.

Or at least, I try to. I don't know that the two cops are former high school football stars. I don't know that every day of their lives is filled with the regret that those glories are behind them, never to be reclaimed. I don't know that Conrad Stenberg was an All-State lineman. All I know is that he hits me with expert precision before I can get away. The jarring tackle brings back all the nausea and dizziness from the concussion, and I go still. I've nothing left in me as he rolls me over and cuffs me.

With one knee in my back, he sends Owen to deal with Marta cowering in the corner of the bedroom. Laia disappeared in the chaos.

"All right, you fucker," Conrad growls. "Let's try this again. Where's the fucking key?" He wraps his fingers in my hair, pulling my head back, and leans down into my ear, which only puts more weight onto my spine. "And you should know Richard Sands's body is due to turn up any day now. Where that happens and who takes the blame come down to the next words out of your mouth."

"Richard is dead?" I ask. It's not the right answer. He slams my face into the ground, and the world starts spinning again. I mentally add one more tick to my lifetime brain injury count.

"I'm running out of patience," he hisses at me. "And I don't give a fuck about your stupid fucking video. We can make that shit disappear."

I'm not sure if I believe him, but I am pretty sure he believes himself, which is all that matters.

"Let me go. I'll give you the key," I gasp, straining underneath his weight.

He releases my hair and eases up with the knee in my back.

"And here my partner thought we couldn't get along," he muses.

I pull in a solid breath. "In my right pocket there's a key chain with a big top hat," I say.

He pats down my leg, finding the keys easily. Hanging from them is my top hat key chain where I glued the second of the two fake keys. He stands up and turns to Owen, who has one arm over the old woman's shoulders, comforting her.

"Let's get out of here," he calls. "We got the key."

Owen ambles over with a smile. "Fuck yeah." He claps his partner on the back. "Let's go get fucking rich."

"And me?" I ask from the ground. "We had a deal." I roll over onto my side so I can look up at the two of them.

Conrad considers the key in his hand. "Yeah," he says. "About that—"

CHAPTER 52

Peter Van Horn, 10:02 P.M.

T he overnight shift sergeant has already been briefed by Sergeant Nowicki when Peter reports for his first night in the filing room. "How's your typing?" she asks.

"It's fine, I guess," Peter says.

"Fucking wonderful. Follow me." She leads Peter to a tiny room in the back of the bullpen labeled RECORDS. The room is barely eight feet to a side and at least fifteen degrees warmer than the rest of the station. Out front are three boxes filled with paper, waiting to be processed and color-coded for urgency. Inside are three computers, one of which is currently manned.

Every interaction an officer has with the public, regardless of how banal or uninteresting, has to be logged. Most officers type their reports directly into the system. To the oldest generation, though, the computers are still not to be trusted. They manually fill out the forms, which then need to be computerized, cataloged, and cross-referenced. That's where people like Peter and his new compatriot, a sallow-skinned officer pushing seventy and currently henpecking his way across the keyboard, come in.

For most this would be a punishment, but there is something about the work that Peter finds soothing. He is putting things in their proper place. It's almost like being a librarian. But Peter can't enjoy it. He needs to get through it. Get to tomorrow. Get back to figuring out what Owen is planning, and how Holzmann, Rye, and the U-Store-It fit into it all.

He does his best to make small talk with his new coworker. His name is Darren, and he joined the force in his forties, leaving a job as a mall cop to do the real thing. He'd wanted to help make the city a better place and wound up here. The department wasn't going to train someone that old up the ranks, and now he's too infirm to do actual patrolling. They can't fire him, and he refuses to quit until he gets his full pension, so they've left him back here.

There is no ventilation in the room, and the body heat combines with the exhaust from the computers to make it unbearably warm, but they must keep the door closed. Company policy.

Between the heat and his lack of sleep, Peter can feel himself fading, so he does what he always does to fill the empty hours. He makes a game for himself. He starts with his chair set to the middle height. With each form that he enters, he counts the number of letters in the final word. If there are an even number, he raises his chair. If odd, he lowers it. The goal is to get his chair either to bottom out or reach its maximum height. He tries not to cheat and look at the last word early, allowing the tension and suspense to carry him through the night.

"You'll drive us mad with that, son," Darren says when Peter lets out a small cry of misery after he nearly reaches the full height, only to fall away.

"I'm sorry," Peter says. "I was just—"

"Just fidgeting," Darren interrupts. "I get it. I've been here long enough. You want to know the secret to making the night pass?" Darren puts the paper he's currently working through aside to hold Peter's gaze.

"Sure." Peter nods.

Darren glances at the door, as though afraid somebody might be listening in, trying to steal his valuable knowledge. He leans in toward Peter, and when he speaks, it is a whisper, barely audible over the humming of the computers.

"Give up," he says. "They sent you here to die. From the smell of you, you're halfway there already."

Darren sits back in his chair, chuckling to himself, and resumes his pecking across the keyboard, laboriously typing in the page, one miserable letter at a time.

Peter tucks his nose into his collar and sniffs. The man is right, but there's nothing to do about it now. Darren might have been sent here to die, but Peter is being trapped. He is being pinned in place so that Owen can marshal his forces and finish destroying him.

In spite of this—maybe the heat and the exhaustion are making him loopy—Peter feels better than he has in years. He did something today. It was a desperate gambit, but it was novel and exciting and it worked. Peter didn't wait for the right person to show up to fix his problem. He went and did it himself. He's a new man with a new outlook. Peter Van Horn doesn't just sit around. No. He does things. He solves problems. And right now, he stinks to the high heavens.

So he heads to the locker room. He doesn't have a change of clothes, but there are at least showers. He's not supposed to shower during his shift—company policy—but he's not the sort of person who cares about that. Not anymore.

The cold water shocks him awake, and he scrubs away the stink of failure that he's been stewing in for the last few days. He'll shower when he needs it, and he'll burn the overhead lights while he does it. It's invigorating. The most thrilling moment of his life. He won't let himself dwell on what that says about him. He's too busy getting things done to be self-pitying.

Once he's cleaned and dried, he pulls his stiff, putrescent clothes back on—he briefly considers returning to the records room with only the towel wrapped around his waist, but decides that might be too much, even for this new him—and strolls back to the overheated room and the piles of reports. He grabs a handful of forms from the lowest priority stack. If the department wants to railroad him, then he's going to do the least important work he can.

CHAPTER 53

Barrett Rye, 11:56 P.M.

The holding cell is a rectangle of cement in the back of the police station that reeks of piss and vodka sweats. There's a steel toilet in the corner and benches along the wall. Four cells are back here, all identical. I'm in the one for the sleepy drunks.

Owen tells the officer on duty that they picked me up outside a bar where I'd been getting handsy. Nobody wants to press charges, so I'll be spending the night here before being released in the morning. I try protesting my sobriety to the officer, but my eyes, still struggling through the concussion, won't dilate properly.

A clock on the wall above the officer's desk tells me it is just before midnight. I promised to meet up with Cass and help her steal the safe. I promised Holzmann that I would get him back the key that Cass now has. I cut a deal with Laia to betray Holzmann and take the prize for herself. And it would appear that these two cops—who I have also now sworn the key to—struck out on their own as well. A lot of pissed off people are about to get a lot more pissed off, and every single one of them is going to point the blame at me.

I'll be in this cell for seven more hours. By then, whatever is going to happen will have happened. There's nothing more I can do. Whoever comes out on top will find me here, and I'll take whatever punishment they mete out. Jonny Boy and Pickens are both on their own.

Great fucking job, me. You thought you could be someone else. You thought you could be Barrett Rye, confidence man. Instead, you've done the only thing you ever do: get people killed and ruin lives. Well fucking played.

CHAPTER 54

Twenty-Seven Years Ago

When I was eight years old I saw a magician doing rope tricks at a birthday party. The magician cut the rope, and he restored it. He cut it again. He restored it again. He remade the world to suit his whims. He bent existence until the errors of the universe were made smooth and whole. I swore that I would learn the secret.

The internet was still in its infancy. I couldn't go to YouTube and watch somebody explain, so I went to a magic shop. The owner, a middle-aged man with a comb-over and an oiled beard, was excited at my enthusiasm but told me I was too young to be doing the restored rope. He said I didn't have the dexterity to pull it off, and he tried to sell me the balls and cups instead. I had no interest in the balls and cups. That was a child's illusion, and I had already mastered it.

He asked me to show him, and so I did. I took the three inverted cups and placed them on the counter with one little rubber ball. The ball went beneath one cup, only to disappear and reappear beneath another. I ran through the variations, producing the ball repeatedly beneath the same cup, splitting it into two, three, or four copies of itself, and causing it to pass through all three cups when stacked on top of each other.

It was trivial, but the shop owner smiled and laughed at each reveal. Once I finished, he took the illusion away and told me that I had real talent. He asked me if I really wanted to learn the secret of the rope, and I nodded yes. Absolutely. Desperately. I trembled as he took out a ball of twine and cut off a length to demonstrate. I had proved myself worthy, he said, and he would now bestow on me this great boon.

He performed it for me first, and it was just as wondrous as I remembered. He stretched the twine out and tied the two ends together, forming a loop. Scissors, produced from nowhere, cut the loop and then disappeared, leaving two pieces of string tied in the middle. His fist closed around the knot, and when he removed it, the knot was gone. The string was whole again.

I understood illusions. I knew that I wasn't making a little ball teleport from beneath one cup to another. There were multiple balls, and I chose which one to reveal when. But this was not an illusion. This was true magic. What else could it be? The shopkeeper broke something and then, through an act of overwhelming will, caused it to be made whole. I squealed with delight and demanded he tell the method.

After he did, I went home and cried for an hour.

The rope wasn't restored. It never was. Never could be. Once he cut it, the two pieces could never be put together again. The trick was that he didn't cut it in half. One of the pieces was cut to only be a few inches long. When he grabbed the knot, he gathered up that little fragment and palmed it away, leaving only the one longer piece behind. An audience won't notice that a few inches have been taken off a four-foot rope, so they think that it's still whole. But it isn't. It is less than it was before, and each time you perform the trick, a little bit more of the rope goes away until all you're left with is a pocketful of scraps. Some things are simply broken, and nothing can change that.

MONDAY

CHAPTER 55

Seventeen Months Ago

was in the hospital, and the nurse told me I had a visitor. I wasn't expecting anyone, but I caught sight of him through the window of my room, and he had a bouquet of yellow and white flowers and that crooked smile, so I told the nurse to let him in.

"My guys really did a number on you, didn't they?" he said once the nurse left and the door was closed.

"They did what they had to," I said. I wanted to shrug stoically, as though it was no big deal, but it hurt too much to move. "That guy was willing to hire hitmen. Now he doesn't think I'm part of the group that screwed him over."

"Even so," Mickey said. "You helped me out, and it landed you here. I owe you."

"You shouldn't be here. We're not supposed to be talking to each other."

His smile fell, but his eyes didn't leave mine. He put the flowers down on the table and stepped back.

"Do you want me to go?" he asked.

He was nervous. I was used to people being nervous around me, but this was something else. He wasn't scared of me. And I didn't want him to leave.

"Were the flowers too much?" he asked. I hadn't answered his question, and his nerves now made him fill the silence. "The flowers were too much."

"The flowers are lovely," I said.

The smile broke open across his face again. "Oh, good," he said. He looked at his hands, and he blushed. "You know there used to be a whole language of flowers? People had entire conversations through nothing but bouquets."

"What do these mean?"

The blush spread down his neck, and he muttered something about not knowing. He'd just seen them in the gift shop downstairs. I asked if he wanted to sit, and he did, and we talked about nothing in particular until I grew tired. I don't remember him leaving, but when I woke up it was night, and visiting hours were over. He was gone, but the flowers were still there.

My phone told me the yellow ones were daisies, which could represent innocence or true love, but could also be sent as a message saying *I will keep your secret.* The white flowers were peonies, an emblem of bashfulness and apology.

The next day I checked myself out. I should have stayed longer, but I didn't want to keep the bed from someone who might truly need it. As I was being discharged, the nurse told me my boyfriend was waiting downstairs to take me home. I didn't correct her. Mickey was there with a wheelchair, and I let him push me around. It made him happy.

"Make sure he gets plenty of rest," the nurse said. "Lots of soups and liquid foods."

"Yes, ma'am," Mickey said with a salute and a grin, and he wheeled me out of the hospital.

"I looked up the flowers," I said as we approached his car. I don't know why I said it, and as soon as I did I realized I might have embarrassed him. He'd told me those things in code so he wouldn't have to confront them, and now I'd thrown it in his face. He didn't say anything, but he moved his fingers from the wheelchair handle to my shoulder. They were warm through the cloth of my shirt.

"You don't have to do this," I told him, once he'd gotten me back to my apartment. I was sitting up in bed with my back to the wall. A can of chicken soup was warming in the microwave. "You don't owe me anything."

"Of course I do," he said, and he sat in the bed next to me and took my hand. His fingers looked tiny and fragile. "But that's not why I'm here."

Blood pounded in my wrist. I wanted to ask more, but I was afraid.

"You're not like anyone else I know," Mickey said. He was talking quickly. The words raced to get out before his brain could catch up. "You're not like the other guys who do this work. I'm sorry if this is forward, but I feel like if I don't say it, it's gonna burn inside me, and I'll never forgive myself, so here I go. I don't have anyone to talk to. Anyone who understands me. I'm lonely, and I'm miserable, and I have a whole host of issues, and if that's too much for you, I get it, and I'll leave as soon as you eat your soup and I'll never come back. But if you're OK with it, I'd like to stay, and I'd like to get to know you, because I think that maybe you feel a little bit the same way."

He looked me in the eye, and his hand shook against mine. I didn't know what to say. I had resigned myself to this life. I didn't enjoy it, but I was good at it, and I had nearly convinced myself that being good at something was the same as enjoying it. I could tell him to leave and go back to that lie, and eventually it might become true. Or I could tell him to stay, and I would never believe it again, but maybe I wouldn't have to.

The microwave dinged, and I still hadn't said anything. His hand slipped away as he stood and walked to the kitchen. He found the drawer with the spoons, brought me the soup, and put it on the table beside my bed. He looked at me, giving me one last chance, and I said nothing. I wanted to be brave, to do what he had done, but I didn't know how.

I could see the regret in his eyes. The shame. He shouldn't have said anything. It was too much, and he'd scared me off. I wanted to tell him it wasn't. He hadn't. I was right here. But I didn't say anything.

"Take care of yourself," he said. He was standing at the door, about to leave. And then he was in the hallway. The door was closing, and I was too late.

"Wait!" I called, and it hurt my ribs to be that loud, but I didn't care.

The door was about to latch. He caught it and pushed it open again, and he stood there looking at me. I smiled, and I asked him a question.

"Do you want to see a magic trick?"

He could have left. So many times he could have left, and he never did.

CHAPTER 56

Peter Van Horn, 12:39 A.M.

P eter is halfway through copying the report into the computer before he realizes what he's looking at. It's an intake form describing an interaction with a belligerent leading to a drunk-and-disorderly arrest. But that's not the important part. What's important are the names of the belligerent and the arresting officer. Barrett Rye and Owen Oster, respectively. Peter still doesn't know how Barrett is connected to all this, but he is a part of it, and he seems to be out of favor with Owen.

Peter is supposed to be keeping his head down. The union is buying him time. That's what they said. The old Peter would have listened to Ally. He would have quietly typed up the report and filed it away.

But if Peter hadn't gone to the bar, that footage would have been erased.

The smart thing to do is forget he ever saw this paper. Don't rock the boat. Let the union do their job. But Peter isn't smart. He might never have a better chance to get answers. He feels in his pocket for a quarter. But he doesn't pull it out. He knows what he's going to do.

◆

"On your feet, Rye," the officer on duty calls to the big man sitting in the back of the holding cell. "It's your lucky fucking night."

"What's happening?" Barrett asks.

The officer just opens the cell and gestures Barrett toward Peter, waiting at the door.

"Would you follow me, Barrett?" Peter asks. He signs a paper on the officer's desk, then leads Barrett through the back hallways of the station.

"What's going on?" Barrett asks again.

"It seems there was a problem with your paperwork, so we're cutting you loose early," Peter says.

"You're letting me go?"

"That's what the piece of paper I just signed says." Peter takes Barrett to the heavy door that leads out to the motor pool. His heart is pounding. He can barely speak for the dryness in his mouth. This plan seemed a lot better thirty minutes ago. Until now he at least had the defense of true innocence on his side. Professional Oversight might not care, but he had honestly done nothing wrong. Now, he has intentionally falsified paperwork. When Owen and Conrad report for their next shift, they will know, and it will all be over. Owen won't need to frame Peter for a thing.

Unless this gamble pays off.

Unless he can convince Barrett to help him. To give him what answers he has and assist in finding those he doesn't. Assuming Barrett has any answers. Assuming he would be willing to provide them.

Barrett steps to the door and puts a hand on the push bar.

Peter tries to clear his throat, half to draw the big man's attention before he disappears forever and half to get any air moving through it at all. Barrett stops at the half-strangled croak.

"Why?" he asks.

"Because I need your help," Peter forces out, his voice cracking around the words.

Barrett chews his lip, but he doesn't take his hand off the door. Peter has nothing to keep him here except his pleas and his hope. If Barrett leaves and Owen learns Peter forged his name on a false report, that's the whole ball game. The union can't delay that. He will be immediately fired for cause. He has no savings. He'll be evicted at the end of the month, and the bank will come after him in earnest. And good luck finding more work. A cop fired for beating a suspect can go one jurisdiction over, but mess with the paperwork and you're unemployable.

"It won't take long," Peter says. "Please."

If this perfect stranger doesn't help him, then Peter is homeless and bankrupt before the end of summer. He should have thought this through. He should have waited. Should have listened to the people who knew better.

"I'm in a hurry," Barrett says, and Peter knows it's lost. "There's somewhere I have to be."

CHAPTER 57

Barrett Rye, 1:52 A.M.

Laia is waiting for me behind the police station. I push through the door, and there she is, leaning against a pole, like she's only out for a smoke break. Floodlights burn overhead, illuminating the motor pool in hard blue light.

The lot is locked up for the night. Spools of razor wire top the fifteen-foot fence, and the only gate in or out won't open for anyone without a badge. I don't question her presence, though. Why should this being a police station be any deterrent to her getting in? When she sees me, she smiles and pushes off from the pole with an agile roll from her hips up to her shoulders.

"Ready for Chicago, big boy?" she asks me.

"I'll get you paid," I say. "Just give me the night."

"Too late," she says with a helpless shrug. "You got arrested, and I got impatient."

"You're giving up millions."

"So you say. You're a good enforcer, Barrett, and you're cleverer than I thought, but this—everything you're doing here—is a shit show. Plus,

278

I've always been more of a cash-up-front kind of girl. Scarpello paid. Holzmann paid. You haven't."

I'm exhausted. The tank is empty. I'm not going to try to fight her again. I know how that ended last time, and she's rested while I've only picked up more bruises.

"Just give me till morning," I plead. "If you don't have the money by then, you can take me back to Chicago. I won't fight you on it."

Her answer is simple. "No." No elaboration. No avenue for me to try to convince her otherwise. She gestures for the gate. "Let's go."

"I'll get you the money, and I'll still come with you. Just—not until morning."

She pauses to consider me. "You don't want me to let you go?" she asks.

"Of course I do," I say. "I'd rather do just about anything than go back, but I will if you wait for morning."

"Why?" Money she understands. Self-preservation she understands. But this makes no sense to her, which means there must be a trick.

"I just need to finish something," I say.

"And then you'll go with me? Easy as that?"

"Easy as that."

"Why should I believe you?" she asks.

"I'll give you my word." I've nothing else left.

"Not good enough," she says, and she tosses me a pair of handcuffs. "Put those on. We're heading back now."

And that's it. It's over. I can't beat her, and I can't convince her to let me go. If she really wants the money, she can sell me to Scarpello, then come back and take out Holzmann's entire operation on her own. I'm offering her nothing but risk.

"I'll swear on him," I say. "On Mickey. On his memory. If I survive the night, I'll surrender myself to Scarpello, or whatever else it is you want me to do. Just a few hours. That's all I want." As a show of good faith, I put the handcuffs on anyway.

It tears at me to give her this power, to allow his name to be spoken with the same air she breathes. But this is the cost. I must burn everything that I was on the altar of change.

She considers me for a long moment. She's already rebuilt her picture of me once tonight, but this doesn't match either version of who she thinks I am. She needs more. A little bit of truth to help it all go down.

"Do you ever regret it?" I ask her. "The things we do, the people we hurt. Do you ever wish it could be different?"

She runs her fingers through her short hair, genuinely considering her response. "No," she says. "Those people don't care about me. They're not gonna give me anything I don't take for myself. The world owes me nothing. I don't owe it anything in return."

"Maybe," I say. "You're probably right. But I did something—hurt someone—and maybe I'm an idiot for trying, but I want to make it right. Just give me a chance to do that, that's all I'm asking for."

"The big guy?"

I don't think she understands why I'm trying to do what I'm doing, but at least, maybe, she understands what it is.

"Yeah. I've got a plan. I just need to find him."

"Well tonight is your lucky night, then," she says as she tosses me the keys to the handcuffs. "He's sitting on a bench right out front. Been there for hours waiting for you. And tell him I'll want my car back when this is all done."

I feel like I should say something. I should thank her. I open my mouth, but when I reach for words of gratitude, all I find is anger. She has given me a chance, but she has destroyed too much. I have no thanks for her. I manage the strength to say nothing.

CHAPTER 58

Barrett Rye, 1:58 A.M.

ast night's storm has cooled the air, and there is a freshness to the
breeze, though the petrichor has long since fled. There is a small
green area in front of the station, not large enough to be called
a park but too elaborate to be mere sidewalk decoration. A couple
hundred square feet of grass and a trio of elder trees, their small white
flowers just starting to yellow and droop. Sitting on a bench beneath
the nearest tree, his head heavy in his hand and his eyes slipping toward
sleep, Jonny Boy keeps watch.

I clear my throat as I approach, not wanting to startle the large man,
and sit down beside him. He blinks slowly, seemingly beyond surprise.
He looks to the front door, then to me, and finally to the screen of his
phone, checking the time.

"How'd you get out?" he asks.

I lean back into the wooden slats of the bench, feeling them flex
beneath our combined weight. I want to enjoy this moment. A few
seconds of freedom before I throw myself back into the fray. I could
leave. Laia would find me, but I would have some time before she

did. For the first time, though, the temptation is gone. I observe the option of flight, but it holds no appeal. This is the path I will take, regardless of the cost.

"I came out the back," I say, ducking the true question Jonny Boy is asking.

"Oh," he says. "Right. I'll let Cass know you're out. She's around the corner with the car." He starts hitting buttons on his phone.

"I just want to sit here a minute," I say. I put a hand over his, stopping him from dialing. "If that's OK with you. Just to catch my breath."

"Sure." He pockets the phone again.

"It's nice," I say. "Just sitting in the quiet sometimes." I watch the flowers rustle overhead in the breeze. "If I try real hard, I can let it all fall away. All the bullshit of the world. All the people I've pissed off and let down fade out, and it's just me and the quiet and the dark, and I can pretend my life is anything other than what it is. For just a minute at least. I just want to enjoy that for a sec before Cass gets here and brings it all back."

I close my eyes and hear Jonny Boy settling into the bench, leaning back beside me.

"She's not very quiet," he says with a small laugh that does nothing to cover the hurt beneath it. I don't regret what I need to do next. It's the right thing. But I regret the pain that is a necessary antecedent to it. The rotting flesh must be cut away so that the wound can heal.

"I'm sorry about your friend," I say, keeping my voice low and steady, probing around the edges to find where the infection burns. Jonny Boy's breath catches, and he shifts on the bench. I crack my eyes. He is sitting forward, his elbows on his thighs and his head hanging down.

"The cops said they'd take care of him," he says. "We can't claim his body and he's got no family left, so they were just gonna burn him." Jonny Boy's shoulders hitch forward and he pauses. I give him time to regain control. "He wouldn't have wanted that," Jonny Boy continues. I can see his face screw up as he fights back tears. His eyes are tightly shut. If he can't see me, then I can't see him crying. "He'd have wanted a casket and a grave and everyone to stand around and cry and talk about how fucking awesome he was and tell stories of all the great shit he did, and I just—" His voice catches, and the tears come. "I just want to see him again."

This is the other side of sitting in the dark and thinking. I haven't had a moment to pause and let it sink in. Ever since I was lying on the rug of Scarpello's office and Mickey was bleeding out, I've been running. I've been planning, and thinking, and scheming, and fighting. Fighting to keep afloat. Fighting to keep ahead. I never grieved for him. I've never truly acknowledged the permanence of his absence. Never again will he laugh or touch me or yell at me. Crush me in a game of Go, or smile when I finally see something he's been waiting five turns for me to notice. My time with him is done and gone, and it's never coming back.

I put a hand on Jonny Boy's back and feel his lungs shudder as he pulls in air, and we sit in the dark with our grief and our guilt and let the finality of it settle upon us. It's easy to forget the importance of touch. Humanity has been bonding for far longer than we have been talking, and there are moments for which words are insufficient. Spoken language can only take us so far, can only say so much. There are times when we need something deeper, something more primal and immediate and prerational. A touch says I am here. I am in this place with you. It is at once far simpler and far more complex than anything that can be carried with words.

After a time, Jonny Boy's breathing steadies. He wipes at his face and reaches to the ground at his feet. He comes up with a brown paper bag. From inside, he pulls out a napkin that he blows his nose in and a wax paper package that he hands to me.

"Turkey," he says as I unwrap the sandwich. "Extra cheese, mayo. I saw you only had wheat bread at your place, so I got you that." He is looking at the ground, not making eye contact, but I watch him, then take a bite from the corner.

"You're a lifesaver," I tell him, and I see him smile, and he rubs his palms into his swollen eyes, and he turns to me.

"Are you OK?" he asks. A simple question. But as he looks at me, I realize how long it's been since someone asked me that and meant it. There is no agenda behind it. He sees his pain—the pain I caused him, though he doesn't know that—in me, and so he asks, because even if nothing can be done to ease that pain, perhaps in sharing it we can lighten the burden.

"I don't think so," I say. The turkey has gone dry in my mouth, and I swallow it down. "Seems like everybody wants my head these days."

"I punched Holzmann," Jonny Boy tells me. "Pinned him to a wall and hit him in the face. I hit him and held a gun on him. I fucking kidnapped him. I don't think he forgives things like that."

I'm not sure what to say to that, so instead I tear off half the sandwich and offer it to him. He takes it and bites and chews, and after we've each had a bit of food, I ask him, "What do you want to do about it?"

"Cass says we get the safe and fuck Holzmann," he says.

"Sure, but what do you want?"

Jonny Boy takes another bite. As long as it's been since someone asked if I was OK, I'm sure it has been longer since he's been asked what he wants. The bite gives him time to think.

"I don't want to fight anymore," he says finally. "I'm tired of it. Tired of being scared."

"I used to work for a guy," I say, and Jonny Boy looks over at me, unsure why I'm bringing this up now, but curious about what I have to say. "I did shit for him that, well, shit I'm not proud of. It was another life. But guys like us—the world says we're only good for one thing, right? Then one day, I realized they're scared of me, yeah? But they don't see me. Not really."

"Just a scary face with nothing behind it," Jonny Boy says, and I nod.

"Exactly. It pissed me the hell off. I was so angry, and all that I knew how to do with that was what they told me I could do. I was mad they only saw a brute, so I acted like a brute. Then I met this guy, and it was all just—none of the rest of it mattered. All that anger went away because he—and I'll never understand why or how—he saw me. Like, really saw me. Not the goon. Not the size. He saw what I could be. And I knew I had to get away.

"I couldn't keep being this person my boss said I was, but I couldn't just walk either. We needed money. Money to get out. Money to start a new life. So we started working my boss. And he had no clue. It felt amazing. Felt like we were the smartest guys in the room. But there's nothing saying smart folks can't be fucking idiots, and we messed up, and we got caught."

"Shit," Jonny Boy whispers. "How'd you get out?"

"He didn't." I look away now. It's too much to meet Jonny Boy's eyes while I share this. "Not sure I did either. But my point is this. If a man is mad you took a shot at him, I don't think stealing from him is gonna make him less pissed off."

"Cass says she'll keep me safe once we're rich," Jonny Boy says.

"That's what we said, too. We just needed a little bit more, then we'd be safe."

"Cass has a plan. She always has a plan."

"Cass," I say, "her plans—it doesn't always seem like your best interest is her goal."

"She's my friend," Jonny Boy says, and I don't press the point.

"If Cass wasn't here," I say, instead, "and there's no Holzmann and none of the rest of this bullshit, what would you do?"

"I don't want to hurt people anymore."

"That's what you wouldn't do. What would you do?"

He crumples up the paper bag and shoves it into his pocket.

"I like food," he says. "It brings people together, you know? Breaking bread and shit. I want to do that." He holds the last corner of his sandwich up, and I touch mine to his in a toast of sorts.

"That sounds nice," I say, and we each finish our food. He takes the phone back out and sends off a text. We sit in silence, and I watch the wind blowing through the blossoms of the elder tree until the headlights of Laia's little Honda make their way around the corner. Jonny Boy wipes his eyes one final time, then shrugs and stands, and the weight of the situation falls on his shoulders once again.

CHAPTER 59

Cass Mullen, 2:04 A.M.

J ust one more night of this bullshit, and Cass can finally be done. Done being looked down on. Done being pitied. Done being surrounded by simpering fools.

At least Jonny Boy managed to do one thing right after the shit show at Aunt Marta's. Cass had dropped from the bedroom window, scratching the hell out of her legs in a holly bush, and been pleasantly surprised, for once in her life, to find Jonny Boy behind the wheel of this little car. The coward wanted to run.

It was only once Cass pointed out that Vic's body was still unclaimed and they would be breaking their promise to Jonny Boy's new turkey-friend that he'd stopped whining about wanting to leave.

Sticky air floods in as she rolls down her window. "Where's the fucking safe?" she asks Barrett as he leans down to look at her. He frowns, and his eyes cloud for a moment. Even this simple question—the singular query that stands at the heart of their relationship—threatens to overwhelm him.

"That way," he says, looking off to the west. "On a farm. I don't know the address, but I can tell you how to get there."

"Get in the fucking car," she says. The little coupe rolls on its suspension, the springs audibly groaning at the effort, as Jonny Boy clambers into the back, and Barrett folds himself, like some kind of contortionist, into the front. As soon as the door is closed, she hits the gas. There's no reason to spend a second more in front of the police station than she has to.

"I'm not buckled," Jonny Boy calls from the back.

"There's a rifle under the seat back there, Jonny Boy," she says to him. "Our new friend here does anything suspicious, put a round in the back of his head." She doesn't trust Jonny Boy to follow through, but that's fine. She's done relying on him. Whoever's car this was, they left a couple presents in the trunk. She put the rifle in the back for Jonny Boy and tucked a .38 revolver in the door for herself. She's had a hand on the pistol ever since. Barrett only got her gun at Vic's house because she wasn't expecting it. If he tries anything again, she'll get a round off in time.

"We're all on the same side, Cass," Jonny Boy complains.

"It's OK," Barrett says, his voice infuriatingly calm. "I lied to you guys before. Cass is just looking out. Can't be too careful, can you?" He looks at her and smiles, and she wants to punch the son of a bitch right in his fucking nose. Instead, she takes out the revolver and lays it across her lap, casually aimed at his center mass. Barrett's eyes widen, and he sits back in his seat. This is why Cass has always loved firearms. A gun doesn't care how big you are. It'll kill you dead all the same.

Barrett directs her away from the city, and they drive in silence on I-6, heading toward the sticks. The A/C is losing its fight against the heat and stench of the two men, so she rolls the windows down. The blast of air overwhelms any chance at conversation and replaces their sweat with the heady aroma of fertilizer. It's not an improvement, but she can't go back now.

CHAPTER 60

Cass Mullen, 2:39 A.M.

B arrett shouts over the wind that the exit is coming up, or at least he thinks it is. He's only driven the route once, and that was during the day and in the opposite direction. After a trio of wrong turns, they finally head down a road that Barrett declares to be familiar, and as a two-story farmhouse comes into view in the distance, Cass pulls over and shuts off the engine.

Away from the lights of the city, stars fill the sky overhead. The house has a wraparound porch, and someone stands at the front door, giving scale to the building that the size of the open Nebraska plains conceals. At this distance, though, perhaps a half mile, Cass can't make out any details about the figure.

"Why'd we stop?" Jonny Boy asks from the back seat.

"We're gonna walk the rest of the way," Cass says, turning off the dome light inside the car as she climbs out. "I don't want them to know we're coming."

The car's shocks creak again as Barrett and Jonny Boy come out the passenger-side door, the springs apparently as upset to be relieved of their weight as they were to accept it.

"You got a plan?" Barrett asks, squinting off at the house. "Or is it just go in guns blazing?"

Cass draws back the hammer on her revolver, smiling at the punctuation of the ratchet. "Get close to the house, then hit it fast and hard. End the whole thing before they know what's happening."

Barrett nods. "Right," he says, "you know how many men Holzmann has in there? How many guns?"

"I got plenty of bullets to go around," she says, grabbing a box of the things from beneath the driver's seat and shoving a handful into her pocket.

"So did Vic," says Jonny Boy. She can't see his face in the dark, but she can picture the curled-up tip of his nose and the quiver of his jowls as he talks.

"How about the layout of the house?" Barrett asks. "Or where the safe is?"

"You had the whole fucking ride here to bring this up, and you're just doing it now?"

"The wind was too loud," Barrett says with a shrug. "Let me take the lead. Me and Jonny Boy will go in the front and take care of anyone there."

"I don't want to shoot anybody," Jonny Boy whines.

"You won't have to," Barrett says. "Not if we do this right."

Cass snorts out a laugh. "So what—you're gonna flex real hard and hope Holzmann just hands over the safe? Fuck that. The guy only understands one thing. Let's go, Jonny Boy. Get that rifle ready."

"No," Barrett says, putting a hand on Jonny Boy's arm. "We'll go in the front. Holzmann only has two guards in there with him, plus Pickens, who doesn't fight, and the stringer." Before Cass can press him on who the fucking stringer is, Barrett explains. "She's a mercenary, out from Chicago. Holzmann brought her in, but you don't have to worry about her."

"And just why the fuck not?" Cass asks. "I think a mercenary is pretty fucking relevant to the situation at hand."

"Because we'll be distracting her, along with Holzmann and his men. We'll keep them tied up upstairs while you sneak in the storm door, grab the safe, and get out, with them none the wiser, and nobody hurt. Couldn't be simpler."

"And what about us?" Jonny Boy asks. "Holzmann isn't gonna just let us walk away."

"Do you still have the money?" Barrett asks, catching Cass off guard with the non sequitur. "The fifty thousand in cash?" he clarifies.

Cass glances to the door pocket where she had stored her pistol. The cash is in its battered bag there, but she's not ready to tell Barrett about that just yet. "Why do you need it?" she asks. If she gives him the money, there's nothing to keep him from just taking it and running.

"I'm gonna use it to smooth things over. Holzmann thinks we're all trying to screw him, right? That we want to steal the safe?"

"That's 'cause we fucking are trying to steal it," Cass says.

"Sure," Barrett agrees, holding out a patronizingly placating hand. "And he expects nothing less from you, but he thinks he broke me, and I bet he believes that Jonny Boy is scared of him."

"I am scared of him," Jonny Boy supplies helpfully.

"Right," continues Barrett. "So we go in the front door, saying we want to talk—we want to make peace. We give him the money as a sign we mean it."

"Fuck that," Cass says. "That's my money. That fucker wants it, he can try to take it from me."

"I don't want to fight Holzmann," Jonny Boy says. Everything about his voice grates at Cass's rapidly fraying patience.

"We won't have to," Barrett reassures him. "And that money is nothing compared to what you'll get for the safe," he tells Cass. "It's fifty thousand versus millions."

Jonny Boy looks ready to join Barrett on this plan. Cass is close as well. He's almost convinced her. It makes sense, in a way. She doesn't know what kind of forces Holzmann has in there. There could be a dozen men with machine guns, or Holzmann could be all alone, and the plan has an appealing simplicity. She can get the safe and get away clean, and it honestly doesn't matter if Tweedle-Dee and Tweedle-Dum make it out or not, because she'll be the one with the safe and the key at the end of it. Then it's just a matter of getting out of the city and finding someone to crack the box open.

But then Barrett smiles that dumb smile. That smug little smirk that says he knows something she doesn't. It's a smile she's spent her whole life staring down. A smile that says she should stay in her god-damned place like a good little bitch and accept the scraps that the men deign to drop her way. It's a smile she's seen from Richard Sands, from her fence, and even from Jonny Boy and Vic in moments when they thought she wasn't paying attention. It's a smile she's never going to put up with again.

"Fuck that," she says. "I'm done sneaking into places. Holzmann is going down, and I want him and every son of a bitch in this goddamned county to know that it was me who fucking did it. Here's the plan: we go in the front door, guns blazing, and we take him the fuck out. If you're too much of a bitch-ass pussy to follow me, that's just one less fuck to split the payday with. Come on, Jonny Boy," she calls as she strides across the grass toward the farmhouse. "We've got work to do."

She makes it seven steps before the sound of a car door behind her draws her to a stop. She turns, raising her pistol, but Barrett isn't trying to leave. He's standing in front of the driver's side door, holding the bag of cash that she had hidden in the door pocket.

"Put that fucking down," she says, punctuating each word with a long step toward him, her gun aimed straight at his head.

He looks down at her with absolute dismissal, as though he cares for her as much as he would a beetle scuttling across a rock in the park.

"Do not point a gun at me," he says. His voice is flat and cold.

"Or fucking what?"

She doesn't see him move. The first indication that he has is the blooming flash of pain in her wrist as he catches it with his hand, jamming his thumb behind the pistol's trigger to prevent her firing it. He sweeps her hand up and away, twisting the gun in her grip and forcing her to choose between keeping hold of it or keeping her wrist unbroken. It happens so quickly that instinct takes over, and her hand releases the pistol of its own accord. She blinks, too overwhelmed in the moment for even her anger to break through the surprise, and turns to Jonny Boy, but he's just watching, slack-jawed, with his rifle hanging limply at his side.

Barrett lowers the hammer on the revolver. He did all that with just one hand. The other still holds the envelope of cash, which he slides into the waistband of his pants.

"You know, you don't have to fight every fight," he says.

"Fuck you," she replies. "You don't know the first thing about what I do or don't have to do. You want respect, all you have to do is show up in the room. But me? If I ever back down—if I, even once, don't fight the fight, then I'm done. That's it. Every scrap I fought for is gone. So yes, I goddamned do have to fight, and you can just shut the hell up with your feel-good bullshit."

She's not in Barrett's face. She couldn't be, even if she wanted to. The top of her head doesn't reach his nipples. But she is close to him.

Barrett inhales through his teeth, a thoughtful sound, as he looks down at her. She hadn't meant to say that, to tell him those things, to expose herself.

"OK," he says, as he spins the revolver in his hand and offers it to her. "So what's the plan?"

She takes the gun and jams it into the back of her pants. "You take point. Open doors and take out anyone who gets close. I'll be right behind covering you, and Jonny Boy keeps our asses clean. We go fast and take no prisoners."

Barrett nods and sets off toward the farmhouse, moving in a crouch to keep his silhouette as hidden as possible. Cass falls into step beside him, and Jonny Boy hustles to catch up. When they've covered a little more than half the distance, with Jonny Boy's rasping breath growing loud enough to give them away, even with the cover of the crickets' song that fills the night, Cass holds a hand up for them to pause.

"Jesus, Jonny Boy," she whispers to the panting man. "When's the last time you got some fucking cardio in?"

"I walked so much," he gasps back. "Everything hurts." He's bent over, one hand bracing against his knee and the other using the rifle as a crutch.

Barrett's attention has stayed on the house, and he hisses at the two of them to get their attention. "Cass," he says, "the safe is in the basement. There's a cellar door around the side you should be able to get into. If it's guarded, they'll be on your right as you go down. You'll need to cross the cellar to a storage room beyond the furnace. The safe is in there."

"The fuck are you talking about?" she asks. "We're not going in through the goddamned cellar."

"You still have the key, right?" he asks.

She pats her pocket to check that the key is still there, but she doesn't answer his question. "This isn't the fucking plan."

"I'm sorry," he says. "This is the only way. Jonny Boy, you're with me. Don't worry. I'll take care of you." And then he straightens up to his full height and starts walking forward as he calls out at the top of his lungs, "Holzmann!"

"What the fuck, Barrett?" Cass yells after him, but he waves her away.

"Get the safe," he calls to her, then back to the house, "Holzmann! It's Barrett! I'm coming up!"

The guard on the porch snatches up his rifle in one hand and shines a flashlight out across the grass with his other. He yells something back into the house.

"Motherfucker," Cass curses under her breath.

As Barrett and Jonny Boy walk off to Holzmann's house, she's left with only one option. She won't give Barrett the chance to betray her. Let him draw the attention of Holzmann's men. She's Cassiopeia Mullen, the best B&E girl the city of Omaha has ever seen, and she is going to get her fucking money.

CHAPTER 61

Jonny Boy Wright, 3:01 A.M.

J onny Boy can't breathe. He knows he is a criminal. He doesn't like it, but that's who he is. Otherwise, he would have broken away from Cass years ago when she had first led him and Vic to the back door of her neighbor's house.

Jonny Boy didn't like any part of it. He was convinced the Ivanovics would come home, even though Cass insisted they would be out of town for another three days. They'd had the post office hold their mail, she explained, and she found the confirmation in their mailbox the week before.

The back door was locked, but Cass had a crowbar. She handed it to Jonny Boy, insisting that nobody could see them and he just needed to fucking do it. He'd hated it, but as the wood splintered under the crowbar's leverage, Cass and Vic whooped with joy and clapped him on the back. He was the hero of the moment. The conqueror of doors. That thrill carried him through the night, and a month later, when Cass showed up again with Vic in tow and a tip about a classmate being away for a long weekend, it was that much harder to say no, and so he didn't.

296

It wasn't the life he had wanted for himself, but he knew that it was the best he was going to get. He wasn't good in school, wasn't smart enough to get into college or learn a trade. Cass made it easy for him. He didn't have to make any more choices after he made the one to follow her. She took care of all the details, and every once in a while, she'd give him a smile or a pat on the back or a kind word.

There were always nerves at the start of a job. That paranoid knowledge that this was the time that something would go wrong. Even after it had gone wrong a few times, when someone had been in the house and he'd been forced to use the crowbar to break more than a doorframe, it didn't get easier.

It was always bad at the start, but the fear did lessen as each job went on. Every burglary had a rhythm to it, and as Jonny Boy fell into that pattern, he could usually relax.

But not this time. The tension had been building inside of him ever since they first knocked on Barrett's door. There was no rhythm. No relaxation. The fear didn't let go. This would be the end of them.

He had shamed Holzmann. Most of what happened between Vic's death and the fight in the van is a blur of anger and red, but there's a moment that stands out in his memory, singular and perfect. Holzmann is pinned to the wall. Jonny Boy is striking him in the face. There is no art to the blows. It is anger and rage and hurt made manifest. A lifetime's worth of pain, expressed through a fist. What happened next—the shootout at Vic's abuela's, his day on the lam, his capture by the cops and betrayal of Cass—was the world drawing him closer to his end.

When he and Cass fled Aunt Marta's, he knew he wasn't going to make it. He knew that as surely as he knew he was a worthless, fat piece of shit. This would be his death, and it would be painful when it came, but at least then the pathetic life that was Jon Wright would have been brought to a close, and the world would be a little bit better for his absence.

Then Barrett handed him half a sandwich. There was nothing attached to it. No demands or insults delivered alongside the offer. It was just a half a sandwich. And the vise that had closed around his throat relaxed by just a hair. He couldn't explain why, but for the first time in days it felt like he could breathe.

Now he can't. There's a man on the porch shouting at them with a long gun aimed in their direction. The wind snatches his words away, though their meaning is clear enough. Hands up. Move slowly. But Barrett isn't looking at the man on the porch. He is looking at Jonny Boy.

"Are you ready?" he asks.

Jonny Boy knows his face is red with exertion. He can feel the sweat drip from his brow and his cheeks puff with each desperate exhale. Every movement feels like he's doing permanent damage to himself, but there's no point in caring about that anymore. He does his best to control the panic. He's already made his choices.

Barrett puts a hand on his arm, and the man's palm is dry and rough against his skin, but the touch centers him. Barrett's hand slides down to his and gently extracts the rifle from his grip.

"I'll get you through this. I just need you to trust me, OK?"

Jonny Boy nods. He can trust Barrett. The man has always been kind to him.

"I'm sorry I got you involved in all this," Barrett says. Another man—this one with his arm in a sling—has appeared on the porch. Barrett raises the rifle above his head, holding it by the stock.

"You didn't," Jonny Boy says, unsure what exactly Barrett is apologizing for. Richard got him involved in this. Cass did. Jonny Boy got himself involved. Barrett had nothing to do with it.

"You deserve better than her, you know," Barrett says. "All her bullshit? That's her garbage. Not yours." He turns to the house, hands still above his head, and walks toward the two men on the porch. Jonny Boy falls into step beside him. He doesn't know what the plan is, but Barrett does, and Jonny Boy will trust him.

"Evening, Benny. Lang. We're here to see Mister Holzmann," Barrett calls up to the two men on the porch.

"No guns," says Benny, the man in the sling. The enmity he has for Barrett is easy to read.

"That's fine," Barrett says. "We don't need it." He lays the rifle down against the stairs.

"Wade's in fucking surgery right now cause of what you did to him," Benny says.

"I'm sorry," Barrett says. "I didn't want to hurt him. Or you."

Benny gestures for the two of them to climb the stairs, and the other man, Lang, pats them down. The envelope in Barrett's belt gives him pause, but it's not a weapon, so he lets it pass. Once they've been cleared, Benny leads them into the farmhouse.

CHAPTER 62

Jonny Boy Wright, 3:03 A.M.

Jonny Boy tries to focus on anything except what he's doing right now. He studies the peeling paint on the doorframe, the wood of the banister on the stairs. He's not walking to meet the most terrifying man in Omaha. He is just walking through a house. He looks at the wallpaper around the arch that leads to the living room. He traces the pattern, finding the point where it begins to repeat.

Other than the two men escorting them, the house seems empty. There are no soldiers lounging about like there had been at Elkhorn. In fact, this doesn't appear to be a crime boss's home at all. This is just a little farmhouse on the outskirts of the city, a relic of an age when a family could work fifty acres growing wheat or corn and sell to the railroad man at harvest time.

A hallway runs the length of the house, providing a cooling breeze through to the back door. Jonny Boy wouldn't be surprised to find an iron dinner bell hung there to call the workers home from the heat of the day. Stairs lie at the end of the hallway, and two open doors lead off to each side of the house. Jonny Boy and Barrett are led through the first on the left, taking them into a cozy living area. A hearth, currently unlit, is in the far corner alongside an antique upright radio and turntable. A well-worn couch and overstuffed armchair face a heavy cabinet with a small TV. Thick curtains are drawn across all the windows, and a lush rug lies on the floor.

The kitchen stands at odds with the décor of the living room. A shining marble counter rings the room, interrupted only by gleaming steel appliances with minimally designed cabinetry hanging above. A wood-topped island dominates the center of the room, and it is there, leaning against the wood with one hand while sipping from a small cup of coffee in the other, that Holzmann waits for them, and Jonny Boy is forced to return to the present situation.

"Welcome, Herr Rye," Holzmann says, lifting his coffee in a toast. "And Herr Wright, I am surprised you would show your face here." He drains his drink and sets it down before lifting his cane, a solid black piece of wood topped by an iron eagle that can't be comfortable in his hand.

Barrett asked Jonny Boy to trust him. He said he would get him through this. Jonny Boy's mouth and throat are dry. He tries to swallow, to find some moisture. He is sure that if he speaks, his voice will crack and strain, assuming he makes any noise at all. The rap of Holzmann's cane against the ground echoes through him, and he can't look away from the man's pale eyes. Holzmann gives the faintest nod, and Jonny Boy feels a presence behind him. Lang pins him in place with a hand on his shoulder. Jonny Boy can feel the man's breath on his ear. He smells like capers.

"I brought you what you asked for," Barrett says.

"And then a little bit more," Holzmann says, raising an eyebrow toward Jonny Boy.

Jonny Boy turns to Barrett in confusion, but his face is unreadable. Has he been working with Holzmann? Was all this a ploy to get Jonny Boy here?

"I'm sorry, sir," Jonny Boy says. "I didn't mean to hit you." The words spill out uncontrollably. His mouth floods with saliva. "Or shoot at you. Near you. I hope I didn't hit you, sir. We weren't supposed to shoot anyone. I didn't shoot anyone, just so you know."

Barrett catches Jonny Boy's eye. The big man looks sideways at him and takes a deep breath. Be calm, he seems to be saying. Everything is under control. Jonny Boy bites down, stopping his babbling.

"This was not your intention, then?" Holzmann asks. "The launching of a war?"

"No," Jonny Boy answers quickly. "I never wanted to fight you."

"This is a shame. I thought perhaps I had misjudged you. That you might be a man of high ambition, pursuing his aims with audacity and strength of spirit. This is a man I could respect."

"Jonny Boy," Barrett interrupts, "came here to make amends. He made a mistake, Mr. Holzmann. He sees that, and he wishes to correct it."

"I am sure he does," Holzmann says.

"Nobody was supposed to get hurt," Jonny Boy says. "The place was supposed to be empty. Cass said it was empty."

"I am not interested in this," Holzmann says. He dismisses Jonny Boy and focuses fully on Barrett. "Where is my key?"

The hand on Jonny Boy's shoulder tightens, and another grabs his elbow to pull him back. Back through the door. Away from Barrett and the small bubble of safety his size has offered. Toward whatever miserable fate awaits him. A fitting end to a pathetic life.

"I have a condition," Barrett says.

Holzmann's hand tightens around the head of his cane and his lips turn down. "Have I not made it clear to you, Herr Rye? You do not make demands. You do not have conditions."

Barrett does not flinch as Benny comes through the door on the far side of the kitchen and casually draws a gun from his belt. It's an awkward draw with his left hand, but clean enough to carry the point.

"Hurt him, and you don't get the key," Barrett says with a gesture toward Jonny Boy.

"What?" Jonny Boy asks, unable to stop the question.

"Why?" asks Holzmann, offering the more salient query.

"Because that's my price. You don't need to know more," Barrett says with enigmatic finality.

Holzmann runs his tongue along his teeth, considering. His weight shifts, and he leans more heavily into his cane.

"If this is what you must do, then so be it," he says. "You will not have brought the key with you, which means that it is with Cassiopeia Mullen. Jonny Boy"—Holzmann fills the name with disdain—"no doubt knows where she is. How long do you think he will remain silent under Miss Quintana's ministrations?"

Jonny Boy's legs buckle, and Lang groans as he strains to keep him from collapsing.

"Respectfully, sir," Barrett says. "He'll last long enough." Barrett is far more confident than Jonny Boy. "Long enough for Cass to destroy the key, and without Sands you can't get another. Not before somebody bigger from Kansas City, or maybe Denver or St. Louis, catches wind of what you've got here and decides they're gonna take it. The only way you get what's in your safe is if Jonny Boy walks out of here alive, unharmed, and with your solemn vow that all is forgiven. You can get your key or you can get your revenge, but you can't have both."

Jonny Boy can feel the grip on his arm tighten. Nobody speaks to Holzmann like that.

Barrett stands straight and proud, more upright in this moment than Jonny Boy has ever seen him. His right hand calmly clasps the other at the wrist, his elbows lightly bent. But for his massive size, he would appear placid and calm, a petitioner before the court, obsequious but undeniable.

Holzmann is dwarfed by the huge man before him, and yet he gives no ground. He stares Barrett down with the air of a man used to getting what he demands. But Jonny Boy can see him thinking. Weighing his fate. If he relents, then Jonny Boy will live.

CHAPTER 63

Henry Holzmann, 1961

The world was different when Hank's family moved from Kansas City in 1961. His dad worked for a screw manufacturer that needed a man in Omaha to oversee their shipping, so the Holzmanns left Missouri for Nebraska. Hank's mom thought it would be good to be in a city with more of their people than the largely Irish-and-Italian Kansas City. It would let her son get in touch with his family's German roots, and the boy, who had always struggled to relate to his Catholic peers, took quickly to the clear direction of the Protestant spirit.

After the Civil Rights Act in '64, the Holzmanns followed the other white families out of North Omaha, but the business remained behind, and in '69 it burned to the ground in a series of riots following the shooting of a colored girl, Vivian Strong. Hank's father, a Korean War veteran, had gone to the warehouse to defend it, and though there were no reported deaths in the riots, he never returned.

Hank, then a teenager, found that the moral absolutism and implied social hierarchy of Prussian philosophy provided order to a world that was slipping into chaos. He threw himself fully into that identity, embracing its proto-fascism even as the fatherland—or at least the western half of it—did its best to leave it behind. He even went so far as to mimic the accents and speech patterns of recent immigrants.

With German industriousness, he salvaged what he could of his father's business network to establish himself as an independent shipping agent. He promised to move goods through the Midwest faster, cheaper, and quieter than the larger firms.

A decade earlier, the mass arrests at the Apalachin meeting had forced J. Edgar Hoover to acknowledge the power of La Cosa Nostra—the Italian mafia—on the East Coast and devote the FBI's resources to stamping it out. In response, the Italians had been moving their operations west and were now firmly established in Kansas City.

A year after he went into business for himself and not yet having achieved the age of majority, Hank Holzmann received a visit from two Sicilian representatives. Hank had been encroaching on their business, they informed him. He could subsume his operation into theirs, or he could die.

Hank remembered his father, the man who refused to accede to the changing facts on the ground and died to protect eight thousand square feet of screws, and he vowed never to become that.

This is how Hank joined the Italian mafia and became their pet German, Henry Holzmann. Thirty percent went back to the bosses in Kansas City—an expense for which he received little other than their tolerance of his continued existence—but Omaha was his. His independence and non-Italian identity proved an asset for an organization looking to dodge racketeering investigators.

Years passed, and while bosses came and went, Holzmann remained. When they moved from Kansas City to Chicago, he continued on as the linchpin of an organization moving women, drugs, money, and guns across the country, and he did it not as an Italian but as a German. He was careful. He was efficient. And he was left alone. As money came to Omaha, he expanded from transporting goods to also supplying the city's vices. His operation collected power. What he wanted was respect.

The knowledge that he would never grow beyond this city ate at him. He was left alone because he was not only too valuable to offend but also too inconsequential to bother with. He was like the earthworms in the soil. Without them, no plants could thrive, but nobody raises up earthworms with honors and praise. He will be more than this, he swore to himself. He will right the wrong of his nascent growth being clipped.

The egg is his key to that. After everything he has done, and everything he has been through—every injustice that has been heaped at his feet and every time he has had to bow and genuflect—he can swallow a bit more shame. Once he has arrived, he will get his revenge. But first he must get there.

CHAPTER 64

Henry Holzmann, 3:07 A.M.

A ll right," Holzmann says, and he steps back to the island, resting a hand on it to take his weight off the jagged top of his cane.

"I want to hear you say it," Barrett says, pushing the boundaries of what Holzmann will accept. "I want your word, as a man of honor, that Jonny Boy goes unharmed. Now and forever."

Giving his word now costs him nothing and wins him everything. Not a defeat, but a strategic retreat. At his signal, Lang lets the fat man loose, and Benny leaves the room to try to put their two guests at ease.

"You have my word," Holzmann says. "I swear Herr Wright may leave this house unmolested and shall continue to enjoy the forbearance of myself and my men so long as he does not further aggravate me. Now where, Herr Rye, is my key?"

Barrett smiles and relaxes. His hands unclasp and point to the cellar door behind Holzmann. "Cass has it," he says. "And right about now, she should be locking herself in the storage room of your basement."

An angry cry draws their attention through the door to the living area. Cassiopeia, not locked in the storage room at all, makes her presence known.

"You fucking cocksucker," she yells, pushing through the door with a revolver in one hand pointed at Holzmann and a rifle in the other, braced against her body and aimed at Barrett's head. "I fucking knew I shouldn't trust you, you son of a bitch."

Her arms tremble with rage, and Holzmann has little fear for himself. At this range, aiming with only her unsteady off hand, she will not hit him with that revolver, but still he waves for Lang to rejoin him by the island and the pistol hidden in its cabinetry.

Jonny Boy, paralyzed by confusion, looks from Barrett to Cassiopeia. "I don't understand," he mewls.

"Get the fuck over here, Jonny Boy," Cassiopeia snaps at him. She keeps the rifle trained on Barrett, while moving to keep several feet of distance between them.

"Damn it, Cass," Barrett says. "Why couldn't you just stick to the plan?"

It is not enough to have a plan, as Barrett is learning now. You must be prepared for that plan to fail. For your enemies to be strong where they appeared weak and your men to break and run though they have the advantage. This is why Holzmann will win.

"Is she in place?" Holzmann whispers to Lang while their guests bicker. The soldier nods.

Laia Quintana had returned to the farm a half hour before Barrett and Jonny Boy announced their approach, bringing word of what they were planning. Cassiopeia, she informed him, would attempt to break in through the basement with the key. Barrett, in the meantime, would bring Jonny Boy to the front door. Holzmann had concealed his forces, secreting a few men in the basement to capture Cassiopeia while the rest hid in the surrounding fields, ready to move in once the snare had been closed, but not wanting to scare away their quarry beforehand.

Holzmann needed only to occupy Barrett until Cassiopeia—and the key—were taken, or, being unable to follow the simplest of plans, she attempted a double cross and appeared in the kitchen, at which point Holzmann's reserve would step in.

"I had this handled, Cass," Barrett says.

"You thought I'd sit back and let you fucking sell me out?" Cassiopeia asks.

"I was trying to keep you safe!" Barrett shouts back.

Cassiopeia pushes Jonny Boy behind her and toward the living area, but the fat man's retreat is brought up short.

"Regardless," says Laia Quintana, blocking Jonny Boy's escape, "you failed." She stands in the doorway, using one hand to guide Jonny Boy back into the kitchen, while the other holds a pistol at Cassiopeia's head.

CHAPTER 65

Henry Holzmann, 3:10 A.M.

The bitter young woman starts to swing her rifle toward Laia. Lang, ever the loyal soldier, drags Holzmann behind the cover of the island and draws the handgun concealed there. Laia pushes past Jonny Boy and reaches out with her free hand, trying to slap Cassiopeia's weapon aside and strip her of it, but, to the mercenary's clear surprise, Cassiopeia anticipates the move and steps out of her reach.

Which leaves the doorway open, and Barrett, temporarily forgotten, dive tackles Jonny Boy through the door and into the living room. Laia pursues Cassiopeia into the kitchen, darting past the muzzle of the rifle and slamming the butt of her pistol into Cassiopeia's face. The young woman's cheek splits open beneath the metal, and she collapses to the ground, losing both her weapons as she falls.

It only takes a moment—more than a blink, less than a breath. When it is over, Jonny Boy and Barrett are left hiding behind the wall in the living room, Holzmann is crouching behind the island—his hip screams at the awkward position, but that pain is receding with every heartbeat as the endorphins take hold—and both Laia and Lang stand in the kitchen with their weapons trained on Cassiopeia, unarmed and bleeding on the ground.

Cassiopeia breaks the silence first. Her words strain as her torn cheek stretches around them. "Who the fuck are you?" she asks, looking up at the woman standing over her.

"We'll have plenty of time to get acquainted," Laia says with a cold smile. "Get on your feet. You're coming with me."

Holzmann rises from behind the island. "And where are you going?" he asks Laia.

She is confused. He should know that she is taking Cassiopeia to the basement to get the key from her. She opens her mouth to speak. To say these things. To lie to his face. But she says no words.

Instead, she lets out a soft grunt, concurrent with the report of a suppressed gunshot, as a small-caliber bullet enters the flesh of her shoulder, just above and to the right of the vest beneath her shirt. She spins with the impact and falls to the ground beside Cassiopeia. She tries to raise her weapon, but her arm does not move. It hangs limply from her ruined shoulder.

Even injured, Benny is a fine shot.

As Benny steps from the living room to join Holzmann at the island, Cassiopeia glances through the door. "How many fucking people are back there?" she asks nobody in particular.

It was Jim Pickens who had tipped him off and told him of Laia's obfuscations. She knew who Barrett was, had known all along that the man she hunted was an enforcer out of Chicago with a bounty on his head. She had not shared this information.

And then she presented him with a plan that had him sending his troops away. That left him isolated here with just a skeleton crew to protect him as she brought the key and safe together. Scarpello had sent her to him. He must be behind this.

The Italians have never respected him, though they will learn to soon. He tries not to be insulted by it. It is a gift, after all, to be under-estimated. Still, it grates at him, and now they have sent this woman, this Mexican, after him. But no matter. Her schemes have failed, and he has won, as he was always going to do.

"You Chicago folks think you are so much better than we mere plebeians out here in the boondocks," he says. He is not gloating. He is giving her a message to carry home to her employers. Henry Holzmann has arrived. "The fee I have already paid for your services should cover your medical expenses. When you return to your boss, tell him I will not forget this slight."

She glares at him from the ground. Her weapon is nearby, and her left arm still works, but both Lang and Benny are ready to shoot her should she move. She can do nothing but stare and bleed. "You'll suffer for this," she says.

"No, Miss Quintana. I will not." Holzmann sighs. Scarpello will be upset, but Holzmann will soon be wealthy enough to repel any assault he launches, and the Italians are still reliant on him to keep their ship-ments flowing. A fight will come, yes, but it will be short, and when it is done, he will finally be seen for the leader he is.

"Now as for you, Herr Rye," he says, turning to consider the big man who now pokes his head around the door from the living room. "The situation has changed, and I will be amending the terms of our deal. While I should very much like to enjoy seeing you suffer for the difficulties you have caused me, I would enjoy provoking your former employer more. Give me the key, and I will let you go free."

"What about Jonny Boy?" Barrett asks.

"I'll fucking kill you, Barrett," Cassiopeia yells from the ground, as though she still has any power here. Lang cleared her dropped weapons away, but she has been eyeing Laia's abandoned pistol.

"You'll never see him again, sir," Barrett continues. "I give you the key, he leaves the city."

Holzmann could say yes. It costs him very little to let the fat man go. To let Barrett and this sad little pet who he seems to have adopted slink away into the night. But it costs him even less to say no. The house is still surrounded by his men. He has spent his life retreating, giving ground an inch at a time until he was ready to strike.

He is ready now.

"No," he says. "Wright is mine. The key is mine. Give them to me, and I will give you safe passage to wherever you would like to go. A new life, in the destination of your choice. Refuse, and I return you to Scarpello."

CHAPTER 66

Barrett Rye, 3:13 A.M.

There it is. My way out. If Holzmann goes to war with Scarpello, that might give me the cover I need to escape. The man's entire career is built on moving things without being noticed. If anybody can hide me away, it's him, and he's said nothing about the fifty thousand dollars I have in my pocket, more than enough to get started again somewhere new. It is what I wanted. It is why I told myself I came here. All I need to do is give him the key. Give him Jonny Boy. Give him one more scrap of my soul.

Jonny Boy is at my side, leaning against the wall where he dragged himself after I tackled him through the door. His face has gone ashen, and he stares at me with wide eyes.

"Don't leave me," he says.

It would be so easy to walk away. To leave it all behind. But I wouldn't be shaving off another piece of myself to do it. The scraps are too small. If I give him up, there will be nothing left of me.

"Do you still trust me?" I ask him. He hesitates. After everything he has seen me do, I don't blame him that he doesn't. "I'll get you out of here," I promise. "I'll keep you safe."

I don't know that I can, but maybe, just this once, if I say the words, I can make them true. Jonny Boy gives the smallest of nods. Holzmann is still waiting for my answer.

"Cass has the key," I tell him. "In her jacket. Napoleon pocket."

"You fucking bitch," Cass screams as she lunges for the gun.

Holzmann is there first. He slams the heavy iron head of his cane into her hand, smashing the bones beneath the sharp edges of the eagle's wings. As her cries of anger turn to ones of pain, Lang pulls her from the ground and digs his hand into her jacket. He retrieves the little metal fob.

It is such an unassuming thing. A spheroid of polished gray with a loop on one end and a button on the other. It almost seems ridiculous.

Lang hands it to Holzmann, who takes it with reverential care. His fingers close softly around the smooth surface. There is a cabinet built into the island that he opens, and from its recesses Lang pulls the safe. It is a cube of black steel, and he is gentle as he places it on the counter. A set of holes have been drilled into it, and the sharp edges of the silver metal gleam there against the surrounding black.

"Get the locksmith," Holzmann says.

Upstairs, Pickens is waiting, ready to finish his task and finally open the safe. Lang leaves to retrieve him. He gets two steps before he freezes. Before a light from outside snaps on with a thrum of electricity, and he is flooded with blinding white. The light pours down the hallway and through the windows along the back of the kitchen, casting harsh shadows across the entire room.

"This is the fucking police!" an amplified voice booms from behind the house. "Everybody get on the fucking ground!"

For a moment there is chaos. Lang dives back into the kitchen, crouching behind the counter along the rear wall. Benny drags

Holzmann behind the island, taking cover both from the windows and from the doorway that I hide behind with Jonny Boy. Laia, cradling her injured shoulder, crawls for a corner of the room and ducks there behind the solid metal frame of the refrigerator. Cass scrambles for the pistol with her uninjured hand and rolls through the door. She almost makes it look intentional and not like she's slipping across the blood-slicked tile. As she gets her bearings, her eyes lock onto me, and the pistol comes up.

"I have this under control," I say. I know I said a con is all about finding the moment to strike, not executing a carefully orchestrated plan. But that, and I hope you'll forgive me, was a little bit bullshit. It turns out I don't know what the fuck I'm talking about. Because I'm not a con man. I'm a soldier. A goon. I'm a big guy who scares people professionally. That's it. That's all I've ever been, and that's what I should have stayed. I've only run one con before in my life, and it ended with my love getting shot in the back. It ended with me unable to lift my eyes from the carpeting to offer him some comfort as he died.

So I try to force calm into my voice, but I know I fail. I've cut the rope too many times. "I have this under control," I say, but I've been bailing out this ship for days. It's fully underwater, and I have nothing under control.

"The fuck you do," says Cass, and she jams the pistol into my chest. I could disarm her. I could try to talk her down. But that would change nothing. Whether it falls apart now or ten minutes or ten days from now doesn't matter. Cass'll shoot me, or the police when they come in, or Laia or Scarpello or someone paid by Holzmann to do me in prison.

I'm tired of this trick. It stopped being fun when Mickey died. So I say nothing, and I do nothing.

"Cass." Jonny Boy reaches out and puts a hand over hers. "He's just trying to keep me safe. You've still got the cash, right?" He looks to me, and I nod. "OK then. They're all distracted. Let's get the hell out of here."

Cass looks through the door, and I do too, and we see that Jonny Boy is right. Everyone is distracted. Holzmann is yelling orders. Benny is trying to raise reinforcements on a radio.

Jonny Boy grabs Cass's hand and pulls her to her feet by the wall. The police are out back, and right now Holzmann's focus is on them. We can slip out the front and get away.

"Please, Cass," Jonny Boy says, finding more strength in his voice than I could. "Let's just go."

From the other room, Holzmann yells to the police. "Oster, is that you?"

"Send out Pickens with the safe," comes back the amplified answer. The speaker is turned way up. Owen is being louder than he needs to be. I know a misdirect when I see it. There's something else happening. I filter out his and Holzmann's noise. What's left? The faint creak of heavy steps on sunbaked wood. Owen might be out back, but there's someone else sneaking along the porch, circling the house.

"It's too late," I say. "The best you can do is keep your heads down."

"I'm not gonna fucking hide," Cass says. "And I'm not gonna fucking run, either." She shakes her hand loose from Jonny Boy's.

"Cassiopeia is in the living room," Holzmann calls to Owen. "Take out her and her team, and I'll give you half a million dollars."

"You're an asshole, Holzmann," Owen answers. "And I'm done taking orders from a fucking Kraut. Give us Pickens and the safe, or we'll come in there and take them, and we won't be fucking gentle about it."

"You're dead," Holzmann yells back. Or at least, that's what he starts to yell before he's interrupted by three gunshots coming through the window along the side of the kitchen.

There is a single moment after the gunshots. Just enough time for me to wrap myself around Jonny Boy to try to shield him from what's about to happen.

And then all hell breaks loose.

CHAPTER 67

Barrett Rye, 3:18 A.M.

Holzmann's men open up first, I think. Lang with his pistol and Benny with the suppressed rifle. Then the shooter on the side of the house begins to fire as well, joined almost immediately by Owen from the back. When a round goes through the wall above us and smashes into the far wall, Cass reaches around the door and begins to fire into the kitchen.

A few more shots pass overhead, but they, likely fired by Owen on the far side of the house, are all angled upward, and we are in little danger. After ten seconds the guns fall silent, leaving only the piercing ring of tinnitus in their wake. I hear no cries of pain, and a quick survey of myself and Jonny Boy confirms that neither of us was hit.

Gunfights don't consist of people picking each other off with well-placed shots from across a room. In reality, you'll be more concerned with keeping yourself hidden, and what we just had was five people firing blindly through an adrenaline rush toward targets in cover. It would have been a small miracle—or at least a moment of supreme unlikeliness—had a shot actually landed. And now the guns have run dry.

While those with extra clips reload, Cass leans out through the doorway and snatches up the rifle she dropped earlier. She checks the breech, then turns to Jonny Boy. "Let's fucking do this," she yells, screaming to be heard over the ringing. "Grow a fucking pair, and let's get our goddamned money!"

Jonny Boy shakes his head no.

And then a canister about the size of a can of soda arcs through a window and rolls across the shards of glass scattered about the kitchen floor. Another sails through the window behind me, landing on the couch a few feet away. Aluminum powder ignites with a hiss that grows to a deafening boom, and a blinding flash of brilliant white overwhelms the house.

I don't hear the door get smashed in. My vision is barely returning as Conrad rushes in the front. Cass faces him, but there is a flash from his gun, and she collapses to the ground. As he barrels past us for the kitchen, I put an arm around Jonny Boy, and bring him to his feet.

"Let's go!" I yell. I can't hear my own voice, and I doubt he can either, but he seems to understand as we, heads down, make for the broken front door. I don't look behind me. Whatever is happening in the kitchen doesn't matter. What matters is getting out of this house.

I barely feel the first impact. The second one strips all the air from my lungs, and my leg buckles. I shove Jonny Boy toward the exit, yelling into the void for him to keep running. The third spins me and brings me to the ground. I collapse against the couch, facing back toward the kitchen. The couch burns behind me, ignited by the flash-bang, but I'm not too concerned.

Through the door of the kitchen, I see Benny facedown on the ground with his hands out in surrender and Holzmann aiming a gun in my general direction. Or maybe it's Conrad's direction. Probably

Conrad's direction, as the scowling cop has moved to put the island between himself and Holzmann. Blood spreads across my chest. Strange. I don't remember getting hit in the chest.

Owen rushes from the hall and tackles Holzmann from behind. There is a lot of screaming happening in the kitchen, but I can't hear any of it. I wonder if that's a result of the flash-bang or the blood loss. Does blood loss affect hearing? I'll have to look into that later.

Cass drags herself clear of the doorway. It looks like Conrad got her in the leg, but it isn't bleeding too badly. That's good, I think, as my own blood spreads beneath me. The acrylic fibers of the couch give off a terrible smell as they burn.

My arms feel weak as I push off the couch, and I stumble, falling forward, slamming my face into the hardwood floor. I can still see Holzmann, though. I can see his expression as he screams with Conrad's knee in his back. I can't hear his words, but I don't need to. We're both looking at the same thing.

We're looking at Owen, standing in front of the safe. We both watch as he reaches into his pocket and pulls out a small spheroid of metal. He raises it in one hand and holds it to the front of the safe to disengage the security system. Holzmann shrieks, and Owen smiles and grabs the handle. Pickens had made sure everything was prepared. He'd already disengaged the locking mechanism. All someone has to do is turn the lever, and the safe will open, whether they have the key or not. Owen twists, and the door swings aside.

The safe was designed for spite. It was purchased by a man who said that if he could not have the great treasures of the world, then nobody could. It was built so that any attempt to open it without the matching key would cause the priceless egg inside, one of the most storied lost treasures of Western civilization, to be destroyed, reduced to a smoking heap of porcelain, jewels, and metal salts.

All of this, everything that had happened, had been done for that egg. And the joke of it all is that Owen doesn't have the key. The little ball of metal in his hand is just a ball of resin with some aluminum electroplated on. I don't need to hear what Holzmann is screaming because I know what he is screaming. He is screaming the rage of a man that wagered everything and lost, and as he turns that rage to me, I smile, and I look away.

There's a funny thing about being shot. It hurts a lot less than you'd think. I guess, at a certain point, pain just doesn't matter anymore. It's your body's way of telling you that you done fucked up, but if you fuck up bad enough, there's no real reason to worry about it. Maybe it's not the best sign that it doesn't hurt quite as much now as it did a moment before, but I can't muster up enough energy to care.

Jonny Boy sits on the far side of the room, staring back at me. It doesn't look like he got hit in the firefight. He's crying as he looks at me, collapsed on the ground in a damp circle of red. The flickering light of the burning couch has been joined now by flashing red-and-blue sirens. I want to tell Jonny Boy that it will be OK. That he's better than all of this, but I don't have the air, and he wouldn't be able to hear me. Instead, I just look at him and smile. He crawls across the room to me, and he takes my hand as I lie on the floor.

Police pour through the door. The real police. They swarm the house and secure weapons, and I see someone standing over me, shouting into their shoulder radio, but I don't pay attention to them.

Jonny Boy doesn't turn away. He meets my eyes, and he squeezes my hand. He's a good kid. He's better than I was. I wish I could have done more for him.

I squeeze his hand back, and I close my eyes.

CHAPTER 68

Peter Van Horn, 7:19 A.M.

The farmhouse is a zoo. Ambulances fight for space on the broad grass field with cruisers and patrol wagons. Omaha employs just under a thousand officers, and it seems like every one of them is out tonight. Some hang yellow tape in a mile-wide perimeter around the house and sweep the fields for the last vestiges of Holzmann's forces. Others maintain a press area at the head of the driveway, corralling the swarm of satellite trucks that have set up shop.

Following the bloodbath in Elkhorn, the police weren't the only ones to get a sudden interest in the gangs of Omaha. The reporters arrived almost as soon as the all-hands call went out from the dispatcher. Detectives from homicide, vice, narcotics, organized crime, and Professional Oversight mill at the entrance to the house, waiting for their bosses to sort out jurisdiction. Two squads of firefighters stand off to the side. They contained a small burn inside the house and now enjoy the unfolding theatrics. The FBI field office even has two agents on site to determine if they are going to take the whole thing off OPD's hands.

324

Crime scene techs wearing moon suits and plastic shoes mark casings, impact points, and boot prints, trace trajectories, and photograph everything. It will be at least a day before they're done cataloging the scene, so their priority is documenting the bodies and anything in the grass outside so that the former can be removed and before the latter is destroyed by the small army of personnel churning the ground to mud.

"I'm just about done here, if you want to get ready," a photographer says to the assistant coroner standing next to him, waiting with a stretcher. "You're gonna want help for this one."

"You're fucking telling me," she says, looking down at the huge man splayed out on the floor. The techs have already marked where the body fell and the spread of blood beneath it. He seems to have been the night's only casualty, though a slightly older corpse identified as Richard Sands was found in a freezer in the cellar. Her boss is currently processing that body, leaving her to sort out this giant.

With a heave, she and Peter, who was waiting for the tech to finish, roll the huge man onto a stretcher. The assistant coroner counts down from three, and they lift, opening up the legs of the stretcher to wheel the body of Barrett Rye out of the house. He won't fit in a bag, so they drape a sheet over him to protect his privacy, not that he'll care much about that anymore. As they struggle to get him down the front steps, the sheet catches beneath Peter's foot and pulls back.

There is a barrage of camera shutters as the less respectful members of the press fight for a shot of the dead man's face. The assistant coroner reaches out to pull the sheet back into place, but Peter puts a hand out to stop her.

"Leave it," he says. "Just get him to the van." Peter leads them away from the press and around the side of the house.

There, behind a wall of ambulances, a triage tent has been set up to treat those injured on the scene and allow detectives to take preliminary statements. A coroner's van is parked next to the tent, and as they pass, Peter sees both Holzmann and the out-of-town woman look up and notice Barrett's body. They load the stretcher into the van, and Peter climbs up to sit beside it.

"Thanks for your help," he says to the assistant coroner.

"Someday you'll have to tell me what all this was about."

"We'll see," Peter says. "But if I tell you, I might have to kill you."

She laughs and closes the door, leaving Peter alone with the body. As the driver starts the engine, and the van pulls away, Chloe Rutherford turns around in the passenger seat to look back at the two of them.

"All right," she says. "We held up our end of the bargain. You better make it worth it."

Peter looks down at the big man laid out before him. The guy is good. If Peter didn't know to look for it, he'd never notice the shallow rise and fall of the man's belly.

Barrett Rye opens his eyes and sits up.

CHAPTER 69

Peter Van Horn, 7:48 A.M.

I'm in a hurry," Barrett had said, with one hand on the door of the police station, ready to head out into the night. "There's somewhere I have to be."

Peter wasn't above begging. He hated the whine in his voice when he got desperate, but he knew that if he played it right, it could win him sympathy. Something told him that wasn't what he needed now, though. He didn't need to show this man how pathetic he was. He needed to show that he was competent. That he could get shit done. And so, with his last, best, and only hope about to walk out of the station and cement his fate, he reached for whatever reserves of confidence he could, trying to recall the days before his life fell apart and what it felt like to have some control over his own destiny.

"You need help," he said. "Maybe you're not used to asking for it, but I can see it. You've got powerful people after you, and they're not going to give up. They're going to get what they want, or they're going to kill you trying. Maybe they'll do both."

Barrett's hand was still on the door, but he hadn't pushed it open. Not yet.

"I can help you. I can stop them, and there's not another person in this city who can make you that same promise."

"What do you want in return?" Barrett asked.

"Owen Oster and Conrad Stenberg. I want to take them down."

Barrett took his hand off the door.

Ethan and Chloe were a bit harder to convince. Peter showed them the video from the Nine Ball, and they agreed it was strange that Owen and Conrad had lied about where they were, but it wasn't enough.

"I have video," Barrett offered. "The two of them admitting on tape that they work for Holzmann and threatening me if I don't help them in a robbery."

"And you'll testify to this?" Ethan asked, sharing a look with Chloe. "If you can deliver that, we might be able to work with you."

"No," said Barrett, and Peter's heart sank. "But I'll give you the video, and I'll sign something saying what it is."

"That's not good enough," said Ethan. "Without you there to lay foundation, it'll get thrown out of court."

"No, it won't," Barrett said.

"It's hearsay," Chloe insisted. "If you're not in court, the judge will toss it. Oster and Stenberg have a right to confront their accuser."

"Not if I'm dead."

The two detectives fell silent at that.

"A statement I make to you, believing my death to be imminent, can be admitted. Especially if that statement is made against the people who caused my death."

"You want to die?" Peter had asked slowly.

"No," Barrett said. "I want Barrett Rye to die."

Once they'd worked out the deal, the details fell into place fairly quickly. Chloe and Ethan would have officers ready to go in as soon as Owen and Conrad made their move. Command might ordinarily have objected to the cost of the large deployment on such shaky grounds, but with the pressure they were under after the Elkhorn murders, it was deemed a worthwhile risk. Barrett, with a handful of squibs and a packet of fake blood—which he would smuggle into the house inside the envelope of cash—left to bait the trap.

And now he sits in the back of their van, a living, breathing dead man.

"You made sure they saw me?" he asks.

"I gave the press a good view," Peter says. "Plus Holzmann and the woman as we loaded you into the van."

"Good. I'll need my phone."

Chloe hands it back to him, and he punches a few commands into a remote ftp server. "There you go," he says, and both Chloe's and Ethan's phones buzz to punctuate the moment, acknowledging the arrival of the file.

"Well then, Mister Rye," Chloe says after verifying the video, "or whatever it is you'll be going by now, I believe that concludes our business. Is there anywhere we can drop you off?"

They leave him at a bus station with enough cash to get out of town. He says he doesn't need any more when Peter tries to offer it to him. He'll be just fine, he says.

Before he goes, though, Peter has one last thing for him. It's a burner cell phone, bought with cash and untraceable. Just in case he needs to get in touch, Peter says.

CHAPTER 70

Peter Van Horn, Two Weeks Later

Peter is at the courthouse, a beautiful building of gray stone in a renaissance revival style. The first hearings in the still-expanding investigation into Henry Holzmann's operations have just wrapped up, and Peter needed to be there to give his testimony. As he walks back to his car, his phone buzzes. He stopped answering it after the press started harassing him for a statement, but he recognizes the number. He hits the green accept button.

"I was wondering if you'd call," he says.

"How've you been, Officer?" Barrett asks.

"Fine," Peter says. "I got offered a detective's badge."

"Congratulations," Barrett says, but there is a bit of a question to it. He's picked up on Peter's own hesitation.

"I don't think I'm going to take it. I'm not cut out to be a cop. Not really. I want to see what else there is for me, once this is all wrapped up." It's the first time Peter has said it out loud, and he's not sure why he's confiding in Barrett Rye, of all people, but the words feel right.

"And how is the wrapping up going?"

Peter looks back at the courthouse. The grandeur of the building conveys such great purpose that you can almost forget how slowly things move inside.

"These things take time," he says. "But Holzmann will be going away for a while. Owen and Conrad, too. Conrad tried to flip, but the DA didn't bite. The union can't budge them, and heads need to roll after Elkhorn."

"What about the out-of-towners?" Barrett asks. Peter wonders if he should be sharing all this, but figures it's nothing Barrett couldn't find if he looked for it, so there's no harm.

"We couldn't find anything on the locksmith or the woman who got shot, so we had to let them go. We'll keep an eye on them if they ever come back, but I figure they're gone for good."

"It sounds like it's gonna work out all right, then," Barrett says. "Just so you know, after I hang up, I might misplace this phone."

"Aren't you going to ask about Wright?" Peter asks.

"Jonny Boy? Why would I ask about him?"

"Well, it's the darnedest thing. Just before his arraignment, a partner at one of the best defense firms in the city showed up and said Jonny Boy is his client. But the kid doesn't have two cents to his name, so no one on the force knows how he's paying for it."

"How strange," Barrett says carefully.

"He must have a guardian angel looking out for him. A few hours later the DA dropped all the charges against him. Not his partner, though. She took a swing at her public defender for telling her to take a plea deal. Last I heard she's trying to represent herself."

"You know, Peter, there is one last thing I wanted to ask you."

"What's that?" Peter asks as he gets to his car. Sitting in the passenger seat is a small package, about the size of a shoebox and wrapped in brown paper.

"Could you make a delivery for me?"

◆

Jonny Boy is right where Barrett said he would be, in the Catholic cemetery near Saddle Creek. Peter waits quietly, not wanting to interrupt the man's thoughts as he stands over the recently dug grave of Victor Velasquez, laid to rest beside his abuela. It's a lovely spot on the side of a hill. There's a tree nearby, and in the morning the church's steeple will cast its shadow over them both.

Jonny Boy turns and frowns slightly. "Do I know you?" he asks, looking Peter up and down, trying to place the man.

"I'm with the police," Peter says. "You've probably seen me around."

"My lawyer says you guys aren't supposed to talk to me without him here."

"I'm not here about that. I just wanted to give you this. It's from a friend." He holds out the package, and Jonny Boy takes it hesitantly.

"What is it?" he asks.

"I don't know," Peter says. "I'm just supposed to give it to you."

With a shrug, Jonny Boy tears the paper wrapping and opens the box beneath. His face pales as he looks inside, and his brow knits together in confusion.

"I don't get it," he says. "Is this a joke?"

"No," says Peter.

"But—"

"He said you'd understand."

Jonny Boy, his legs suddenly weak, sits down and stares into the box. He reaches inside and pulls out a sandwich in a Ziploc bag with a Post-it Note on top that reads: *You can make the next one.*

Peter joins him on the grass, waiting for the man to tell him to back off, but he doesn't.

"A sandwich?" Peter asks. "Does that mean something to you?"

Jonny Boy doesn't respond. He isn't listening. He reaches into the box again and pulls out a glossy magazine. The cover is a collage of pictures of young people in pristine aprons smiling in an industrial kitchen of gleaming chrome. As Peter looks more closely he realizes it isn't a magazine, but an advertising pamphlet for a trade school, the Chicago Parisian Cooking Academy.

Jonny Boy is openly weeping now as he pulls the third and final object from the box. It's a brown paper lunch bag, thick with some rectangular object inside, which—Peter can't help but observe—is remarkably close in size to a significant stack of money. Jonny Boy doesn't look. He just pockets the bag and turns his attention back to the sandwich. He opens the Ziploc with reverential care and draws the sandwich out. It is turkey on rye, dripping with mayonnaise, and cut along the diagonal.

Jonny Boy laughs through his tears and looks over at Peter.

"He gave this to you?" he asks, and Peter nods. Jonny Boy holds out half the sandwich. "Do you want some? I think he'd like that."

"Sure," Peter says, and he takes the other half of the sandwich. Jonny Boy smiles. A genuine smile that spreads across his whole face, and Peter finds himself smiling as well. The two men sit beneath the afternoon sun, and together they break bread.

CHAPTER 71

Barrett Rye, Some Time Later

The cafe's outdoor seating is empty except for me and Jim Pickens, growing ever so slightly damp in the lightly misting rain as we sip from paper cups of mediocre coffee. There are a couple dozen empty tables on the patio, surrounded by a waist-high fence with a gate leading to the street. A door leads back into the cafe.

Pickens caught a ride back to Chicago with Laia after they'd been released by the OPD. He'd told her our plan, or at least the broad strokes of it. There was no reason not to now that I was dead. I guess Laia didn't think much of it. It wasn't, in retrospect, the best plan. I'm big enough to admit that. There were too many variables to control and no means of doing so. I was too reliant on other people behaving how I expected and too callous to the real pain I inflicted on the innocent—or at least, the less guilty.

Scarpello wanted to speak with Pickens upon his return, and though he was nervous, he told the boss what he'd seen. I was dead, the egg was destroyed, and Holzmann's operation was in shambles.

334

Conrad Stenberg, it turns out, had been one paranoid motherfucker and had meticulous documentation of everything that he and his partner had done. Holzmann's entire business was being dismantled. Shipping across the Midwest would be slow, and the high rollers of Omaha would have to accept a lower class of entertainment until Scarpello could send someone to clean it up.

Between Pickens's and Laia's stories, it looked like Scarpello had bought the big lie that I had been killed in the confrontation at the farmhouse. It wasn't even a lie on Pickens's part. Me faking my death had never been part of the plan, just a fortuitous opportunity that came along. That's what it's all about after all, right? Striking when the moment presents itself.

I couldn't go back to Omaha or Chicago, so I'd reached Pickens through a dead drop Mickey had set up for us online. I wish I could have seen his face when he learned I was alive, but that, alas, wasn't in the cards. When we met up three nights ago, seeing each other for the first time since my escape from Holzmann's basement, I still got a bit of the effect. Based on his expression, I don't think he had actually believed I'd made it through until that moment.

It took a couple days after that to arrange everything else. I had a bit squirreled away—the last of the skim Mickey and I had collected—that went to Jonny Boy's lawyer. Pickens sold his tools, and that cash got us set up where we are now.

I won't tell you where that is. It isn't terribly important. But it's not Omaha. It's probably not even the Great Plains. It doesn't rain like this there, not at this time of year.

We've been sitting here for about half an hour. The barista gave us a curious look when we asked if the patio was open, but, at the end of the day, why should she care if we want to get a bit wet? I'm not worried at the delay, though. We got here early. So I drink my coffee, think about what we're going to do next, and idly wonder whether the delicate legs of this chair will continue to support my weight.

Pickens clears his throat. "They're here," he says, and he lifts the thick briefcase he's been holding by his side into his lap, clutching it to himself.

Five men in suits have taken up positions surrounding the patio. They have the hardened look of professionals to them, but they're not threatening. They're here to observe and ensure safety. I pick out the one who looks to be in charge—he's the only one with an umbrella—and meet his eye. I raise my coffee to him in greeting, and I see his lips moving as he speaks into an unseen microphone.

Thirty seconds later a black sedan, comfortable but not ostentatious, pulls up and he moves to the rear door, holding out his umbrella as he opens it. A fifty-year-old man in perfectly tailored slacks and shirt sleeves climbs out. He eases through the gate, the guard following behind, and joins us at the table. He lays a hand towel down on the chair before taking a seat.

"This is it?" he asks of the briefcase in Jim's lap. There is a faint growl of Russian to his accent, softened by the rounded tones of high street London. I'm not sure which, if either, is the affectation.

"You have our money?" I ask in response.

He gives me a wan smile. "It is already in your accounts."

Pickens pulls his phone out with the hand not holding the briefcase. It takes him a minute to sign in to the banking app. The VPN we're using to hide our location slows the connection, and there are several layers of security to get through before he can see the collection of accounts that Mickey had set up—one last gift, an untraceable home for our future wealth—but once he is in, his breath catches in his throat. He turns the phone to show me the balance. Twenty-five million dollars.

"Just like that?" I ask, looking at the man sitting across from us and preparing for a trap to slam closed.

"Just like that," he says. "We have made a deal. Why should I not pay you? We must have trust in each other. We are all professionals, no?"

"Then this is for you," I say. I look to Pickens, and he slides the briefcase across the table. His fingers linger on the handle for a moment as the man reaches out for it.

The man turns the case to face himself, and his guard moves in closer, using both his body and the umbrella to block the view of anyone who might be watching. We didn't bother to spin the codewheels on the briefcase's lock, so it clicks open as the man presses in the buttons, and he slowly raises the lid.

Inside is the Nécessaire, the lost Fabergé egg from Novak's safe.

The man smiles and closes the briefcase. After a glance at the lock to memorize the combination, he muddles the numbers and lays his hands flat on top.

"I have a question," he says. "You have no obligation to answer. Our business is concluded. But if you would indulge my curiosity—you could have gotten far more than twenty-five million for this at auction, perhaps even twice as much. Why sell it to me?"

It's a fair question. Pickens is silent, waiting for me to respond. The man is correct. I don't have to answer. But I do anyway. I want him—and the people he represents—to feel at ease. They have gotten a treasure at a bargain, and might be concerned. There are very few things in the world that are purely good luck.

"Because we would have had to go public," I say. "As far as the world is concerned, this doesn't exist, and I am dead. I see no reason to disabuse it of either notion, and my understanding is that your client will keep their ownership of this private."

"They will," the man says, and he rises from the chair. "Gentlemen, it has been a pleasure." He offers his hand, and we each shake in turn, and then he leaves. The five men in suits fade back into the mist of the morning rain, leaving me and Pickens alone at the cafe table, slightly richer than we were when they arrived.

"We did it," Pickens says, not quite believing it, hoping that saying it out loud will cement it in the universe as a true statement.

"We did." I smile, but the relief I had looked forward to isn't there. I want to laugh and shout and whoop in celebration, but all I can do is feel his absence.

"What are you going to do now?" Pickens asks.

I have no idea what my plan is. I've spent so long working for this moment, working to be free of Scarpello's grasp, that I haven't had time to think about what comes next. "Go somewhere new," I say. "Try to start over, live the life he wanted for us both."

"He would have been proud of you. You pulled it off. We pulled it off."

"No," I reply. "He wouldn't be proud of me. Not yet."

CHAPTER 72

A Conclusion

S o you might be a little upset right now, but don't worry. It'll
all make sense. The plan really was simple. Pickens would go
and work for Holzmann. He'd get the safe as close to open as
he could without the key, and then he'd wait. My job was to get him
out of there. Get him and the safe to a place where he wasn't observed.
Once he was there—in the bedroom of Vic's abuela's house, as it turned
out—he'd send me a signal, and I'd find him.

He'd done it while Jonny Boy and I talked about sandwiches, and
Cass grew increasingly more nervous that I was just stalling. She was
closer to the truth than she'd thought. I was stalling as I circled the
house, waiting for Pickens's cough, the sign that I and the key I held
were close enough. Then I stood there while he finished opening the
safe and swapped out the real egg. Pickens's drill had been heavier
and larger than it needed to be. Inside it, he was hiding a cell phone
to contact me with and the rest of our money, converted into a lump
of gold and porcelain and a handful of jewels. He tossed that into
the safe, then threw the real egg out the window and into the murky

waters of the algae-filled pool, where it waited for him to retrieve it once everything had settled down.

Then I made sure that when the safe actually got opened, it wasn't the real key that was used, but one of my fakes, and we let the safe's security measures cover up all the evidence of our little swap.

I'm not going to insult your intelligence and say that we'd planned out every step of the whole thing from the beginning. I'll admit it was real fucking touch-and-go for a minute there. Hell, we'd actually meant to give the thing to Scarpello in the end. But you gotta remember, a con isn't about perfect planning. No plan survives contact with the enemy. A con is about improvisation. Recognizing opportunity and daring to strike when the moment is right. Besides, right at the start of all of this, I gave you two things to remember.

Nothing I said was the truth, but nothing I said was a lie. I've kept my word. Go ahead and check. I'll wait.

EPILOGUE

The rain starts in earnest as we walk toward the street. My phone buzzes in my pocket, and I shield it with my jacket as I pull it out. The only person who has this number had just driven away, our business concluded. But he's sent me a text message. Pickens stops to look at me, the concern surely obvious on my face as I look down at the words:

From one professional to another. A warning. You are being watched.

"What's wrong?" Pickens asks.

"Stay calm," I say, trying to get myself to heed my own words. Who could be watching us? Nobody knows I'm alive. Or at least, nobody should. If anyone does, it's going to get back to Scarpello, and then no amount of money, not twenty-five or fifty or a hundred million dollars will be enough to guarantee my safety. If somebody knows I'm alive, I need to find out now and silence them.

I hate the thought. I hate that my mind immediately goes there. This was all supposed to be over. I've not left that life behind for five minutes, and I'm already planning to murder somebody in cold blood.

I force myself to slow down. If someone is watching me, I need to find out who they are without them knowing. I make a show of stretching my neck, turning my head left and right to check over my shoulders. I don't see anyone, but visibility is terrible in this rain, and there are windows all around that could hide interested eyes.

But whoever is watching, my buyer made them, which means I should be able to spot them as well. As I lead Pickens through the gate and out to the street, I take one last look behind us.

The streetlights had reflected off the cafe windows at our table, keeping us from seeing in through them but doing nothing to obscure us from someone inside. From this new vantage, there is no reflection.

Laia Quintana waves through the window with her left hand, beckoning us to join her inside. Her right arm is strapped to her body while it heals from the gunshot.

"How the hell—" Jim starts to ask.

"She's Laia Quintana," I answer before he can finish. "Who knows how she does what she does."

"Do we run?"

"No. There's no point. Besides, if she wanted us dead, we'd be dead."

"Then what does she want?" Jim asks.

"I don't know," I say. "But there's only one way we find out." I close the gate, and we start back toward the cafe.

The cafe is warm and dry, and the barista waves to us as we come inside. "It's a bit wet out there, huh?" she calls. "You guys want a top off?"

I shake my head no, not trusting my voice to stay steady as I walk, dripping slightly, across the room to join Laia at her table. Pickens stays beside me, as silent as I am.

"Hello, Barrett," she says once we've settled in. "I figured Pickens here was hiding something, but I gotta admit, I was not expecting to see your face when I started following him." Her tone is casual, almost friendly, and she keeps her voice low. To anyone walking past, we're just three old friends getting coffee together.

"Does he know yet?" I ask. I want to build to the question more indirectly, but instead I just blurt it out. So much for my masterful subtlety.

Laia laughs and wipes a drip of coffee from her lip. "I hear you two have come into quite a bit of money recently," she says.

"So that's what this is?" Pickens asks. "You're shaking us down to buy your silence?"

She laughs again, as though he told the cleverest joke. It is a strange sound coming from her. "No," she says. "I don't want you to buy my silence. I don't even begrudge you lying to me. I gotta respect the play, though Barrett promising to pay me if he made it out alive was a bit too cute."

She's toying with us. I'm recovered from my concussion. I'm rested, and she's injured. I could end this now.

"I feel like you two have the wrong impression of me," she continues. "I can be a bitch, sure, but only because that's my job. I'm not totally heartless. My friends even think I'm kind of fun to be around." I can't picture Laia Quintana with friends.

"What do you want?" I press her. I don't want to spend any more time with her than I have to.

"I want you to hire me," she says simply, and sits back, folding her hands in her lap.

"To do what?" Pickens asks.

"To give you information. Maybe even to help you out. The two of you are good. You're clever, and you think well on your feet, but you're also sloppy. You're going to need to be perfect if you want to pull this off."

"Pull what off, Laia?" I ask. I'm losing my patience.

"Another heist," she says. "You're going to be stealing something even more precious." She slides a picture across the table. It's a bit grainy, taken in a dark room under less-than-ideal lighting, but I can see well enough what it shows. There's a newspaper, a few days old now but still recent enough. Beside the paper is a man's face. It's both swollen with bruising and gaunt with hunger, and a few of the ever so slightly crooked teeth are missing, but I would know that face anywhere. It has lived in my dreams and my thoughts every moment since I lay on a carpet and failed to look up.

"You see, Barrett," Laia is saying, but I barely hear her. All I can hear is his breathing. His voice. "You're not the only one who can fake a death. And your boy needs help."

It doesn't make sense. I don't know why or how. I can't see the pattern. But none of that matters. All that matters is his face. His eyes.

Mickey is alive. And I'm going to get him back.